# JIM AND HEIDI

## Eric Armstrong

**MINERVA PRESS**

LONDON

MONTREUX   LOS ANGELES   SYDNEY

**JIM AND HEIDI**
Copyright © Eric Armstrong 1997

ISBN 1 86106 400 4

First Published 1997 by
MINERVA PRESS
195 Knightsbridge
London SW7 1RE

Printed in Great Britain for Minerva Press

# JIM AND HEIDI

## About the Author

Having practised, taught and written extensively about industrial relations, Emeritus Professor Eric Armstrong OBE, a highly experienced arbitrator, has recently branched out to become the author of works on other aspects of social history.

# Contents

| | | |
|---|---|---|
| *One* | Chevy Chase | 7 |
| *Two* | Hot Ginger and Dynamite | 14 |
| *Three* | Foreign Parts | 22 |
| *Four* | *Adieux* – And a Mane Event | 34 |
| *Five* | Getting to Know – Who? | 44 |
| *Six* | Night of the Numbskulls | 55 |
| *Seven* | Strolling in the Park | 66 |
| *Eight* | Conversations | 76 |
| *Nine* | Personal Questions | 87 |
| *Ten* | Resolutions | 96 |
| *Eleven* | Powwow in Blighty | 108 |
| *Twelve* | On the Move | 118 |
| *Thirteen* | Back and Forth | 128 |
| *Fourteen* | Go to Gaol | 140 |
| *Fifteen* | Crime and Punishment | 149 |
| *Sixteen* | Icicles and Red Tape | 160 |

*Seventeen*   Last Hitch to Pullenstadt     171

*Eighteen*   Civvy Street     182

*Nineteen*   The Great Paper Chase     192

## Chapter One

# Chevy Chase

It was late afternoon towards the blowsy end of summer. The dense, broad leafed wood seemed to spread itself drowsily across the sharply uneven folds of a rugged hillside. Within the wood's deep shadows a soft stillness prevailed – save for the occasional low buzz of an insect, and a flutter of unseen, fidgeting bird wings. Now and again, a breeze languidly ruffled the sombre, jaded looking leaves of old trees, snagging, tangled bushes and matted undergrowth. Although overcast, the sky was dove rather than slate grey in colour. A mildly warming sun broke fitfully through thin haze, on its slow downward glide towards the tops of the trees. A soothing, sleepy atmosphere pervaded this small corner of England – a corner which lent itself to calm, even melancholy reflection.

So thought the young man who lay sprawling on the still lush but ageing grass beside a strong, thick-set tree.

Jim began to conjure up images of old 'muckers', fellow foot-sloggers who, in their heavy, clumping, hobnailed boots, had 'bashed on regardless' with him along blister-raising roads, lanes and tracks: across energy sapping shingle and shifting sand dunes, fields ploughed and unploughed; through ankle snagging heath land and dense, face scratching woodland; rushing icy streams and slimy, muddy culverts; leaping and yelling through bomb shattered, smoke blackened buildings. Rarely was the weather 'ideal', for such training – scorching sun on the sand dunes made the senses swim and the eyes fill with stinging sweat. Across the hilly moorland swept vicious, piercing winds and lashing, near freezing rain. Almost automatically, Jim rubbed his round, wire-framed glasses at the recollections.

Yes, those old mates of his had intuitively understood how to raise the spirits of a dog-tired, sodden platoon which knew that at least two painful miles remained before the camp of sheltering Nissen huts would be reached. Pain and fatigue from the marching and skirmishing of the day – pain from body-chafing webbing and equipment – with more to come along the last bone and ligament jolting lanes – mostly uphill. Yes, those lads had far more nous regarding morale than the sniffy company commander who occasionally visited the platoon, riding squire-like in his 15cwt truck of course, simply to bleat, "Buck up, chaps, best foot forward now."

Take beaming Ben 'Beanpole' for instance. Steel barrel firmly gripped in his large right hand, Ben would be balancing a Bren gun on his narrow, sloping shoulder as he started to bellow a popular parody of the hymn 'Jesus wants me for a sunbeam'.

"When this bleeding war is over,
Oh how happy I shall be,
When this bleedin' war is over,
No more soldiering for me.
No more church parades on Sunday,
No more asking for a pass,
You can tell the sergeant-major
To stuff his passes up his..."

"Weskit."
"Jumper."
"Drawers, cellular."

Roars of tired laughter – and panted mutterings of, '*nil illegitimo carborundem*' – the 'illegitimo' ranging from officious lance corporals to armchair warriors at the War Office.

From the head of the platoon would come a clear call of, "They're going to pull the pub down."

"Boo-oo-oo!" prolonged, voiced the rest of the platoon.

"But they're going to build a new one."

"Hooray!" the cheers were even more prolonged.

"The barmaid's going to have a baby."

"Boo-oo-oo!"

"You've been at it again then, Smudger."

"A baby Guinness."

"Hooray!"

Cue for a rollicking rendering of 'The barmaid of the inn at Inverary'.

Good old Beanpole. How and where was he now? Having become browned off with strenuous but repetitious infantry training, with only a mock enemy lurking in ambush, Ben volunteered for the 'real thing' and joined a unit fighting in France. His great mucker, happy go lucky 'Roughnut' agreed to go with him. In early August Roughnut had written to Jim,

'Ben has been wounded in both arms... shrapnel from a mortar bomb. I got a bit of shrapnel from a hand grenade in my forehead... I was in hospital for a few days'. Not so very long afterwards, Roughnut was reported 'Killed in Action'. He could have paid no higher price for having wanted to be with his more headstrong friend in the thick of battle. Perhaps there had been a strong protective streak in his make-up? Jim wondered about that. Roughnut had previously experienced desperate action as a commando and was subsequently transferred to an infantry battalion training for overseas service – for a 'rest cure'! And now – just one more RIP.

Jim shifted his position in the cool grass around the tree roots, turning to support himself on his left elbow as he picked up a silvery looking detonator.

Was it right that he, Jim, should be where he was at this time – a twenty-one year old corporal in an English wood with the Second Front well under way? He had asked himself a similar basic question many times. Could he, should he, do more for the war effort, and maybe for his own sake, than he had so far done?

His thoughts drifted back to an earlier stage of his service with the battalion. Yes, he acknowledged he had been the quiet, relatively unassertive one among several young lance corporals in the same company – all of them with a grammar school background.

Dave was the calm, self-possessed but devil-may-care member of this better educated group, a bunch of one-stripers far less dependent on a flow of obscenities in their conversations than were the men in the sections they led. Quite a character this tall, slim, curly headed Scouser who mixed Liverpudlian wit with his own distinctive brand of 'older than his years' cynicism towards life. Like fellow Liverpudlians in the company, he kept a small, battered tin of 'doofers' – a collection of dog ends. Why 'doofers'? 'Cos they'll do fer tomorrow – have one?'

Dave enjoyed a number of qualities which enabled him to take chances with an equanimity that aroused not only Jim's strong admiration – but a sizeable measure of envy as well.

During balmy summer nights, Dave thought nothing of 'sleeping' away from the billet in order to tumble an amorous ATS girl in a local haystack. He was never caught 'off-limits', never late for parade, never found with a wisp of hay on his uniform or about his person. Lucky (and methodically efficient) devil! His was the personable, streetwise nature that could often turn adverse situations to its own advantage. It was like a law of nature that Dave should go to OCTU, gain a commission, and, as a lieutenant, eventually lead with distinction and imaginative audacity, his own platoon in France.

There had been Ted as well, the first of the group to leave the battalion. His was a complex character indeed. The highly articulate son of a collier, Ted was outwardly buoyantly extrovert but inwardly, from 'confessions' in his letters to Jim, too often volatile, his moods swinging between 'terribly happy' and 'the very depths of despair'. Jim never fully understood why – assuming Ted's self-analysis to be accurate.

Outwardly, Ted was plainly warm-hearted and emotional. With his broad grin, cheerful and confident manner, he was good company. He had courage too. In a commercial theatre, packed with not easy to please troops, Ted had done a ten minute turn as a stand-up comic. The applause had been modest and Jim himself hadn't rated the jokes very highly – but Ted had stuck gamely, wearing the same broad grin, to his challenging task.

His many faceted courage could be allied to compassion and the development of self knowledge. Ted formed one of a small number of volunteers whose task was to clear away from bloody sands, the gobbets of raw flesh and splintered, white bone of the shattered bodies of ATS girls who, while carrying out PE on the beach, had been mercilessly strafed and physically ripped apart by an enemy aircraft.

Then again, Ted, the coal miner's son, had shown the temerity, dash it all, to fall in love with a colonel's daughter. Emma returned that love. Did Ted feel the need to 'prove himself' in the eyes of a radically different social class? He certainly had the drive, the will to succeed and the spirit of adventure. Whatever his mixture of motives, Ted volunteered for the paras, made the grade and dropped into France in the early hours of D-Day. In a farewell note on leaving the 'old' battalion, he had urged Jim, in effect, to take his finger out and do something more ambitious.

Jim hadn't, so far, reacted in a way of which Ted would have approved. He had stayed with the old mob. After all, his pals had chosen to move away for reasons of their own, expressed and unexpressed. No, he'd take his chances with this battalion. No one could claim that it would be a picnic fighting the Japs and that was what the battalion was training to do. And it would not be just a matter of fighting, but coping with the loathsome miseries of the fetid jungle, the horrific leeches and other slimy, creeping evils.

Ah, better get on with it. This 'jungle' would soon be alive with the ear-bruising explosions of 'battle'. A serenely tranquil corner of a 'green and pleasant land' would undergo a brutal violation by noise. Files of tired out, stumbling squaddies, rifles held at the port to aid speed of firing action, would be urged by bellowing, yelling, near hoarsely screaming senior NCOs and officers, to follow a narrow, winding trail through the wood.

"Sniper in tree half left!"

"Keep yer bleedin' eyes peeled!"

"Go round that, you dozy lot!" (A partly camouflaged pit of pointed stakes).

"Enemy strong post forty-five degrees right!"

"Look out for tripwires!"

"Keep moving, keep moving!"

In its way, the incessant clamour would signal the peak of the confusion tactic – 'Get 'em so they don't know whether they want a shit, shave or shampoo!'

Rifles firing blanks would crack sharply, thunderflashes, thrown in all directions, would explode with stabs of flame and venomous blasts of sound; heat, sweat, pungent smoke, acrid stinks, noise, confusion, noise – the bedlam of the testing finale to a long hard day of skirmishing and marching. Trembling with fatigue, eyes smarting from exertion, sweat and choking fumes, the toll taken of 'Jap' snipers by these bewildered squaddies would have caused no loss of sleep for Hirohito.

Jim himself had several times led a section of men along that 'zap the Jap' trail. It was part of a week long training exercise. Jim was now gaining further experience of setting booby traps. A cushy number really – provided that you always paid close attention to what you were doing.

A tripwire, just about ankle height, had been stretched tautly between two trees. An igniter, safety pin firmly in position, had been attached and now – just place the detonator, on a length of fuse, into a stick of explosive and the job would be almost done. Jim paused. He wondered if Dave and Ted had killed anybody today, and what it must be like to kill a fellow human being even if he was one of the enemy. But brooding like this would set no booby traps. Get on with it, man.

'Funny, deceitful stuff that,' Jim thought looking at the short, greyish yellow, waxy looking material. A bit like harmless plasticine in appearance. But when fired by the detonator, it would explode with startling suddenness, noise and ferocity at the side of the trail – when the tripwire was disturbed, the safety pin having previously been carefully removed. For a few seconds, tired bodies and harassed senses would be out of control as the panting, stumbling file of men staggered past.

Jim, still sprawling, turned slightly on his left hip and began to crimp the open end of the silvery detonator around the fuse, attached at its other end to the igniter. 'Must be plain barmy those chaps who do crimping with their teeth,' he thought.

Crimping completed, Jim laid detonator and fuse on the ground between his legs. He picked up the explosive in his left hand and the detonator in his right. Then, carefully, he began to move his two hands closer together.

CRACK!

"Christ almighty! What's happened?"

Jim experienced an acutely sharp, stinging, burning sensation. Gingerly, he slid his trembling hands inside his khaki denim trousers and inched his slightly splayed fingers carefully, slowly southwards. He began to shiver slightly for in the FFI inspection area (free from infection/fit for insertion) his fingertips encountered a spreading patch of sticky moisture. He gave an involuntary gasp – and prayed.

"Oh dear God, don't let me be invalided out as an eunuch especially as I've not been on really active service! Oh please, please, please!"

Jim withdrew his fingers, dripping with bright scarlet blood – into the warm summer air. His trembling increased. Only now did he realise that had the detonator been fixed to the explosive, then in all probability he would have been a goner. Saved by what? A couple of inches separation – a second of time? Shakily he rose to his feet.

"Nearly lost your manhood there, corporal."

"Yes, sir."

The MO, his back bent, continued dabbing yellow aquaflavine on the numerous small craters in Jim's flesh, and then straightened up.

"There, that should do the trick. Are you married, corporal?"

"No sir."

"No doubt you will be, one day. Anyway, England's future should soon be all right again. Meanwhile, I'll put you on light duties for a couple of days. But you'll find yourself walking about like a small boy who's peed himself."

Waddling gloomily back to the bliss of his blankets and *palliasse* on the concrete floor, Jim reflected on life. It was all very well for the MO to talk, a good humoured, mischievous smile on his face, about 'the future'. Back home, no ardent, liberally minded sweetheart was waiting for Jim's return. Not even a warm-hearted girlfriend with whom he might hint at delicate matters. And he had no wish to go a-'whoring'. Indulging a fantasy, he could not imagine, even if he got to first base, that Mae West would show the slightest interest in him. He nodded off, a wry smile on his lips.

'Light duties' – that was a laugh. Straight back to setting booby traps – but naturally with a much higher degree of concentration. He still wondered whether the igniter had been faulty. Somehow, the safety pin must have dropped out. Maybe he'd been careless, become blasé? Anyway, handle with great care from now on. You bet. He was grateful for still having a future.

The MO had been right about the wet underpants walk though. Still never mind – soldier on! if only for a little while at a soggy pace.

## Chapter Two

# Hot Ginger and Dynamite

"Hey, sarge."

"What now, you peddler of piffle?"

"Heard the news?"

"What news? Let me guess – you heard it from the company clerk, who heard it from his oppo in the Orderly Room, that we're flying out next week."

Jim injected a note of sarcasm into his voice, for the scrawny Nobby was a notorious rumour monger.

"No, no – nothing like that. No, a dirty great bomb has been dropped on Japan. There's talk it might knock the stuffing out of them."

"It'll take a lot of dirty great bombs to make the Japs give up."

"But this bomb is something special, I'm sure it is." Nobby sounded far more excited than he usually did when he had a titbit of gossip to drool over – or a 'heard it on the grapevine' nugget of information to relate and embellish.

Jim put down his spare jungle-green underwear that he was carefully folding in readiness for kit inspection.

"Spill the beans then, Field Marshal Slim."

Jim propped his 'jungle dancer' lightweight, stubby rifle against the pole of the bell tent and listened to Nobby's account of the damage done to Hiroshima.

"Well, even if this new bomb has near enough flattened one Japanese city, I can't see the Japs giving up on that account. Can't have been many Jap soldiers killed in that raid. Jerry wasn't bombed into submission – and neither were we." Jim started to clean his rifle.

"But, you have to admit, sarge, this bombing does seem different. Anyway, it would be great if the Japs did surrender and we didn't have to go out East – and probably West into the bargain."

"Amen to that. Meanwhile, you'd better look sharp and get your kit ready."

"OK, sarge."

A few days later and another 'dirty great bomb' had been dropped – this time on Nagasaki.

All Jim knew of Nagasaki was what he dimly, and probably inaccurately remembered of a comedy song – played by Harry Roy's band and jauntily sung by bouncy, pop-eyed Harry himself.

'Down in Nagasaki where the fellers chew tobaccy, And the women wikky wakky woo...' at least that's what it sounded like.

'Wikky wakky woo' a racy euphemism perhaps. But for what? Surely something pretty 'oojah cum spiff' as the saying went.

'Hot ginger and dynamite...' Jim could remember no more of that 1930s silly song but he would never forget the appalling association between a bit of harmless nonsense and the most devastating weapon mankind had so far invented.

A few days more and the war against Japan was at an end – to be quickly followed by VJ day. Jim didn't much mind that he was detailed to be battalion orderly sergeant on that day of general rejoicing and widespread jollification. He had little taste for boozing to the point of stupefaction. The nearest town was miles away and he would have felt uncomfortable at gatecrashing a street party where everyone was a stranger to him.

Home was two hundred miles distant – where bonny lassie Ellen had been 'snapped up' by some persistent chap working in the same office. Willowy, dark-haired Julie was also spoken for. As for Mary, well, he saw her so infrequently. She had become so 'distant' in every way, treating him more like a cousin than a former sweetheart who, deep down, yearned to rekindle the flame of the 'divine pash'.

Where, oh where could the love and the bluebells of yesteryear now be found? (Well, of May 1939 to be exact). Six years on, just bitter sweet memories. Soon it would be Mary's twenty-first birthday. Jim had received an invitation to her party – at some swank hotel. It was a nicely printed card – but sent to how many other young men? He reflected. No, he couldn't possibly seek special leave on 'compassionate' grounds. (Compassionate – ha! ha! – often longhand for the 'passionate' – very). No, not a chance either for the leave – or the passion.

No, all pleasure and romance factors considered, he didn't much mind being on duty on VJ Day. In any event, as probably the youngest and almost certainly the newest sergeant in the battalion, he could rightly expect to 'cop for it'.

Anyway, he quite enjoyed slipping on 'the mantle of office', a bright red sash stretching from shoulder to opposite hip, an imposing baldric forsooth – with a tassel! He took pains not to puff out his chest too often in the self-glorifying manner of a bantam cock. (He was still only five foot six and a half inches in height – but perhaps a few pounds heavier than the one hundred and twenty-six of 1942 when his 'maximum chest' had been officially recorded as thirty-four inches).

VJ Day – to celebrate the victory of liberty over tyranny – would surely be the worst of all possible days in which to carry out 'good order and military discipline' duties with the 'insolence of office'. (He still remembered his Sixth Form *Hamlet*).

So, Jim strolled self-consciously about the large tented camp spread over park land, striving to look as dignified as his boyish twenty-two year old appearance would allow. He took considerable care not to have his seeming poise ruined by tripping, arse over tip, over one or more of the many taut guy ropes that lay in malevolent ambush for him. A veritable playground here for Laurel and Hardy antics.

But it wasn't all beer and skittles being a sergeant – no, sir. A few days later, Jim's face became a great deal redder than the baldric he had so recently worn with such glowing pride. Duty this time – sergeant of the battalion HQ guard. Dithering inwardly but trying to appear calm and assured, he marched the squad of men briskly towards the line painted on the asphalt where they were to halt and dress ranks.

"Squ-a-a-d. Halt!"

The men snapped smartly to a stop – but a disastrous six inches beyond the line! Hell's bells and buckets of blood!

'Tara, Tara-sem' the RSM (Regimental Sergeant Major) nearly exploded with wrath. "Six bleedin' inches, or thereabouts *before* the line was where you should soddin' well be!" Men, in the front rank, at the appropriate command, could then have shuffled forwards until the toes of their highly polished boots just touched the line. Shuffling forward dead right. Shuffling backwards – *verboten*, totally. Who wants soldiers swaying about like a line of bleedin' fairies or poncey chorus boys? "Take the men back, sergeant and try again."

Wrong – a second time. Oh hell!

Sweating, scarlet faced with exertion, vexation and humiliation, Jim finally judged timing and spacing just right at the third, heart in the mouth, attempt.

To help pass the time and to divert his troubled thoughts from the 'right dress' – and the 'right dressing down' fiasco of a few hours earlier, Jim decided to write a poem. Brow furrowed, he gazed at the Nissen hut ceiling for inspiration.

> Guard Commander 0100 hours
>
> Whitewashed corrugations.
> Stilled imaginations.
> No noise, it's Regulations,
> In the Guard Room.
>
> [...]
>
> A bugle mute suspended.
> Stale bread not much commended.
> A night that's never ended.
> In the Guard Room.

Ah well, he was capturing something of the monotony of guard duty and it was better sitting at a wooden trestle table with the Muse than standing 'alone and palely loitering' outside. Not long to go before he had a spot of leave. Clean white sheets, bacon and egg as only Mom could fry it. The company of Ellen, or Julie or Mary or Anne Other? No such luck.

On his return from a leave void of romance, Jim wrote home in somewhat jaundiced vein.

'Training of a kind is still going on' but he anticipated several days of 'bull' as the colonel of the regiment was planning to visit. 'No doubt he's coming to sympathise at our disappointment in not now being able to liberate Singapore, at not being able to add another battle honour to the regimental list.

'I also had a letter from Ted's wife. Ted has been promoted to CQMS but is now well on his way to India. And he's been 'in' since the outbreak of war and before, being a "terrier".'

Yes, Ted had won through, as Jim had always thought he would, and married the colonel's daughter. A sign of changing times Jim hoped, this erosion of toffee-nosed social barriers. Jim himself had not swerved an inch from the bedrock family tradition of 'vote Labour, support Aston Villa and shop at the Co-op'. In the recent general election he had gleefully added his own vote to the many others for Clem and his lads – and a few lassies. Ted, he knew, would have done the same. What a wonderful and spectacular victory – Labour 393 seats, Tories 213. To blazes with Eton and Harrow and like centres of gluttonous privilege. But it did seem so unfair on Ted, to post him now to India. Still, he would probably be well up the list for 'demob'.

Demobilisation had become a major topic of animated conversation and discussion. In fact, as a theme, it had become as popular as football and fornication, especially among the older and longer service men. But tricky times lay ahead. Civilians in uniform, which is what most servicemen and women were, accepted, albeit with good-natured grumbling, the need for military discipline and rigorous training when there was an enemy to fight. But with the war won, troops might become restive unless they had something worth while to do. Morale might sag unless far-sighted policies were brought into being and effectively carried out.

Far, far more would be needed, for example, than extending the hours for which housey-housey could be played in the NAAFI. Some squaddies were bound to lose more money that way and so become even more browned off. Yes, that was the nub, or was it rub? Nub and rub perhaps. How did you prevent squaddies from becoming browned off in peacetime when most of them were aching to be in civvies and back home again? A sergeant, being close to the men, needed to know.

Such weighty thoughts were trundling through Jim's mind when he was smartly struck behind the right ear by a rosy red apple.

"Sorry sarge."

"You will be if you miss your aim again. On a fizzer as sure as your name's Perkins."

"But my name's Baker."

"I know."

Baker grinned.

Jim grinned.

Both men were up a tree, not the proverbial adhesive kind but a sturdy English apple tree, one of many in an extensive Kent orchard. In neighbouring trees, men of Jim's platoon were well below sweating level, busy picking apples and tossing them into baskets. Necessary, useful – and boring work – but a heckuva sight better than square bashing. Providing a reasonable weight of apples was picked for the farmer, men could skive relatively easily. They could not disappear however, for there was nowhere to go except other orchards, all, seemingly empty of hearty land army girls.

Yes, it was a jolly rum business perching in one apple tree after another, musing about life – and death. During his boyhood in Birmingham he had never had the chance to climb an apple tree, lamp posts yes, but they were barren and flecked, not with moss, but with rust.

Jim savoured the sweet juices as he bit into his third crisp apple of the morning – and reflected, as he wiped his moistened chin.

Just about twelve months now since he had nearly blown himself, or rather, rather precious parts of himself to Kingdom Come. Fortunately, no lasting damage had been done, but it had been a near squeak, indeed it had. And now – he took another good bite from the apple – his own life and the lives of many, many others had probably been spared through the destruction of two Japanese industrial cities – and some estimated two hundred thousand of their citizens. It seemed the very grimmest of ironies, many lives preserved, including Japanese, through the massive devastation wrought by just two, only two mark you, atomic bombs. Jim experienced a pang of sorrow, not a deep or lasting one, for all those Japanese killed or still suffering from horrific burns.

After all, Japan was so far away, its culture so alien to Westerners. While Jim had thoroughly enjoyed his old school's production of *The Mikado* (the headmaster had rightly played Pooh Bah) his 'willing suspension of disbelief' had finished with the final chorus.

No, the real Japs were given to lacquering everything in sight, eating huge quantities of raw fish and torturing the feet of their womenfolk. Earthquakes, paper houses and geisha girls, pretty as dolls, but give him a tomboy like Mary any time. Oh hell, why didn't she seem to care.

Jim was highly relieved that he would not now have to meet Japanese soldiers in a jungle clearing – round eye to slit eye. It didn't do to be captured by the slit eyes: some British POWs had received scarcely credible brutal treatment at their hands, fists, boots and bayonets. Yes, a cruel, sadistic lot, for all their toothy grins.

So he brooded, and rejoiced, over the literally fresh lease of life that atomic bombs had given him. Just one snag, though. He thought he might always have some regrets about not having been in action. Perhaps enduring air raids in Birmingham would count for something. Anyway, he had not 'dodged the column', simply accepting willingly or unwillingly what others had decided should or should not happen to him. Except once, and that recently.

He had, before shinning up trees, been interviewed in London to see if he might be a suitable student to take a crash course in Japanese at the School of Oriental Languages. It could have been most interesting he thought. Just one drawback, a major one too – successful applicants had to agree to serve an extra six months beyond the still unknown date of eventual demob. Not on your Nelly! Far too risky! 'No', his immediate answer. End of interview.

Yes, he probably would retain regrets about his lack of battle experience. Still, like his old, middle-aged Mom, and many of her cronies said,

"What can't be cured must be endured."

\*

"Watch out, Sarge!"

"What for – some rare bird, or any old bird at all?"

"No, no such luck. I just thought you were nodding off and about to drop off – your perch."

Baker cackled at his witticism.

"Cheeky young sod – I was just day dreaming."

Baker sought safer ground.

"Are you in the Battalion rifle team next week sarge?"

"I am – and in the Bren team."

"Think we'll win?"

"We stand a damn good chance."

They did win the inter-unit shooting competition. A posh, commercial photo was taken of the successful sharpshooters. Jim took good care to turn the left sleeve of his well pressed serge blouse towards the camera. Even the dimmest of dimwits could now see that he was a sergeant.

\*

Jim shivered a little. Recently, the evening breezes had begun to take on a chilly edge.

"Hey, Nobby – it's getting a bit parky these days. When are we going to fold our tents and steal away into some decent billets? What is the latest gen on the grapevine?"

Nobby assumed his 'only a chosen few of us are in the secret' look, sucked air through his uneven, tobacco stained teeth to heighten the tension beloved of 'those in the know' and said portentously, "Well, word in the cookhouse is that we'll soon be off to Dover – then embarkation leave – and then..."

"Where, weasel face?"

"No, I can't tell you that. The cooks themselves aren't sure. The barber says he doesn't know. But the CO's batman says he's heard Aden mentioned."

"Garn. He's pulling your leg. For one thing, we haven't had the right jabs and for another we haven't been issued with khaki shorts."

"Give us your best guess. A fag each from the five of us." Nobby grabbed the clutch of Woodbines and Players and began to sidle towards the tent opening.

"OK. Well, I think it'll be..." he paused for effect, then blurted out, "...up the Khyber!" and rapidly disappeared into the deepening twilight.

"You bleedin' swindler!" yelled Baker.

Nobby was right about the move to Dover though. Snug but rather claustrophobic billets – man-made caves, roughly the shape of Nissen huts, hewn out of the cliffs on the landward side. It seemed harder than ever to raise the bleary-eyed platoon at *reveille*.

Jim bawled, at his brightest and best, "Wakey, wakey, rise and shine – out of those wanking chariots, you idle lot!"

But it remained hard work.

Nobby was right about embarkation leave too – given before going to see what remained of the Reich that was to have lasted a thousand years.

## Chapter Three

# Foreign Parts

*Dear Mother and Dad,*
*Part of the cake came in very handy on the railway*
*journey today.*

Good old Mom, she remained chronically mistrustful of the
Army's ability to feed her son properly. Jim grinned, realising that
Mother's Union 'Mater' would blush to the brightest beetroot hue if
she only knew what, dependent on the context, was commonly
understood by – 'getting your rations'.

> *Our short stay in Ostend found us in one of the big*
> *transit camps, where the Sergeants' Mess equipped us*
> *well in the way of food and recreation. Belgian girls*
> *acted as waitresses so for an experiment I tried out my*
> *schoolboy French. To the amusement of all present at*
> *the table, she replied in English, that she didn't*
> *understand French.*

Eventually, the centime dropped in Jim's buzzing head. That was
it – the pretty little minx in her becoming black and white uniform
was probably Flemish. Not to worry, she had recognised his first,
real life '*parlez vous*' attempt as being broadly intelligible.

So, there he was, aged twenty-two, abroad for the first time in his
life – among lots of Johnny Foreigners. He felt excited, curious but
not the least bit homesick. How would he react, he wondered, to
being in ex-enemy territory? How would he behave in his first
meetings with Germans? He wasn't at all sure, but thought much
would depend on the formality or informality of such encounters.

What he was sure about was that unlike some folk, he felt quite
incapable of hating – or loving, a whole nation, people or race. He

knew enough history to accept that many of the seeds of the Second World War had been sown in the punitive Peace Treaty of Versailles at the end of World War I. Of course, the injustice of that settlement together with mass unemployment, dreadful, degrading poverty, the lack of a democratic tradition did not, most emphatically did not justify what followed – brutal, merciless persecution of the Jews and other peoples. But such vicious extremism fed off earlier degradation and humiliation.

Not only that, Jim believed that Britain had helped Hitler to power. And why? Because too many of those with power, great wealth and influence in Britain had feared Uncle Joe Stalin far more than they had feared Adolf. Yes, any analysis of the 1920s and 1930s had to be complex if it was to have any validity at all. Complexity could be puzzling, disturbing, unsettling. So some people opted for the strength and clarity of the simplistic viewpoint (reinforced in some cases by personal sorrows) that '...the only good German is a dead German'.

No, it wouldn't wash. Jim was clear in his mind about that and stuck to his parents' approach that 'you should try to judge people as individuals'. So, he might come to hate some Germans, some most likely in an impersonal way – those found guilty of war crimes for instance. But whatever the nature of his future feelings, these would be centred on the individual, not on the mass.

The train stuttered on its slow, clanking way – start, stop, stay – start, stop, stay – through the dark November night, hampered in its spasmodic progress by shot, shell and bomb damage.

'Accounts of devastation in the German cities have not been exaggerated... we passed into the Ruhr area by way of Essen and Gelsenkirchen and finally to Hamm, our detraining point. Small wonder this city featured prominently in air raid bulletins.'

Gazing across this vast marshalling yard Jim went back to thinking about Germans.

If he didn't hate, did he dislike 'the Germans'?

As a small boy, he had played at 'English v Jerries' in the school yard – boisterous, noisy, simulated aerial dogfights. As an older boy he had read many stories which featured the Hun, the Boche, the Krauts – some of the characters cowards and bullies, some absolute *Schweinhunds*, and some courageous and chivalrous, especially the 'knights of the air'.

Uncles who had served in the trenches during the Great War had spoken well of the Germans' fighting abilities but had not expressed hatred or loathing dislike of Jerry. Not even gentle Uncle Frank who, as a soldier, had been badly gassed, and as a civilian had died prematurely from toxic 'war wounds'. A half-brother Jim had never known had been killed in Flanders in 1918 but while their father harboured deep bitterness about the loss of his eldest son, the bitterness vented itself not against the enemy, but the folly of war itself – and the follies unabated that occurred within war.

With a smile, Jim asked himself, 'Do I have prejudices, then?' and answered, 'not 'arf, and all of 'em 'ealthy.' To wit: public schools; London football teams, especially Arsenal; Tory politicians – Churchill apart, Eden as well perhaps; those junior officers who with snooty accents led by exhortation rather than example, snotty nosed little buggers usually 'carried' by their senior NCOs, the very antithesis of Dave who had lived the life of a squaddie, of a lance corporal and who moved justifiably upwards; those GIs who were far too free with their money and their nylons; and sulphur tablets. All, in their various ways 'stinkers'. As for Germans he'd try to keep an open mind.

Time to detrain; into '3 tonners' and away from the fields of ruins (*Trümmerfelder*) of Hamm towards the hilly countryside. The long convoy pursued its slow, grinding gear changing way along narrow, winding and rising roads, past reservoirs and long stretches of dense, dark, dreary conifer trees. 'Don Rs' on their motorbikes scooted with brash, noisy, self importance back and forth along the snaking line of lumbering lorries, fussing rather like well-trained sheep dogs anxious to keep the flock moving at a steady pace and with appropriate spacings. These dispatch riders had news, joyful to many, to impart. Requested or volunteered, the message could not have been clearer. Loosely translated from the coarse Anglo-Saxon vernacular, it meant that German womenfolk were both plentiful and warmly accommodating.

\*

"A and HQ companies debus here."

'Here' constituted a small, attractive village set in a slender fertile valley and shielded by undulating wooded hills rising on either side of the straight 'main' road. Away from that central thoroughfare wriggling minor roads, lanes, tracks, stretched, in loose network patterns, up the hillsides. No obvious battle scars here – maybe psychological and emotional damage but no buildings smashed to rubble by shell or bomb. The valley's *Felder* seemed designed for haymaking, cattle grazing, maybe some crop growing. One field was self-evidently marked out as a football pitch. Quite a decent flat pitch at that, with its goal posts intact. An admirable prospective arena for a needle match.

Mixed groups of black and white timbered, brown and white timbered, brick, and concrete faced houses stood in pleasing jumbled and scattered patterns throughout the village. Close to the centre, in chummy proximity, lay the savings bank, the primary school and the church – Roman Catholic naturally in such a rural heartland. Between '*Kinder*' and '*Kirche*' rushed the icy waters of a broad, crystal clear stream, bouncing pell-mell over rounded pale grey stones down towards the lower, calmer reaches of the valley. At the top of a rise, perhaps a ten minute walk from the church, and at the edge of a wood, stood the *Pestkapelle*, a tiny chapel built to commemorate the victims of a plague of long ago.

Within a couple of days of arrival, Jim felt as snug as a bug in a rug. With five other sergeants and a CSM, he had taken up residence ('billeted' carried far too many uncouth connotations) in a modern, substantially built house. Such a contrast to the down at heel, pokey, brick built terraced house back in Brum where he had lived with his Mom and Dad before Hitler began mucking up people's lives.

Such richness of space in 'Stillroamin' – all of it well furnished and maintained. Attics, ground and first floor rooms and large cellars. A solid, detached house, concrete faced, its lines rather severe to British eyes, but a 'highly desirable' property with spacious gardens front and back. This cushy billet for sleeping, messing and messing about formed one of a short row of eminently respectable properties worthy, probably, of the local bank manager, dentist, lawyer, Nazi official – those middle class sort of chaps. Now, 'Stillroamin' served as the temporary home of a clerk, a butcher, a barber, a factory chargehand, a shipwright... in Tommies' uniforms. So, like old Will had so rightly said with his customary perception:

'Thus the whirligig of time brings in his revenges.'

Routine military duties had still to be established and a free and easy atmosphere seemed to develop quite naturally. But a few days later – what a radically disturbing difference. Jim found himself, if not head to head, or face to face, then certainly sideways on to – evil.

Walking to the appointed building to take his appointed seat, Jim carefully picked his way through grim and battered streets, looking up occasionally to admire the skilfully engineered, unique overhead 'hanging' train – technically the Barmen – Elberfeld mono railway system which had run for part of its eight mile route, lengthwise above the river Wupper. Human ingenuity approaching its best. A few minutes more and it would be a case of human ingenuity allegedly approaching its worst.

Jim presented his ticket to the redcap – 'Admit (Jim) to War Crimes Court Wuppertal'.

Jim stared bleakly at the five German men in the dock in an effort to make out whether they looked markedly different from the man on the Clapham bus, who was not given to torturing his fellow passengers. From where he sat, he did not have a close view but their faces seemed lined and they often frowned – but then, they were concentrating hard on the evidence being given.

Because of language complications and the newness of the war crimes trial procedure, proceedings were inevitably slow – but, as far as Jim could tell, painstakingly fair.

By comparison with what was going on down in Nuremberg where ex-national figures – Goering, Hess, Keitel, Doenitz, Streicher, Ribbentrop, Von Papen were standing trial, this Wuppertal business was far less dramatic. Yet it served to illustrate that a culture of 'man's inhumanity to man' could and did permeate various levels of a militaristic dictatorship. A British newspaper reported:

### FIVE HOUR HEAT TORTURE OF POW!

...the cell became hotter and hotter (the WO – RAF) took off his clothes and lay on the floor with his mouth a few inches from the bottom of the door to get some air. Finally he was overcome by general weakness.

Next day, for a period of five hours, he was given the same excessive heat treatment.

Fellow POWs testified to similar ordeals. Posing as members of the Red Cross, the interrogators had unsuccessfully sought to extract information about RAF operational matters.

On his thankful way back to the purer, bracing air of Kerzenbaum, Jim tried to resolve, to his own satisfaction, another puzzle. Would/could some British servicemen/women behave as those five Germans almost certainly had? He found he couldn't give an unequivocal 'no' to the question.

He thought it possible that in a few instances of aberration, British personnel could behave brutally – but not on a widespread, systematic official or condoned scale. After all, Nazism was an overtly and viciously 'might is right' creed, much given to the end justifying the means. British democracy, though still imperfect and lop-sided in favour of privilege, did not sustain itself by fear, by the knock on the door in the night and silent disappearances. No, in Britain a stink could openly and often legitimately be kicked up, about alleged injustices.

Even so, Jim shivered slightly at the recollection of one of the airgraphs he had received a year or two ago from an old mucker then serving in North Africa. Bob had mentioned a certain 'Darter'. Jim himself remembered the chap – a bit of an odd 'un.

One dark but dry night on the East Coast, the company had been slowly crawling under a large area of low strung barbed wire, carefully probing into the racecourse turf with their skewer like bayonets, for enemy mines. A short distance above their heads sang volleys of live bullets, including tracers, fired from machine guns mounted on tripods – very firmly mounted, hoped the turf prodders.

Bringing up the rear, as he usually tried to do, Darter had literally given vent, to his party piece – a totally unique rendering, in Jim's experience, of a readily recognisable version of – 'um tiddley batch cake brown bread' by a series of melodic farts.

In North Africa, Darter, a committed German hater, had got himself arrested for shooting newly captured prisoners in the back.

*

Phew, it really was refreshing to return to the charm, the slow pace of Kerzenbaum, even prettier now it was covered with a light coating of snow. Acres upon acres of dark, frowning trees had been magically transformed into sparkling white as signals of impending Christmas cheer.

It was time to show the flag though, to undertake patrols among the many, widely scattered, tiny farming communities in the company's allocated area of occupation forces responsibility. It would do the locals no harm to be reminded that British soldiers might turn up unexpectedly. Show 'em that Tommy was alive and well – but kicking only when it was really necessary.

Given the terrain, and the weather, Bren gun carriers were handy for this sort of work – reasonably quick, nimbly manoeuvrable – and gratingly noisy. They served as a warning from a distance. That might scotch a few black market deals. But it was the greedy big fish who needed to be caught. Modest black marketeering and barter were quite often essential to the survival of ordinary folk. No need to be heavy handed with the small entrepreneurs.

"Sergeant Norton."

"Yes, sir."

"I understand you know some German."

"Yes sir, but only what I learned at school."

"That will probably be good enough. I want you to take a driver and the 15 hundred weight out tonight to patrol round here." The captain indicated the designated area with a pencil. "Bit too much black marketeering going on between these two towns. Check any suspicious looking vehicle. Take a couple of reliable chaps with you."

\*

"Stationary Jerry lorry up ahead, sarge."

"I see it. Pull up in front of it."

"*Was ist hier los?*" (What's the matter?)

The slim, wiry German driver, in shabby clothes seemed a surly devil and gave a truculent reply.

"*Ich habe eine Panne.*" (I have a – what the devil was a *Panne*?)

Jim sieved rapidly through his German vocabulary – but he could recall no *Panne*. Quite absurdly a love poem flashed through his mind.

"*Du bist wie eine Blume,*" (You are like a flower)

"*So schön, so rein und hold,*" (So lovely, pure and charming)

"*Du bist wie eine Panne,*" no, ludicrous, couldn't possibly be.

A flash of inspiration.

"Show me!"

A second of wild panic; what if *Panne* was some disgusting physical condition of the driver's?

The German driver began to walk in lethargic, sullen fashion, a hint of defiance in his dragging footsteps, to the far side of his battered truck.

"Quick, Baker, nip round to the left and you, Tomkins, come with me to the right. This bolshie blighter might be leading us into an ambush."

No, the blighter was quite alone. He pointed sneeringly to a sad looking, crumpled tire. So that was it – a *Panne*, simply a puncture!

Oh well, '*man lebt und lernt*'.

Nothing worth bothering about in the back of the canopied truck – but a few days later came a much better haul. Following a tip-off, the empty upstairs rooms of a large house in the village were raided and searched by Jim with a small patrol of squaddies. Hefty floorboards were carefully prised up and eventually a large number of official looking cardboard files were lifted out of their sheltering cavities between the joists. The documents included page after page of names in neat, hand-written lists.

"This Nazi bumph seems to have something to do with the Hitler Youth Movement – records of some sort. I expect 'I Corps' will want to take a dekko at them," murmured Jim to Baker.

"Hang on a minute, there's something else."

Jim slowly brought into view a large, slightly tarnished, cube shaped tin – a pressed in circular piece of metal serving as its lid. No labels, no identification sign, just a heavy tin, full of something or other.

He sniffed at it carefully. He didn't really think it was a crude, home made incendiary device, but it paid to be cautious, especially when you've experienced one near, well, very near, miss. He sniffed again and, with his head turned away, smartly raised the lid with his penknife.

Yes, he had been right the first time, it was cocoa, about seven pounds of it he estimated. The 'authorities' could have no possible need of that. He put the tin to one side. It might well come in handy.

Partly through the diplomatic good offices of a German local government official, some of the German villagers and some of the

British visitors came to understand each other a little better and to gain a slightly more enlightened insight into their nations' differing interests and customs. But viewpoints fell into a special and troubling category.

For the Germans, fear of the knock on the door in the night had worked as a malignly powerful inhibitor of free speech, of expressing anything the least bit out of line with Nazi doctrine. Even under the benign regime of the Tommies, it would take time and patience for Germans to develop the habit of freely speaking their minds.

As for the Tommies, they could make no direct link in their minds between an obviously caring and care worn mother and the sadistic, satanic horrors of Belsen. So the lads in khaki tended to stick to homes and families for their gesticulating, well intentioned comments. "Here is a photo of my – er – *Kinder. Schön, ne?*" (Pretty).

Jim was invited to a home where three young children lived. Their mother, like many German women, still didn't know whether she was a wife or a widow. Her husband had been serving '*im Osten*', a phrase always spoken with dread, meaning terrifyingly barbaric Russia. And now? Karl might be a POW in that nightmare land waiting to be released. It was the most she dared hope.

The three children, two boys and a girl, all well scrubbed aged between about five and nine, sat in a wriggling fidgety row on a shabby, battered, but well-dusted sofa. Pinched cheeks flushed with excitement, the children giggled and whispered rapidly among themselves, a little apprehensively Jim thought, their eyes round and large with the sense of wonders to come.

Suddenly the clump of heavy boots sounded on the stairs. To the sharp, clear peals of a hand bell, the door to the small living room was flung wide to reveal a tall imposing figure wearing a bishop's finery, supplemented by brightly rouged cheeks and a splendid cotton wool beard – the august Saint Niklaus himself. Behind the saint bounded his servant, Ruprecht the Knecht, a terrifying apparition clad completely in black, his eyes glinting through slits in a mask. The quaking children were closely questioned and confessions of bad and promises of good behaviour were exacted. (Such disguised adult neighbours would know a great deal – the good, the naughty and the in-between – about the local children). Then in an act of affectionate reassurance, Saint Niklaus emptied a small sack onto the table of apples, shortbread biscuits in the shape of angels, horses and owls, and, most wonderful of all, a bar of chocolate.

Jim went back to join these charming nippers on several occasions, principally because the little blighters so enjoyed beating him at *Mühle* (Mill). This was a game of some skill played with counters on a board. Jim still hadn't fully mastered *Mühle*'s subtleties by the time he left Kerzenbaum.

Shortly before Christmas, a company based mission of goodwill towards children was organised. In faltering German Jim explained, as best he could (he was always over-concerned about his declensions – getting his word endings right, a legacy from grammar school days) why this group of clumping Tommies had come to this village hall to give away chocolates, sweets and biscuits, pieces of fruit cake, to young German children. He was heard in polite but seemingly controlled silence – a right eerie business he thought to himself.

The mothers, grandmothers, the aunts and older sisters seemed uncertain what to do. But the eyes of the children, dulled by long years of war and material shortages, soon began to glisten and sparkle as only the eyes of children can, when the presents were handed over to eager but never ill-mannered little hands. Slowly the two groups of recent enemies began to mingle, albeit self-consciously and awkwardly. '*Dankeschön*', '*Vielen Dank,*' and '*tank you – vielmals*' could be heard among hesitant murmured exchanges.

From his battle dress blouse burly Corporal Hickson drew a creased, much handled wallet and proudly produced for display a black and white photograph, "Tony, my little lad – a real imp 'e is, and no mistake!"

The snap was carefully passed around, the women's friendly smiles betraying their anxiety to say the right thing. An imp? A soft voice murmured, "*Ein kleiner Schelm.*" Puzzled frowns dissolved in the spontaneous laughter. "*Ja, mein Sohn – also imp.*" More laughter. Jim silently blessed the unknown interpreter.

The time came for '*auf wiedersehen*'. Jim turned and made for the door. As he did so, a pale faced young woman hurriedly left her companions to press what felt like a small, plain paper bag into Jim's hand. Jim quickly spun round but the young woman had been quicker, concealed now as one of a nearby group of smiling mothers.

Outside, in the invigorating frosty air, Jim opened the little bag. Inside lay a varnished wooden star, a tiny peg at its centre to hold the slim red Christmas candle enclosed in a folded sheet of note paper. Jim opened out the paper to read (the words were neatly typed in English):

>*Your goodness for the little ones is like this small light in the darkness of our time and therefore I wish you a merry Christmas and a happy New Year.*

To disguise the lump in the throat reaction, Jim yelled for the driver of the Bren gun carrier to hurry up and start the engine.

*

A few days later came a Saturnalian Christmas feast for A and HQ companies.  A celebration after the manner of Bacchus rather than Christus.

One day later, a tonic mixture of booze and bruise – the eagerly awaited match, on the football pitch, between the sergeants' mess and the officers' mess – a mixture of rugby, football and all-in wrestling, some of it in rich, ripe, cloying mud as the early snows had melted in the valley.  Perhaps that old buffer Freud would have explored, in tedious detail, why most of players, including Jim, were clad in motley, ill-matching arrays of women's clothing, much of it of a rather sturdy peasant lingerie pattern and quality.  Still, a well padded, generous sized bra did put a useful spin on a chested ball.

In a desperate rearguard action, the officers whistled onto the pitch a Bren gun carrier which, as it slewed this way and that on its caterpillar tracks, spewed up thick showers of mud.  Cads at heart, the officers.

At the touch lines, first aid was frequently required and endured with fitting manly fortitude.  No embrocation, no liniment, no aquaflavine to ease the pain; just gin, whisky, brandy for steady and generous application – internally.  The score?  Who cared?

A few German spectators had turned up – mostly elderly men, youths and boys.  They stood totally bemused, but agreed on one thing: the veracity of the description *verrückte Engländer:* crazy English.

Jim indulged in the fanciful thought that had the Germans developed and genuinely enjoyed the British type of humour, the world might well have been a damn sight better place than it had been during the past twenty or so years.

'Sans fairy Ann' he'd be off to Blighty shortly.

*Chapter Four*

# *Adieux* – And a Mane Event

Jim lurched and staggered down the gangplank. He wasn't tipsy, just struggling to keep his balance on the steep slope to dry land. His kit bag, lodged on his left shoulder, really was bloomin' heavy – but then, it was stuffed stitch straining full of bloomin' good swag, to be shared with the 'old folks at home'. He stepped onto English concrete.

"Just a moment, sergeant."

Jim looked up at the tall, fresh-faced stripling redcap.

"What's the matter?"

"Have you got your blanket with you?"

"No."

"You know you're required to carry one?"

"Yes, I know the order. But I haven't flogged it. I just thought I could do without it on this journey."

(In the unlit train carriage with its many jaggedly broken windows allowing very free circulation of the chill Winter air, Jim had experienced momentary regrets at having travelled blanketless from 'Stillroamin'. But he was fully prepared to forgo 'comfort' for greater swag bearing).

"You realise that I'll have to put you on a charge?"

"That's up to you."

Jim wasn't much bothered about being placed on a fizzer. He could well imagine the CSM's reaction when the 252 reached him. A snort of derision, the sound of paper being torn – the debris dropping into the company office's litter bin. The CSM knew that Jim had not set off home with a blanket, so he couldn't have flogged one to a black marketeer during the journey. The redcap couldn't know that, and was only doing his duty, if a touch officiously, but he'd learn.

Home to smiling faces, warm greetings and a blazing, roaring, room stifling coal fire. On the old square table a well roasted, succulent fowl, lay ready to be expertly sliced by good old Uncle Les, a broad grin on his cheerful Fred Astaire face, his shirt sleeves rolled brisk and business-like to the elbows.

Beneath the slippered feet of Jim's Mom and Dad spread small, fleecy, slightly off-white sheepskins, the essential padding for the safe transit of the main bulk of the swag hauled lovingly home from foreign parts.

On the small, highly polished, mahogany-coloured dresser stood, with round-bellied pride, five bottles, the dancing firelight glinting enticingly in the coloured glass. Three bottles of champagne, decidedly the pukka stuff, one of French brandy and one of Kümmel – as yet, an unknown, untested type of hooch.

By half past three, Jim's Mom was back in her shabby, winged arm chair, mouth open, snoring gently. Ten minutes later, after his last slurred attempt at 'Tis the last rose of summer', Wilf reverted to his favourite valedictory, "Like I 'orl," he giggled, "'orl," a snigger, "'orl lays shlay: fair play's a jooel."

He chuckled and dozed off.

With a grin broader than ever, Uncle Les set off to meet his bird of the month. Jim, after clearing the table as quietly as possible took himself off for a walk in the 'replete with memories' Handsworth Park. What was he going to do once he was back in civvy street?

*

"There's some mail for you."

Jim glanced quizzically at the CSM who had spoken in a most off-parade voice.

"Sorry, one letter looks like bad news."

Jim picked out the black edged envelope feeling more curious than anxious. His parents had not told him of anyone in the immediate family who seemed to be near death's door. Suddenly he was gripped with a stomach churning sense of dread – oh hell, it must be a friend, someone he really cared about and not just one of numerous, fairly distant relatives. Hell.

He read the words but at first they seemed so matter of fact, so empty of emotion: 'killed in an air crash'. Then the dam of rationality burst asunder and Jim found himself assailed by a surging, swirling tide of strangely mixed emotions: aching, sickening sorrow at the loss of a good pal; warm, welling sympathy for the Dad, aunt and sister; fierce, resentful anger that death had struck in this way, at this time with the war over for several months; and troubling stabs of guilt that he, Jim, remained unscathed.

Syd had become the second of his two closest friends from Sixth Form days, to be killed. Dashing, highly intelligent Doug, a Sopwith Camel 'pilot' pal of primary school playground days, had been killed in March 1945, in a crossing of the Rhine. And now Syd, a fellow evacuee and boon companion of many a schoolboy lark in Stroud, was no more. To have survived the war as a Warrant Officer navigator in the RAF, and then to be snuffed out in this idiotically wasteful way, was monstrously cruel.

With blurred eyes, Jim re-read a letter he had received from Syd as recently as mid-December. In his phlegmatic, good-natured way, Syd had bemoaned his luck at having to kick his heels on an isolated airfield in Norfolk knowing that with just a few colleagues he would be stuck there, on duty, during the Christmas period.

'I am now convinced that my luck in any sort of draw is a large minus quantity'.

A premonition? Jim dismissed that as fanciful, unworthy of pursuit. Rage and sorrow stormed within him. Oh sod war and sod all its principal perpetrators. And sod the random nature of ill luck.

He trudged angrily through the thick snow to the *Pestkapelle*. A solitary place, a quiet place in which to try and calm tumultuous thoughts. Eventually he began to focus on what he would write to Syd's Dad and the loving, doting aunt who had taken the place of the mother who had died when Syd was a young boy.

A change of duties helped to ease the way back to a calmer acceptance of fate.

Although the BAOR's (British Army of the Rhine) main duties remained those of an occupation force, the emphasis within the soldier's life began to shift, just a little, away from keeping civilians in uniform up to military scratch, in the direction of helping soldiers to turn themselves into useful civilians.

Along with another sergeant, Jim was placed on educational duties – a right cushy number. 'Mac' and he were allocated the interconnected rooms in the top storey of the school in which they were required to push back the frontiers of ignorance.

Mac, a suave sophisticate from Leeds, with an Errol Flynn moustache, and relaxed and self-confident manner, taught chaps how to drive and how to fathom the mysteries of the internal combustion engine. Jim, a gauche, 'still nobbut a lad' from Brum, offered beginners' classes in French and German. Mac's classes were always over-subscribed; would-be civilians could see the sense of learning to drive. But French and German? Well, a bit of German might come in handy for a while, but French? Useless, unless you were swotting for some exam or other.

So, in pushing back the frontiers Jim enjoyed many periods of private study, free of order giving and order taking. Ample time to gaze across the rushing stream to the sober and sedate savings bank opposite. Time to muse.

Would there come a day when he wasn't short of money when, swag apart, his parents could enjoy modest luxuries, such as a hot water geyser over the battered old kitchen sink – and in the wildest of supposes, a bathroom? Were toilet rolls, instead of torn up newspapers, too much to ask for?

Would his bachelor uncles, those who had given him his first sight of the sea back in '37, ever find themselves hooked? On his recent leave, there had been dark rumours and much leg-pulling – a jolly, rosy-cheeked widder woman for the one, and a spirited factory machine operator for the other. If weddings were nearing in their offing, would his dear old Ma finally get her teeth fixed?

Why did Jack Southern only have gin, and neat gin at that, for breakfast? Did he have secret sorrows? First line of enquiry: *cherchez la femme*. Jim wondered if he would ever hear from Mary again. Unlikely.

'We were once sweethearts, but what are we now?'

A nice melody that. But he wasn't sure any more what his true feelings for Mary were.

'Happy go lucky you and broken-hearted me'.

The first bit seemed true but the second? Overstating it that. What about: 'You're just looking for romance and I am looking for love'.

Much nearer the mark.

Then there had been Jane, who, as a no-nonsense Wren had brusquely but humorously dismissed his plaints and complaints on the lovelorn theme. Perhaps he had overdone it a bit, that 'melancholy strain' approach.

Slowly, he became aware that someone was trying to attract his attention. That short, dumpy, round faced, black-haired girl in the bank. She was waving vigorously, her broad smile quite plain. By her side, a younger, taller colleague, a pretty girl with fair hair was also waving – but rather shyly. Their boss, a man, must be out, thought Jim.

He could well imagine the two girls egging one another on 'Go on, you wave, he seems a nice young Tommy and looks as though he might be homesick.'

Homesick – no. Lovesick – quite possibly but for no one in particular. Jim strained his eyes to take a better look at the younger girl. Yes, definitely very pretty, *sehr hübsch* in fact and Jim was confident he wasn't indulging in wishful thinking.

So, from waving to talking, irritatingly too often with both girls rather than the blonde, attractive Trudi alone. But talking only led to baulking – to a frustrating nowhere. The flirtation, principally motivated as Jim supposed, on the girls' part by curiosity, remained just that, flirtation. Jim struggled, too impatiently perhaps, to make headway. But Trudi became alarmed, fearful of the possible repercussions especially back in her home village, where her father and most other menfolk took a harsh view of *Mädchen* who fraternised with British soldiers. It would indeed be a deep love that prompted a girl to accept the risk of having her head shaved bald – the badge of fraternisation shame.

Jim respected that fear, but resolved nevertheless to visit that village of primitives, but without calling on the girl or even acknowledging her should they by chance meet. His opportunity came in a curious fashion.

"Any of you chaps ever ridden a horse?" A slight supercilious twitch of the nostrils from the new subaltern.

None of the sergeants thought fit to reply. All were wary of this particular snotty young bugger who gave himself such airs.

"I suppose you're all townies, what?" it was all that he could do to keep the sneer out of his voice.

"Yes sir."

It was broad shouldered Ernie Griffiths, a butcher in civvy street, who spoke, just a quiver of suppressed anger in his voice.

"Coventry, Birmingham, Wallsend, Watford..."

"Yes, yes, yes, I don't need a geography lesson. Have any of you ever been on a horse?"

Jim took half a pace forward. He had no option. He had just been shoved hard in the small of the back. 'Blast you Jock,' he thought. He was sure it was the dark Mexican moustachioed Scotsman who had 'volunteered' him. 'I'll get even with you. Maybe I'll give that precious, prized moustache of yours a good short back and sides when you're snoring away.'

"What, you, Norton? Can't be many racehorses in Birmingham, eh, what?"

'God almighty, what a preciously reared twerp you are,' thought Jim.

"How many times have you ridden a horse?"

"Just two or three on a friend's farm in Worcestershire."

That was the plain truth. No need to tell this one pip officer and five star pipsqueak that the friend had been Mary, former schoolgirl sweetheart. On her parents' farm, Mary had become an accomplished horsewoman and, yet again, through the bewitching use of those golden hazel eyes, she had landed Jim in trouble.

Once in the saddle, Jim had tried to follow Mary's brief, giggling instructions but the horse more or less cantered its own way around the extensive paddock. At unpredictable intervals, the malevolent beast would change gear and gallop full tilt towards a large apple tree, and dash wildly under a low hanging bough with the obvious intention of having Jim swept smartly out of the saddle. As he ducked, and felt the apple leaves swish against his back, Jim distinctly heard Mary's clear laughter.

Crikey, she was more mettlesome and possibly more mischievous than the horse. He felt distinctly uneasy about what the nature of a binding relationship with her might be. Perhaps a couple of more 'lessons' followed – and that constituted Jim's total riding experience.

Pipsqueak tossed the reins of a large chestnut gelding to Jim and said airily, "You take this one, he's a bit sprightly, and allocate the remaining four to the other sergeants. See you're back here no later than 1500 hours."

Pipsqueak slapped his thigh with a riding crop and strode off.

"Mon, ye'd think he was the bluddy laird."

"And the soddin' nags aren't even his – they've been commandeered from Jerry."

"Come on, Jock, you have this one."

Jim had chosen the horse that of the remaining four looked the most vicious – a bay with a black mane and menacing glint in its eye.

Jim's plan was simple: a steady trot to Trudi's village, a drink of beer in the local *Wirtschaft*, and a steady trot back home.

His decision to take a short cut nearly led to a disaster of broken limbs. The narrow footbridge (just wide enough to accept a horse) over a raging, swollen stream, was unevenly studded with clods of ice and frozen snow. Leading his nag by the reins, coaxing and cursing in a bizarre mixture of English and German, Jim finally urged his wild-eyed, frightened, slithering, shivering beast over that near deafening torrent of the riders' Rubicon. That hazardous process was repeated four more times. The posse then rode on, not best pleased with its leader.

But spirits soon rose again as the five horsemen of the 'ippolapse' trotted on to 'Trudiheim'. It was a dull day but free of rain, the air fresh but not bitter. The novice riders shared a sense of exhilaration in their novel experience.

Having hitched their horses to nearby trees, the sergeants clumped into the gloomy but clean pub. The buzz of animated conversation stopped suddenly as if a radio had been hurriedly switched off. The few Germans who had been near the bar edged back to their compatriots sitting and standing deeper into the room. The Woodcutter's customers were soberly dressed farm workers, woodsmen, maybe a shopkeeper or two – it was Sunday.

The British sergeants turned their leather jerkin clad backs to the wall of silence, standing shoulder to shoulder at the bar. Their foam-headed beers were served in a neutrally polite manner. Whatever the eyes staring into their backs might be revealing – hate, suspicion, indifference, curiosity, anger, bitter resentment, the sergeants deliberately drank their beer unhurriedly, chatting casually to one another before leaving. Not a word of German had been spoken except when ordering the beers.

"Yon lot were a wee bit dour," said Jock as he wiped a trace of froth from his splendid black moustache.

Nothing the least bit dour about 'Fritz Blitz' as Jim had dubbed his horse. No sooner in the saddle than Fritz bolted off like a spirited colt at the start of the Derby. Jim almost lost hold of the reins. What had got into this handsome chestnut devil? Had some spiteful German saboteur placed burrs under the saddle? Jim had no means of stopping the horse to find out.

Now in full unrestrained gallop, nostrils flaring, eyes glaring, frothing at the mouth, Blitz thundered at frightening, breakneck speed along the relatively straight and flat valley road, the steel shoes ringing as they struck the icy ruts and ridges. How Mary would have laughed, Jim thought grimly, at this unsought attempt to place John Gilpin among the also rans.

Clutching desperately at the shortened reins and the horse's thick mane, Jim dimly sensed that despite the slippery, icy patches on the road, it was probably safest to let Fritz run himself to a trembling standstill, flanks heaving like over worked bellows. He glanced over his right shoulder, Jock's horse had also bolted, serve the hairy blighter right. He was the one really to blame for this whole farcical episode. From much further back, he could hear faint laughter as the rest of the cavalry troop trotted sedately along.

"Well, for non-riders you seem to have given the horses a good work-out. Anything to report?"

"No sir," Jim smirked, for he had seen Jock of jolted bones give a sharp wince.

"Well, Jock, I don't suppose you'll be doing much riding in Pullenstadt."

"Nae on a bluidy horse, mon. Neigh, neigh," he whinnied and chuckled.

Jim laughed.

"Although I'm a townie like Pipsqueak said, I shall be sorry to leave here. I like this countryside and the fresh air – not a factory chimney in sight."

"Aye – but you were mebbee gettin' o'er fond of that lassie, yon fair Trudi."

"Yes, I suppose you're right, you canny old porridge basher."

Indeed, it was time to lock the schoolhouse door, hand over the key, blow a discreet kiss to Trudi peering through the bank window, and climb into the waiting truck.

*

Jim's first impressions of Pullenstadt turned out to be more favourable than he had anticipated. No depressing *Trümmerfelder* to be seen. No immediately obvious war damage. But then this town, unlike neighbouring Essen, Dortmund, or Gelsenkirchen had not been a major centre of industrial production essential to the German war effort. No Krupps factory here.

From the fair-sized, neatly cobbled square (fronted by rather blank-faced new and old shops, cafes, pubs, a departmental store and private houses) ran narrow roads and alley ways, many of which contained older, partly timbered houses sorely in need of a good wash and brush up. Rather like the warped spokes of a distorted wheel, the horse and cart lanes and *Gassen* led to a wider circular road along which ran single-decker trams, usually pairs in tandem, their livery badly faded, their warning bells almost feeble. From this inner ring road, the tram lines branched away through various suburbs to outlying pit villages.

Almost at once Jim sensed the greater sophistication of this town compared to Kerzenbaum. More often than not, passers-by hardly glanced at chaps in khaki, whatever the numbers of stripes on their sleeves. Peasant suspicion and mistrust and surly resentment seemed to have been replaced by a poised acceptance of the inevitable.

Jim fancied he could almost hear the good burghers arguing: 'Well, you know, the British aren't so bad, we don't get on with the French, we fear, loathe and despise the Russians and as for the Yanks, well they may be free with their candy and nylons but they're a bit too free and easy with our women. At least, many of the British seem to be good-natured lads with a sense of fair play.'

'So what was the battalion here for?' Jim wondered. An early duty, or rather the reaction to it, Jim found grossly repugnant. He didn't know the details, but volunteers were sought to form a firing squad. The required number was greatly over-subscribed. One of the brutalising effects of war, to be so ready to take a life in cold blood? The great GB didn't know it, but Jim went along with Shaw – slap a child when you're angry, not with calm calculation.

Of course, there would be guard duties. A few miles out of town sprawled a huge internment camp full to bursting with some five thousand Germans, men of the automatic arrest class – high Nazi officials, high ranking Army and Luftwaffe officers and industrial bigwigs – important cogs in the Nazi apparatus for war. Let 'em cool their arrogant heels in primitive and uncomfortable conditions for a while.

Jim looked out of his billet window, to his right and across the road. Some forty yards back from the kerb stood the impressive town hall – *das Rathaus*. A very different and unmistakably foreign type of *Rathaus* from that of his native Brum, where past civic dignitaries had opted for the rather incongruous outward pretensions of a Greek temple, set in a cramped position in noisy, milling traffic conditions.

No, this Pullenstadt building looked just right in its surroundings, set back from the road with an expansive, well swept forecourt. From the back of the building stretched a park containing both formal and informal areas – flower beds, lawns, gravel paths, meadow lands, stands of tall trees and a large, clear and clean pool. All things considered, the park looked only a little down at heel, but it was still only mid-February, damp, grey and dreary. Come springtime, it might well be transformed into a place of delight, idyllic for strolling lovers. 'Stop romancing, you ass, you know well enough you had your best *Knospen* chance back in May '39. But the words still came unbidden from his memory.

'*Im wunderschönen Monat Mai,*' (In the wonderful month of May).
'*Als alle Knospen sprangen,*' (When every bud was breaking).
"Dreaming again Jim?"
Jim gave a start. He had not heard Mac enter the room.
'Wearing his brothel creepers again,' thought Jim.
"I hear you're off to Ghent. Lucky beggar. I've heard there are plenty of cat houses there."
"I don't see you've got much to grumble about – you seem to be doing very nicely already – as the actress said to the bishop." Mac gave a self-satisfied grin and smoothed his neatly trimmed moustache.

## Chapter Five

# Getting to Know – Who?

With its fine old, presumably Gothic inspired, buildings, wide canals, graceful bridges and workmanlike if shabby boats, historic Ghent impressed Jim most favourably. Such a pleasing style of architecture, so old worldly foreign, so interestingly, picturesquely different from, say, the Black Country's waterways moving sluggishly through a landscape of drab industrial grime.

By contrast, the Ghent College of Agriculture seemed, well, anonymous, 'modern commonplace', a low brick building, appropriately framed within a dreary, dull grey February sky and slightly dingy, boot-trampled snow.

But within that modern factory like shell, a cheery hive of industrious learning and imaginative teaching was happily a buzzing. For Jim, his three weeks in the classroom constituted an intellectual rebirth. If university life was something like this, he thought, then he would eagerly take a crack at a degree course – if, of course, the government would play its part with a grant. It now looked as if Dave, his great pal, would be going to Cambridge in October – on a two year 'crash' degree course. And Dave, Fleet Air Arm sub-louie hadn't even stayed on at school to get his HSC! Jim's hopes rose.

A regimental instructors' training course was the official title for what Jim was attending – in plain, specific terms, 'learn how to teach a foreign language', which was in this instance, German.

What a startlingly refreshing contrast, these direct teaching methods, from those of learning by flaming, chanting rote, oh way back in '36 in Remove C.

In Ghent, young, enthusiastic teachers in officers' battle dress taught almost exclusively in the German language itself. Students themselves had to prepare and present lessons to their classmates. Jim enjoyed exercising his imagination to explain, for example, knotty points of grammar.

A) *Die Katze kommt in das Zimmer.*
(The cat comes into the room.
Ample scope for chuckle raising drawings or mime or both.)

B) *Die Katze liegt in dem Zimmer*
(The cat lies in the room.)

Spot the difference? Of course, when there is movement towards whatever the preposition 'in' is followed by the accusative case for the noun following; if there is no movement, as in B, the dative case is used. Still a lot to be learned by heart though, *zum Beispiel*, whether a noun should be prefixed by a der, die or das. Pragmatic English was far more economical and simpler – just a 'the' for the three German definite articles.

Yes, it was good intellectual fun, designing a way to get the point across.

Good fun, of a different word play kind, was frequently to be found in the mess – plenty of booze to accompany a hearty sing-song around the Joanna, including a fair bit of the witty bawdy – repeatedly concerning the amorous adventures of three German officers who crossed the Rhine; the big wheel; a great kidney bean and, naturally, that good old favourite 'Cats on the roof tops'.

Cats on the roof tops, cats on the tiles,
Cats with syphilis, cats with piles,
Cats with de dum...
As they de dum...

The hippopotamus is a solitary moke,
He seldom has a grind and rarely has a poke,
But when he does, he lets it so o oak,
As he revels in the joys of copulation.

Wildly enthusiastic cheers for the hippo's success.
"Come on 'Shorthouse' – a recitation!"

A tall, slim warrant officer rose languidly to his feet and, in a passable imitation of the drawling voices of the Western Brothers, informed his attentive, literate audience that:

The sexual urge of the camel
Is greater than anyone thinks.
One night in a fit of passion
He tried to dishonour the Sphinx.
But the Sphinx's connubial passage
Had been blocked by the sands of the Nile.
Which accounts for the hump on the camel,
And the Sphinx's inscrutable smile.

More appreciative cheering, followed by more vigorous thumping of the piano keys.

Oh landlord have you a daughter fair,
With lily white...

With mild surprise Jim noticed that the lustily singing pianist was a sergeant, an ATS sergeant. What would the nice church going girls back home have made of her, he wondered.

Then a Saturday night hop – not quite like those of '40 and '41 in the church hall back in Brum. Ah, those dances with Ellen, Hilda, Julie – no strong drink but who cared? The atmosphere was heady enough what with young love and 'Californian Poppy'.

A nifty quickstep, a languorous slow waltz could well be interrupted by a wailing siren, the crump of an exploding bomb. But even after Hitler's worst to wreck the evening those 'goodnight sweetheart' kisses would still survive. 'In my dreams I'll hold you, goodnight, sweetheart goodnight'. Sing it again Al.

For the Ghent Saturday-nighters, local girls were invited to come along and many turned up in pairs, just like at home. Jim soon got to know a plump-faced Belgian girl, a nice enough lass, but legs not quite as shapely as he would have wished. Her disposition was a touch melancholy, too. Still, the conversation never flagged.

During a pacy quickstep Jim, while simultaneously concentrating hard on his footwork and being distracted by the big round eyes of blue so near to his bespectacled own of hazel, strained his ears to catch the drift of Anne-Marie's rapid French. A word something *polon* – something kept being repeated. A dance, a kind of sausage?

Breathing hard and sitting out the next dance, the meaning of Anne-Marie's *polon* something became clear. She had been referring to a *polonais*, a Polish soldier in the British Army, to whom she claimed she was greatly attached. But '*Polon*' wrote too infrequently and never seemed able to get leave to visit Ghent – *le pauvre garçon*. (Girlie, you're being strung along, thought Jim. Or was this just a ploy to keep 'Tommy' at a proper distance? You never could fully fathom out a woman's motives, could you? Never.)

Anne-Marie spoke and wrote good, clear English and together she and Jim walked and talked, in equal step for walking, and at a ratio of about, oh, seven to one in talking and ten to one in words spoken. They visited the Ciné Rex together: *Le Diable s'en Mêle* (The Devil and Miss Jones). '*Film parlant anglais, sous-titres français et flamands.*' Anne-Marie and Jim did not hold hands. It didn't really matter, Jim's attention was fully held by one of his favourite stars, the husky-voiced, delectable Jean Arthur.

Because of the gadabout pace of this social life, Jim's cash began to run low. It was time to tap the resources of the black market. Accompanied by a fellow student, Tom, a sergeant in a similar plight, Jim sought contact with the seamy side of *la vie Belgique*.

With an air of bravado, Jim drew back the heavy, dusty curtain and stepped into a large, ill-lit room smelling of stale tobacco smoke, cheap scent and just a hint of what might have been carbolic soap. He formed a vague impression of well-worn, shabby, sagging chairs and couches about the place, their once gaudy fabrics now badly faded, frayed and stained.

He approached what appeared to be a writing table where business might be done, thinking to himself;

'Crikey, if this is the oldest profession, then these three must be among the founder members!'

The head girl of the three crones, all heavily rouged, thickly powdered, crudely lipsticked, motioned the two sergeants to sit down.

"You boys early – but you want jig-a-jig? We can do – but will cost more. Very good this time of day jig-a-jig."

She leered, her teeth showing brown, stained and uneven. No smile appeared in her dull, red veined eyes. Her ghastly companions leered and snickered in unison.

"*Mais oui, très bon after le petit déjeuner – le jig-a-jig.* We fix – but cost you more."

"No thank you."

The raddled dames raised their plucked and painted eyebrows in what seemed genuine surprise. They thought of another tack.

48

"You boys are boys who like help yourselves? We can help – nicely."

One crone, inspired by that thought, picked up a wooden ruler at one end, and, with her other lightly clenched hand cupped around the exposed centimetres, she began to move her painted talon fingers rhythmically up and down.

"What we want is money. We have soap and cigarettes to sell." These precious items were placed on the table and bargaining began.

Reasonably well pleased with the exchange, Tom and Jim paused as they left 'the premises', to take in great gulps of purer air.

"Beats me how chaps do it, even when they are partly drunk, to make so called 'love' to such hideous hags, who have obviously been laced more times than an old boot."

"Well, Jim, you know what some of them would say."

"What's that?"

"You don't look at the mantelpiece when you're poking the fire!"

\*

Back at Pullenstadt Jim prodded suspiciously with his fork at a mess of moist, dark green vegetable on his otherwise appetising plate.

"What the dickens is this, Duffy?"

In reply the sergeant cook, red and merry of face chirped, "You may know a fair bit of German, Jim, but some things you know sod all about. That's spinach."

Spinach, eh. Well, his uncles and Grandad had never grown it on their allotments. His Mom had never cooked it – he would have remembered. Still, if it was good enough for Popeye, Jim Norton would give it a go. Yes, it did taste good, another mouthful – yes, very good.

"That should put some lead in your pencil – and more twist to your table tennis wrist. You'll be at the club tonight?" Jack Southern, who had now given up hard liquor, at least for breakfast, had put the question.

"You bet."

Jim greatly enjoyed his off-duty visits to the Sonnenberg, the only drawback being that its facilities, a good, well-stocked bar, a small dance floor, table tennis tables, had to be shared with the riffraff WOs and sergeants of other units stationed in and around the town.

The small country house type premises had once housed the best restaurant in Pullenstadt, for the members of the German professional classes, lawyers, doctors, senior bureaucrats, and later, higher ranking officers in the forces. Some of that lot, thought Jim, may well be down the road in the internment camp. No need to dwell on that. It was much pleasanter to play table tennis and to take a leisurely, appraising look at the fillies in the paddock, the four German girls who hurried and scurried about with heavy trays laden with full or empty glasses of beer. It was part of their job to sit and chat civilly with the soldiers within the four walls. Outside those walls, fraternisation, for the girls, remained a risky business.

Each of the four, all in their early to late twenties, was attractive in her own way. For a start, the becoming black and white uniforms caught the eye - not least the black stockings readily visible to the knee, so emphasising shapely calves and trim ankles.

Take Freda, for instance, by far the oldest, pushing thirty, Jim thought. Bold black eyes, bubbly of manner, black-haired, wilful and temperamental. Yes, fiery Freda, a buxom wench with sparrow thin ankles - funny, he'd noticed that combination of features before. Freda was married with a young daughter, but as a mother like many others, she still didn't know whether she was wife or widow and what's more, didn't seem to care. She'd take from harshly bruising life anything from which she might benefit. She and Mac became bosom, well, big bosom pals.

Freda appeared to bully, cajole and sweet talk a younger girl, Heidi, in the bossy manner of an older sister taking advantage of a younger. Heidi, the shortest of the four had gentle, pleasing features, a trim, nicely proportioned figure, hair of a light gold colour, and clear, honest grey eyes. She seemed far less worldly than the other three waitresses, possibly vulnerable to exploitation, but, instinctively, so it seemed, good-natured.

Thea looked to be broad shouldered, or perhaps it was just oversized shoulder pads that created that impression. You never knew your luck, there might come a chance to find out. Thea was certainly the tallest, the most sturdily built, with fresh, rosy cheeks, sparkling blue eyes, a happy grin and very sturdy legs. She looked like the healthy daughter of a healthy farmer. With brown hair piled high above a broad forehead, she looked as though she would stand no nonsense from anyone, including a brood of children she had the hips to bear.

Sweet-faced Gretchen was arguably the prettiest of the four. Just a touch of coquettishness about her shy, sly smile and slight ducking of the head as she looked from under her raven-dark eyebrows at those around her. Her deep brown tresses hung thick and lustrous, her eyes shone a deep liquid brown. A comely girl to cuddle and cherish – for there would be competition. 'I'll bet there are some rum aspects to her character,' thought Jim, 'never forget the old adage: still waters run deep.' He thought of Julie and '41.

Such were the sketches that Jim made in his mind of the girls who carried the drinks, engaged in small talk and looked with some interest, at least for the first time, at snapshots from back home in Britain.

Of course, Jim acknowledged, I could be completely wrong about any one or all of them. He wondered if the battalion would stay long enough in Pullenstadt for him to find out. But what the dickens – his appraisals didn't really matter anyway.

Duties called – away from the beauties to the 'beasts' in their internment camp. After being served by pleasant German girls, it became Jim's turn to mount guard over surly, resentful German men.

Such a dispiriting, depressing place that CIC. Whichever way the guards or the guarded looked, high fences of meshed barbed wire confronted them. Between the inner perimeter of the compound and an outer wire fence ran a strip of cleared, bare land, some forty yards wide. At strategic intervals stood the standard issue wooden watch towers of the conventional prison camp. These rough and ready structures gave good vision across the camp and along the sanitary cordon, and could provide a good field of fire, if need be, along that cross-me-at-your-peril strip of bare earth.

The paramount duty for the guards was to prevent any prisoner from escaping. To assist the edgy watchers, a special squad of soldiers had been formed, men carefully chosen for their pronounced lack of refined manners. The 'Ferrets' job was to make surprise raids on the prisoners' huts and search with a due measure of vigour and uncouthness, for signs of possible escape attempts.

In the warm sun of early spring, some of the prisoners, in civilian clothes, strolled about, bare to the waist. Some among them had obviously lost weight, rather dramatically at that. Ample, and probably boast-worthy belly blubber had once been theirs. The blubber had gone and the skin that had once smoothly contained it now hung in loose repulsive folds. Jim felt no twinge of sympathy for such men. No doubt their earlier grossness had derived from the fleshpots' dividends of the Herrenvolk creed, the plundered goods of conquered peoples, the surpluses produced by slave labour. Let 'em lour and glower – such men fully deserved their comeuppance and their come down in the world.

There came a period when ordinary German workers began to be awkward, especially the coal miners. It was alleged that under Communist influence, the *Bergleute* were operating a go slow. How to improve productivity? Look tough – send squads of senior NCOs to stroll about the pit heads armed with Sten guns, loaded magazines purposely just visible, projecting from between the centre buttons of battle dress blouses.

The sergeants concerned, Jim included, felt a bit 'silly' at carrying out such a duty.

"I reckon they'd work harder if they had more grub," growled Jack.

"Aye, more snap, schnapps and sausages could do the trick," murmured a sergeant who lived near a Nottinghamshire coal field.

A day or two later, there followed another productivity improvement drive in a large, meat products producing factory – mainly churning out sausages.

Jim didn't much care for the walk through a long narrow passageway, open to the sky, but bordered on either side by shallow, wooden, roofed over stalls. From the underside of the jutting, sloping roofs hung the carcasses of large animals, some with sizeable streaks of blue-black and purpley flesh, suggestive of death by old age. Jim could have sworn that a few of the unhealthy looking carcasses were those of horses. In a moment of wild fantasy, he sincerely hoped that one of them did not belong to Fritz Blitz. It could never be right for such a fine animal to end up inside wurst. Jim was glad that Jock, just a few paces behind him, had not given his imitation of a whinny.

Whew, what a relief it was to return to Duffy supervised cooking.

"The new club opens tonight, Jim. Will you be going?"

"Sure thing. Pity we had to leave the Sonnenberg, though. Some fiddle there, you can bet."

"Well, it won't be far to stagger home from." Jim and his fellow A Company sergeants were now lodged above a cafe. A large comfortable lounge, well furnished and boasting a piano, hosted many an all male boozing party cum sing-song.

Oh, what do they do for a sing-song in Sing Sing?

And,

> Susie, Susie sitting in the shoe shine shop.
> All day long she sits and shines,
> Shines and sits, sits and shines.
> Susie, Susie sitting in the shoe shine shop.

"Come on, young Jim, you know you can sing it faster than that. Don't be so bloody fussy with your pronunciation. Speed it up a bit. Have another whisky to oil your tonsils. Give old 'Crackerjack' (the pianist) there another drink. Oh, and while you're about it, one for the pianner as well." Bill was in an expansive mood that evening.

Crackerjack duly received two lots of beer. With the slow, careful deliberation of the semi-drunk, he carefully emptied one large glass through the open lid of the up-right, into the heated innards of the pianner.

"Here, have another?"

He struck a note with one finger.

"Don't mind if I do, shez the pianner."

"Get on with it, Jim, let Susie rip."

Jim, slurring some words, sang at a good round pace with the customary mirth making transpositions of sh's and s's that inevitably followed increased speed.

Bill, now approaching the maudlin state, requested, "One for the ladies – bless 'em."

A ragged chorus followed,

"Goodnight ladies, goodnight ladies, we're going to leave you now."

Actually, the three ladies had left hours ago – a German cook, a German kitchen maid and the German kitchen maid/waitress, still a maid, or so she made out, the redoubtable Helga.

Bonny Helga, another rosy faced, sturdy, peasant type girl with a wide mouth, somewhat coarse features and a disposition that veered capriciously between innocence and the ardent desire to be something less than innocent. For one thing, she wanted to learn, to understand Tommy's sense of humour. (A tall order, Jim thought). Helga usually knew when she was being teased, she could answer back with sharp elbowed jabs but not with sharp tongued words.

In his clumsy, rather severe Scots Presbyterian way, Jock took a shine to Helga and intervened protectively, if he thought the bantering teasing was getting too near the knuckle.

One day at the kitchen table, Helga was vigorously but vainly trying to shake free from its clinging round tin, some kind of gelatine laden mess of pressed meat. Only slowly did the mottled brown cylinder of part of a dinner to be emerge, the tin to be shaken yet again.

In her loud, slightly hoarse, slightly rasping voice, Helga asked, "Vot the English for vot I now do?"

A cockney voice immediately replied, "Helga, you're wanking it – just great."

"Vanking?"

"Nae mon, that's nae fair."

Jock's voice held a tremor of anger.

"Sorry – just kidding, only kidding."

"Vot is vanking. Vot is kidding?"

A bit too 'abstruse' all this – even for the direct method.

Jim dodged away.

*

So, from the saloon of the 'booze bashed ivories' to the new club, Kaffeekanne. Not a patch on the Sonnenberg, of course, for grandeur, size or elegance but this new club generated a snugly *gemütlich* atmosphere, most emphatically so. Although not very wide, the room stretched a fair distance from its inviting front (near the town square) way back to where another large window allowed a clear view of a grim looking church standing in an expansive paved area.

The town side of the room was filled with good quality cafe, say Kardomah standard, chairs and tables for both serious but more often merry making drinking – and raucous singing. On the forbidding church side, where perhaps the floor was a yard higher, smooth parquet blocks provided an area for the musicians and the dancers.

As Jim arrived, the highly skilled professional pianist was darting his hands about the keyboard to present a rippling, catchy tune,

Si, si, si sing your love song for a penny,
Si, si, si just a penny serenade.

Yes, quite the wizard on the ivories, the blond, bland, perpetually smiling Hubert. On gala evenings like this, he would be joined by a fiddler and an accordionist. Great survivors, thought Jim, these professional musicians – probably all consumptive though.

He glanced around the room. Hubert and his oppos were now playing a waltz, not the strenuous galloping kind, but a slow waltz – a pleasingly dreamy German tune that Jim later learned was called 'Melodia'.

Looking pensively at the dancers, seemingly free, for the moment, of hurrying and scurrying, Heidi stood tapping one slim foot. Jim, a bit rusty in his dancing technique since Ghent, 'stiffened his sinews' and all the rest of it, and asked Heidi to dance with him.

Heidi gave him an abstracted smile and fell lightly into step. After a few pleasing turns around the dance floor, she stopped, pushed Jim in the direction of Thea, who now seemed to be free, and said, "Sorry, I have duties. I am needed at the bar." Thea with her broad, farm girl like hands grabbed Jim and nearly swirled him off his feet. Despite the spinach intake, he still weighed only about ten stone. Oh well, on with the dance.

## Chapter Six
# Night of the Numbskulls

"We want you to carry on with educational duties – especially teaching German. You will be with Sergeant McDonald as in Kerzenbaum. Sergeant Bates will also be joining later. All three of you will answer directly to Captain Morgan, the unit Education Officer. Of course, you will still have to carry out guard duties as required, both at HQ and at the CIC. Understood?!"

"Yes, sir."

You bet, sir – three bags full, sir.

Jim certainly understood – and greatly rejoiced. What a cushy number, a real doddle, a piece of cake. So much free time to mooch about the town centre, to wander through the extensive park nearby, to suss out the whereabouts of the open air swimming baths reported to be a couple of miles from Battalion HQ, now stationed in a fairly large, modern, municipal office block. Of course, the transfer would mean leaving the old gang of Jock, Ernie, Jack and the others to join HQ Sergeants' Mess. Still, here was a good reason for a boozy farewell party. The Joanna should be dry by now.

The HQ sergeants, mostly specialists, seemed just as convivial as those in A Company: Mick the medic; Dick in charge of the navvies (the pioneers); Ken, Motor Transport; Duffy, of course – the cook radical who had introduced Jim to spinach, the only sergeant who, by his appearance, suggested what his trade might be. Round and mottled red of face, his ear to ear grin caused his eyes to screw up to the apparent size of currants, warmly glistening black currants. Here was a man of natural joviality, surely destined to become a popular pub landlord. Even in battle dress, the signs of a swelling beer and plum duff belly were plain to see.

Just one snag though about this good-natured, easy going but efficient group – Tara would be its boss! Tara the terror, the formidable, ram-rod straight backed regular soldier RSM. Would he have forgotten, forgiven Jim's lamentably inept, first attempts to toe the line, that blasted line on the asphalt, when mounting HQ guard for the first time, oh way back, when the two dirty great bombs had been dropped on the Japs? Would Jim find himself constantly ribbed about those literal *faux pas*? Jim didn't relish the prospect. But he needn't have worried.

"Hey, Duffy, is Tara joining us?"

"No, not this evening. Got his hands full again I shouldn't wonder."

A roar of laughter arose around the mess table, with only Jim not joining in. He looked puzzled.

"You'll understand in due course, Jim."

"Oh good."

"Yes, he's got his hands full alright – and not just with regimental duties."

Another burst of laughter followed.

On the occasions when Tara did join the mess for meals, he seemed far less intimidating, far less terrifying than on the parade ground or at ceremonial duties. Quite like an older brother in fact, wise in the ways of the military world, a brother who took a marginal but kindly, if slightly condescending interest in the follies and ignorance of a still wet behind the ears stripling. He made no allusion to the 'Who do you think you are, the bloody Duke of York, marching 'em up and down this ruddy slope' incident.

But it needed quite an effort of will on Jim's part to bottle up the bubbling laughter when he realised the nature of 'his hands full again' joke.

Tara, middle aged romantic that he proved to be, had formed a deep, and apparently genuine, attachment to a lonely German lady of lusciously ripe years and proportions. Would Junoesque be the word? Stately beauty – most decidedly. Tara liked to share, even to dwell on, his admiration for this mature popsie's plenteous physique. With near poetic fervour he described the lady's breasts as being 'as smooth and as white as alabaster.' Such a refreshing change from the coarser prose of the barrack room's 'nice pair of tits'!

*

Jim smiled at that recollection of a recollection as he placed a single daffodil in a vase on his desk – a touch of spring colour in otherwise drab surroundings.

The education unit, now in easy, languorous swing, stretched through a number of rooms set immediately beneath the roof, dormer windows affording a view of the battalion's trucks parked in the yard below. Mac, looking as dapper as ever in shirt sleeve order, at last had some good gear with which to work, including cut-away sections of engines so that their crafty inner workings could be better explained.

In addition to classrooms, a small library was provided and, what luxury, a room fitted out with easy chairs, officially the 'Quiet Room' for contemplation and study, unofficially known as 'The Flanker's Retreat'. Altogether, a doddle of a place in which to carry out a collective doddle of duties.

Jim looked at his watch, soon be time for grub, maybe accompanied by another spicy, illuminating account of 'the deep division of prodigious breasts'. Good for Tara, and his lady love, that he had such large hands. So, with such pleasing thoughts, spruce up, Jim me lad, knot the tie carefully, and saunter off to the Kaffeekanne, imaginatively rechristened the Hammer-On Club. No longer a case of 'hammer on regardless', of military perils and trials but rather 'hammer on for demob', with approximate dates now known for the return to civvy street.

Club membership was slowly dwindling. Ernie and the CSM would soon be making tracks for Blighty, back to being butcher and barber respectively. Jim's demob number was 45 so he expected to be home around November. And then what? Time enough to think about that. Anyway, his last employer would be duty bound to offer him some sort of job.

"Where's Jock tonight?"

"Oh, as per usual, making sure that Helga doesn't seduce Jack and that Jack doesn't corrupt her English – which isn't bad for a Scotsman."

Jim grinned and looked around. Yes, all four waitresses were on duty, all looking a snip in their crisp black and white uniforms. Most of the Hammer-On regulars from the battalion had also reported for duty – to John Barleycorn, or rather his German equivalent. A few chaps from other, by definition inferior mobs had also turned up.

Through the open doorway that led to the bar limped a WO II from one such mob. He made his steady, assured way to a round table at which two of his buddies already sat. 'Limper' drew a fourth chair to the table, sat down himself and with the smile of accustomed authority motioned Heidi to join 'his' group of drinkers. Light of foot, and eager to please Heidi quickly threaded her graceful way between jumbles of chairs and tables, took the order and soon returned to Limper's table. At his self-satisfied invitation, she sat down on the vacant chair and began to smoke the proffered cigarette.

'She really does have a very nice profile,' thought Jim, 'a slight upward tilt to the nose, fine spun, blonde hair cascading in soft waves down to the nape of the neck. Compared to her colleagues she seems quite dainty, nothing like as coarse grained as fresh faced Thea.'

Heidi tilted her head back slightly, puffed out blue grey smoke and gave a few gentle coughs.

'But she's no smoker,' mused Jim who, while never having smoked himself, had remained a close observer of other people's smoking habits. 'She's faking it, just like Dad does. She's trying to appear sophisticated and worldly but I can't believe that is her true nature – or that she's enjoying that cigarette. She's basically the innocent type, I'll bet – but is she gullible?' He remained troubled about Limper's possible designs on a 'really nice girl'.

Without making it too obvious, Jim continued his careful watch on Limper's table. Limper was doing most of the chatting. 'Coming the old soldier' Jim thought, as the WO II turned soulful eyes in Heidi's direction. Her expression seemed friendly and sympathetic. 'I wonder what bullshit he's spinning her now? Graphic details of his war wound and how it came about? Will she fall for it, all this spaniel-eyed flannel?'

As Limper occasionally tapped Heidi's slender forearm, presumably to emphasise a particularly poignant point in his harrowing life, Jim felt a surge of rage and jealousy course through him.

'Well, it's her own lookout. She seems basically free, she's wearing no engagement or wedding ring, she's certainly white – a pleasingly softly pinkish white really – and almost certainly twenty-one or over. No, it's no business of mine.' Suddenly, Hubert the bland and Fiddler Fritz struck up 'Melodia'. Jim's mood changed abruptly.

'Just for a lark, let's put the bugger (he meant Limper of course) to the test. I'll ask Heidi to dance. If he says Heidi's already promised to dance with me – then his limping is exaggerated or a sham. Let's find out.'

Heidi seemed mildly surprised at the invitation but made no move until Limper, frowning slightly and not looking best pleased at the interruption, had given a permissive wave of the hand.

"I like this tune – it's pretty."

"Yes, it is."

"Are there any words to it?"

"Yes."

"Perhaps you'll tell me what they are some time?"

"Perhaps, if I have time."

Heidi looked anxiously in the direction of the bar. Jim twirled her so that the bar was kept out of sight.

"You do more than your fair share of work, you know." Heidi flushed slightly.

"What makes you say that?"

"Well, I've watched how you girls work with one another. The other three spend far more time chatting at the tables than you do – especially Freda. In England we would say 'you are the willing horse' always ready to fetch and carry more trays than the others."

"Villing horse – vot does that mean?"

Golly, was there an equivalent German expression?

"Well, if there is someone who..."

The music stopped. Heidi quickly freed her hands from Jim's and darted away.

During the following week, on several evenings Jim wangled a dance or two with Heidi. Hubert wasn't above a spot of bribery and for a few fags would play the occasional reprise of 'Melodia'. (*Hörst Du mein heimliches Rufen?* Do you hear my secret call?)

Heidi began to thaw slowly, oh so slowly. She would now spend a few minutes at Jim's table, asking the occasional question about his home life, life in England generally, striking up the kind of conversation a traveller might share with a total stranger in a railway station buffet.

Jim enjoyed these quiet, stumbling exchanges with a gentle-natured girl. But his efforts to fathom the thoughts behind those clear grey and oh so honest eyes, met with no success.

Then came the night of the numskulls to throw everything out of kilter. And to make matters worse, Limper had played no part, well, no apparent part, in the primeval proceedings.

There was nothing unusual about the start of that evening but for some inexplicable reason it was as though everyone had decided to go on a classic bender – to musical accompaniment.

> Sons of the seas,
> (Bobbing up and down like this)
> Sailing the ocean,
> (Bobbing up and down like this)

At the first 'b' of bobbing, and at every subsequent bobbing, each soldier would rise quickly from his seat, sit quickly, and then rise again always with his glass in hand – until the final 'this' was reached. The more vigorous the bobbing, the greater the spillage, and the greater the frequency of refills. *Prosit*! *Zum Wohle*! Down the hatch! Bottoms up! *Gesundheit*! And no one was sneezing.

> No you can't beat the boys of the bulldog breed
> (For bobbing up and down like this)

Breathless laughter and warm applause followed the cease-fire and heave to.

The theme didn't need to be nautical, oh no, for another round of joyful bobbing to begin.

> My old man said foller the van
> (Bobbing up and down like this)

A romantic favourite could become mirth raising.

> Daisy, Daisy give me your answer do,
> (Bobbing up and down like this)

As the evening staggered forward, a sentimental, slightly maudlin mood affected some of the topers;

> Underneath the lamplight by the barrack gate,
> Darling, I remember the way you used to wait;
> [...]
> My own Lilli Marlene.

Jim hummed to himself,

Vor der Kaserne, vor dem grossen Tor
[...]
sie bliesen Zapfenstreich.

'Blimey,' he thought, 'try and say that with a hot chip in your mouth!'

*

"Right, thash enough of that, I want Ave Maria."

"Randy little sod," came a muttered chorus.

"Hey, Hubert and fiddler man – Ave Maria and no messin' about."

A wiry sparrow of a sergeant took off his shoes, clambered laboriously onto a table and, swaying slightly, gave a fine, reverential, if shlightly shlurred rendition of the holy song. He was heard in respectful silence broken by a storm of cheering when he fell silent, his eyes moist with tears.

By this time the waitresses had retreated behind the bar, passing in trays of drinks as required. Not that anything offensive, crude or of a rough house nature had so far taken place. But the girls knew from their experience with their own former German customers that strong drink could affect weak men in many different ways – some of them decidedly unpleasant.

After Ave Maria came a general mood change, from the reverential sentimental to challenge and show-down.

"Hey, Nobby, me old mate, I'sh brought the bisc... bis... bis... queem kwackers. Wot about it then?"

'It' meant challenge. Two men sat facing one another at a table. Before Nobby was set a glass of beer and a teaspoon. In front of Dusty, the challenger, lay two dry biscuits. Nobby had bet that he could drink his glass dry simply by using the tea spoon before Dusty could finish eating the two biscuits.

"Right, let battle commence."

Nobby set quickly and rhythmically to work totally absorbed in his task.

"Hey, Nobby – you look a right old Charlie." Dusty coughed explosively, laughed and spluttered all at the same time, showering biscuit fragments all around him. He couldn't eat. He could only rock on his seat and laugh.

Therein lay part of the drinker's success. Only accept the challenge when the opponent is sufficiently squiffy that he's ready to laugh at almost anything – the dry biscuits would do the rest. Jim knew from experience. He had won one such contest as the drinker, a week or two earlier, when still with A Company.

'But, crikey, how squiffy am I now?' he thought, his face hectically flushed, his senses swimming. 'I'll bet some swine has spiked my drink.' He glowered across to where Limper had been sitting.

He giggled, frowned, wiped his eyes and concentrated with unconvincing gravity at the unfolding scene. Chairs and tables were being pushed back to the highly polished, waist high wooden panels of the walls to create a clear space in the centre of the room, a splendid 'arena', ringed by cheering soldiers, for the battling rams.

"Right, Muttonhead," yelled the short wiry sergeant of 'Ave Maria' acclaim, now reshod, as he glowered defiantly at his opponent standing at the opposite end of the empty oval space.

"Right, you little cockney bleeder," bawled Muttonhead, a burly man, not much above middle height, but with a short, thick, muscular neck and strong corrugations in his low beetling forehead.

Between them, but to one side, stood Ernie, soon to be back among the carcasses of his butcher's shop.

"Right, when I say 'Go' you both charge. Got it?"

"He'll get it alright," muttered Cockney Bleeder.

Muttonhead contented himself with, "Cheeky little sod." Waiting for the signal, both men started to snort loudly and to scrape the soles of their shoes on the wooden floor in the rhythmically menacing manner of bulls preparing for a spot of bother. Each man held both arms stiffly parallel to a slightly forward leaning trunk, head forward but erect. Muttonhead's stoop was the greater in order to maintain eye contact with the shorter Cockney Bleeder.

Bedlam, cheers, stifling heat, an atmosphere charged with the visceral thrills of violence. The girls, bemused but curious, strained to see, between khaki shoulders, what was happening. From the corner of his eye, Jim saw Heidi turn her head away.

"Go!"

The rams set off at a wavering slow trot but steadily gathered momentum.

C E R R A C K!!

A full head to head collision.

Bleeder staggered back a few paces, looking dazed, and fell onto a chair thrust rapidly beneath him.

With all the grace of a dropped sandbag, Muttonhead sat down where he had stood, looking mildly surprised.

A storm of cheering erupted.

"A draw!" bawled Ernie, as cool as if he had been wrapping up Mrs Ramsbottom's sausages.

A positive hurricane of cheering followed.

A few moments later, Muttonhead and Cockney Bleeder were sitting side by side, one of Muttonhead's great paws resting, friendly like, on Bleeder's narrow shoulder.

"Hey, Tich, do you know," he paused to emphasise clearly the words "that old fashioned mother of mine?" Tich frowned and winced.

"Corse not – never bin to that 'ell 'ole of Oldham."

Muttonhead blinked, looked puzzled, then grinned.

"No, you bloody fathead, the song."

Tich frowned again – and winced again. His look of sozzled concentration yielded to smiling recognition.

"Gorrit. I'll give it a bash when me bleedin' 'ead's stopped throbbin'."

He softly began to croon

"She wears no fine clothes, no rich silken hose..."

'Time I wasn't here,' thought Jim, 'shust like to get my head down in the old flea pit, the good ol' flea pit, the goo, ol' char, char char – what – ah, charpoy. Shlow me the way to go home, I'm tired and oh God, I'm tired and...'

He walked unsteadily into the night air to find the world reeling about him in a dizzying blur of cobblestones, pavements, tipsy leaning buildings that closed menacingly upon him. After deep breaths of the mild, early spring air, and a steadying grasp of a lamppost, "Golly, you've lost a bit of weight, Lilli!" he sniggered and lurched off with uneven steps in the general direction of his billet. Who the hell had slipped him that Micky Finn? Oh, God he did need to get his head down, but not in the gutter, no not that, please not that. He wearily shook his head a few times and staggered past shabby old houses that fronted a winding narrow lane with even narrower pavements. All was still and quiet, except for the sound of his own softly echoing footsteps.

Suddenly, he felt his shoulder tapped. He swivelled slowly around, managing by an immense effort of will to stay upright, vaguely curious to identify the tapper.

*"Komm, Liebling,* you are tired. Come – and rest with me."

The voice was warm, inviting.

Once more a slender arm and slim fingers beckoned. Jim went closer but couldn't make out the girl's features or figure in the dark, unlit interior of the room.

What the hell. He knew his defences were down – so might be, in a few minutes, his trousers, to be followed by his regulation issue drawers, cellular. What a lark. He giggled.

*"Komm Liebling, komm."*

Ponderously, Jim applied his Higher School Certificate noddle to the problem – how to cross the threshold to bliss. Now, the window sill was what, oh something less than three feet above the pavement. All he had to do was to raise his right leg, sit on the sill, raise his left leg – 'oh, do the hokey, cokey' – he giggled again, and then topple down onto the floor of paradise.

Okey, dokey – let the cokey begin. Several times he raised his right leg to a horizontal position, but couldn't get it resting securely on the sill. He tried from the other end of the sill lifting his left leg first. Still no good. He tottered back, spluttering with mirth.

"Blimey, can't get my leg over to get my leg over! Bad show, what!"

The girl was patient.

*"Komm, Schätzlein,* try once more. It's not high."

"No, me old darlin', but I'm as high as a kite."

*"Bitte?"*

Still, ever polite, Jim did try to please the lady. For encouragement, the girl pressed Jim's face against her warm, soft breasts.

"Crikey, nothing of an alabaster nature there."

Jim tittered and struggled for air.

*"Komm,* sweetheart, *schnell."*

The girl leant out of the window, bent over and kissed Jim full on the lips, a long lingering kiss – a real, tingling smackeroo.

'Golly her breasts smell lovely but her breath isn't very fragrant!' thought Jim, trying to identify through his fuddled senses, the nature of the odour. 'Got it – must be that bloody garlic some of our chaps rave about. Knob something in German – ah yes, *Knoblauch*. Bet this wench has enjoyed a good few knobs in her time.' He giggled. 'With knobs on!' he giggled helplessly.

"Ish no good, sweetheart, I'd be no good. Probably fall ashleep as I fell inside."

He staggered to and fro – and waved a slip–shod farewell.

"Not tonight, Josephine or Hannelore – or whatever your name is."

He wended his wavering way towards that blessed charpoy and flopped luxuriantly into the arms of Morpheus.

'Goo ole Morph', she sought nothing in return for her bounty.

## Chapter Seven

# Strolling in the Park

Just a few hours later, that same day, Jim was gently brushing his teeth, grimacing as he did so, for a whole division of miniature road workers was frenziedly attacking the underside of his skull with their tiny, merciless jackhammers. Suddenly, he stopped, partly because of the blinding pain, and stared stupidly, sottishly at his brush. It was flecked with bright blood. He carefully washed the brush and then, with even slower care, resumed brushing. More blood among the tooth paste. Had he damaged his gums by his clumsy, half sozzled efforts at oral hygiene? He washed a little finger and ran its tip carefully along his gums. Yet more blood.

With a jolting, sickening feeling of dismay and self-disgust, Jim recognised the cause of the bleeding. Gingivitis! That was why 'Josephine-Hannelore's' breath had smelt so peculiar at the time of the smackeroo! Nothing to do with garlic but a great deal to do with her graceless 'love' life.

Jim felt too ashamed to contemplate at all seriously the sensible idea of going to see the MO. As his fuddled, whirring thoughts struggled to find a focus for action, he suddenly remembered 'Granny's remedy' for sore throats and the like, to wit rinsing and gargling with a solution of household salt and water. He resolved to give this remedy a good try – and did.

As his reeling, throbbing headed thoughts steadied a little, he realised how narrow had been his escape from catching a 'dose' of the dreaded clap, the fearful pox. He shuddered outwardly and inwardly, to think of the misery and mortification that would have followed what would have been, for him, a physical and moral catastrophe. He had not been among the jeerers, the piercing whistlers, and ironic cheerers when prophylactic films had been shown to warn squaddies of the dangers of VD. Such noisy, boisterous reactions to the shots of grotesquely distorted privates' privates suggested futile bravado. Ugh! He shivered at his recollections of the obscenely ugly results of one night of 'love'. Thank the Lord, and the powers that might be, that the 'dire warnings' had not been filmed in 'glorious Technicolor – or colour'.

Still, his luck was in, just as it had been at the time of the exploding detonator in the Northumbrian wood. Then, an inch of space had saved him from disaster. And now, just think, had the wooden window sill been an inch lower, or the pavement an inch higher, he might well have fallen victim to an 'explosion' of filth in his body. He shuddered again.

He vowed never to find himself in such a sottish state or potentially perilous situation again. No, he wouldn't go TT, that would be overdoing things. Besides, he readily conceded that he had gained something in self-knowledge from the excess drinking spree. It would seem that too much alcohol did not turn him into the garrulous, argumentative, aggressive 'wanna fight?' type – but placed him well within the giggly, sentimental, sleepy school of topers. He reached for another glass of salt water.

He acknowledged it wasn't just his own self respect he was concerned about. No, he wanted to gain the respect, even the affection perhaps, of a nice girl – say someone like Heidi. He didn't believe she was the prudish kind but he had already formed the impression that the sort of crude language and behaviour that Freda would have laughed at and brushed aside, Heidi would have puzzled about and possibly found offensive.

Yes, he did want Heidi to like him. But why? He wondered about the source of her charm. She seemed kind and considerate, spontaneously so by nature, not by studied artifice. Much of her appeal, he decided, lay in her natural quietness and what he took to be an instinctive aversion to 'showing off'. And dammit, yes, although he hadn't made an attempt, he had so wanted to kiss her. But the night of the numskulls had firmly put the kybosh on that alright. He rinsed his mouth again.

For several evenings Jim kept away from the club. The saline mix seemed to be working. The bleeding became less and finally stopped. To be on the safe side though, Jim waited another couple of days before returning to Hammer On.

As he entered, Heidi, returning a tray of empty glasses to the bar, nearly collided with him.

"Oh, it's you. We thought you had left us."

"No, I've been rather busy – and, well, I wouldn't go away without saying *auf wiedersehen*."

Heidi looked at him just a little quizzically but said nothing.

Jim glanced away, feeling uncomfortable. He was glad when saucy Freda came to join them.

"Nice to see you back, Jim." She smiled archly at her friend. "Heidi's missed you." She rattled quickly on to prevent a denial.

"Now you, *Kinder*, why don't you join Mac and I tomorrow afternoon. We're just going for a stroll in the gardens, the ones by the *Rathaus*."

In his eagerness, Jim forgot his manners and quickly answered first.

"Well, I'd certainly like to – but, of course," he added somewhat sheepishly, "I can't speak for Heidi."

Heidi looked vexed, a little troubled at becoming the one placed 'on the spot'.

"Well, I've got a lot of ironing and some mending to do and..." She saw a look of disappointment cross Jim's face, and hurried on "but I dare say it will keep a day or two."

So began a short pattern of foursome strolls, followed by a slightly longer one of two by twos. Then, when debonair, 'England's women need me', Mac was suddenly posted back to Blighty, Freda, never one to be a gooseberry, took up other pursuits, so releasing Heidi and Jim from a mesh of idle, flirtatious chatter.

Slowly and cautiously on Jim's part, slowly and timidly on Heidi's, the strollers exchanged information about their respective lives and countries. Each wanted to avoid wounding the other by a careless comment or question about the war, Hitler, Belsen, or loyalty to one's country.

"My mother is not happy that I go for walks with a Tommy."

"I can understand that. But you know quite a number of Tommies and we're not too bad are we?"

"No, that's what I tell her – and that one particular sergeant Tommy is quite nice."

She gave Jim's arm an affectionate squeeze.

"And what about your Dad?"

"What do you mean?"

"How does he feel about his daughter *spazieren gehen* with a Tommy?"

"He's not so strict as Mom and he trusts me."

"And do you trust me?"

Heidi hesitated.

"Well, only up to a point."

Her grey eyes danced with mischief. She gave him a winning, winsome smile which he took to mean 'come on, try and kiss me'. But he held back. His gums now had not bled for some ten days but best wait a couple or more days before taking this sweet girl in his arms.

They walked on for a few minutes in silence, Heidi looking just slightly miffed and a little puzzled and Jim slightly embarrassed.

"By the way, what does your Dad do for a living?"

"He's a coal miner and he spent much of his working life underground. But since he developed what we call *Steinstaublunge* he's been working at the pit-head, in the open air, in the saw mill."

"His lungs are badly clogged with coal dust?"

"Yes, his breathing is very wheezy and he coughs a lot. Mother is always on at him to give up smoking – or at least cut it down. He likes a drink too."

"Well, I suppose he feels a few fags and the odd drop of schnapps are modest enough pleasures for a man whose illness is only liken to worsen."

"Yes, there are lots of men in our village in a similar state. They meet and compare notes with one another about their failing health. It's very sad really."

"Would you like to give these cigarettes to him?"

Jim fished a packet of twenty from his battle dress blouse pocket. Heidi appeared flustered.

"It's all right. You needn't say they're from me if it causes complications. Use some of them on the black market if you like. Go on, it's all right, really. I don't smoke as you know, but I still take my fag ration. Please take them, do." Heidi dropped her head and lowered her eyes.

"You are a kind young man, Jim. Thank you so much."

She picked up the packet and placed it carefully in her overcoat pocket. The spring air was still nippy.

"Now tell me something about your Dad. What does he do?"

"Well, he trained as what we call a gem setter in the jewellery trade – rings, brooches, that sort of thing."

"Please, what is 'gem'?"

"*Edelstein*. But what with the economic depression of the '30s and a serious illness, he was quite often without work when I was a boy. During the war he worked on security jobs, as a kind of guard or watchman, in munitions factories. Now, of course, he's an old man, nearly seventy."

"Is your Mother that old as well?"

"No, she's oh, some fifteen years younger. My father was a widower when he married her. So I have three half brothers and a half sister, and some nephews who are nearly as old as myself. Dad's eldest son was killed in France in 1918 just before the Great War ended."

"Killed as a soldier?"

"Yes, on the Western Front."

"Does that mean your Dad hates Germans?"

"If he does, he has never said so. At least as far as I know. He's bitter about war, about Capitalism and about John's death."

"My younger brother, Hans, was also killed in France, in the spring of last year. He was only a boy, just nineteen."

"I'm very sorry."

Jim put a comforting arm around her slender shoulders.

"My parents don't say much – but I know they grieve deeply. They miss Hans terribly. We don't know for sure where he is buried or even if he has a grave. Not knowing makes my parents feel awful."

"You have no other brothers or sisters?"

"No."

"Well, with you as their 'only chick', as we say, it's natural that your parents should be very concerned about your welfare."

"Yes, that's true, but I try to be a dutiful and conscientious daughter. I hope I am."

"Yes, I'm sure you are. You're certainly very conscientious at work."

Jim squeezed her shoulder.

"But I still want to lead a life of my own."

"Of course, don't we all? Any way, that's enough serious talk for a bit."

There was a pause, then, "Right, young sergeant, Jim – I'll race you round the pool. Just give me twenty metres start."

"OK, off you go."

Heidi darted gracefully away with Jim hot on her heels, keeping just a metre behind so that she remained well aware of his nearness. He took care not to overtake her and at the finishing line, she turned to face him, her cheeks flushed, her eyes sparkling from the cool air, from exertion and the thrill of the chase. Jim waited a few seconds until she had regained her breath, then flung his arms about her and kissed her warmly – *einmal, zweimal – und noch einmal*, for luck.

Heidi gently released herself and together they walked back in silence to the Kaffeekanne.

\*

As he had done in years past, Jim rejoiced in observing how trees and shrubs first budded and then broke into the freshest of fresh green leaves. Nature could be so enchanting, so beguiling at this season, especially when you were in the company of a young attractive girl – a Mary for example, and now a Heidi.

> In the Spring a young man's fancy
> lightly turns to thoughts of love,

That old josser Lord Alf had got that much right, except perhaps for 'lightly'. Why lightly? Thinking about it, Jim supposed lightly was spot on, say for a seventeen year old, a sixteen year old even, as he himself had been during that magical, memorable May of 1939. What wonderful times he had shared with Mary in that enchanting bluebell wood. He smiled and then frowned. Now it was March 1946. All those cherished adolescent memories seemed part of someone else's life in a distant land. Mary had been only fourteen at the time. Jim recalled he was now approaching twenty-three when you couldn't, shouldn't take things so lightly. Nor too sombrely either. He was quite ready for another race around the pool.

"Penny, as you say, for your thoughts?"

"No, they're worth rather more than that."

"Will a *Groschen* do?"

"No, ten per cent of a mark comes nowhere near the mark." Heidi smiled, a little puzzled still by the curious English habit of playing with words. There had been nothing eccentric like that in her Lutheran schooling.

The pair walked on in silence in the direction of a rustic bridge.

"Jim, don't you have a girlfriend in England?" Women were the very devil sometimes. They did seem to possess a special intuitive sense where possible rivals were concerned.

Jim swallowed hard.

"No – at least not in the sense that I think you mean girlfriend."

"But you have had girlfriends?"

"Yes, but not many. To be honest with you, I was very fond of one particular girl but I was only fifteen, sixteen at the time, and she was only fourteen. It was a situation of what we call in England calf love."

"I think I understand. What was her name?"

"Mary."

"And what has happened to Mary?"

"I'm not really sure. I think she may be training to be a nurse."

"You didn't see her on your last leave?"

"Didn't even try to."

"And who came after Mary?"

"No real girlfriend, but several friends who happened to be girls, you know, someone to go to the pictures with, or to a dance."

"I quite thought there'd be some nice English rose longing for the day when you left the Army."

"No such luck."

"I wonder why. You seem to be a nice enough young man?"

"Why thank you, but then I'm possibly pretty choosy."

"At least I can believe you are not married. You have no ring on your finger."

"That's no proof. In England plenty of married men do not wear a wedding ring. For all you know, I might have a wife and several children."

Heidi pouted slightly – but delightfully.

"Now I think you tease me. You English always want to what you call it – pull the leg?"

"I suppose we do. We do it all the time to one another. Perhaps too few foreigners understand that."

"You won't tease me unfairly, will you? Please don't."

Heidi's voice sounded anxious.

"No, I can promise you that. And if I think others are teasing you too much, I'll stop them."

They paused to look over the rail of the bridge at the clear stream below and the young willow trees on either bank.

"Tell me please, why didn't this Mary stay your girlfriend?"

"It's difficult to say in a few words. We were very young, I think she tired of me and then the war came and, as in so many cases, we drifted apart."

"Was she anything like me?"

"Not really."

They were now walking alongside the pool.

"I'll give you an example. If say, Mary and I were walking like this, and if she's much the same now as she was at fourteen, she might suddenly dig me in the ribs with her elbow and shove me down the bank, perhaps hoping that I might slide into the water."

"What a strange girl, your Mary."

"Not really – she was only fourteen and what we would call something of a tomboy."

"Tomboy?"

"Yes, a high spirited, boisterous girl who likes to take part in boys' games, in fact behaves rather like a boy – until she falls deeply in love. Now you wouldn't push me down this slope would you?"

Jim affected mock apprehension.

Heidi affected hesitation and gave him a shy kiss.

"And now *Fräulein Neugier* 1946 – Miss Nosey Parker – what about your boyfriend? You are pretty and pleasant enough to have had plenty of young men following you around. Plenty of the chaps at the club seem to like you. Come on now, I have been frank with you."

Heidi's face clouded even though she knew such a question was inevitable.

"Like you, I have been choosy."

"Not good enough, I want to know more."

Heidi remained silent, thoughtful, wondering what to say. Suddenly she blurted out, "I was once engaged."

"I'm not surprised, but I'm not happy."

"Well, you did ask. Yes, I was engaged to a tram driver. So now you know."

Jim experienced a sharp spasm of deep loathing towards all German tram drivers.

"So, why aren't you still engaged – or perhaps you still are?"

Jim felt quite sick at that thought.

"No, I'm quite free, I broke off the engagement."

"Care to tell me why?"

Heidi paused to think hard, very hard. "No, I'd rather not."

And there the tram driver was left, at his terminus. Well almost so.

"Only to say that he was a friend of my brother who was an apprentice carpenter with the same tram company before becoming a soldier. Anyway, it's all in the past."

With a sudden change of direction away from the pool, Heidi, equally suddenly, switched to a different topic.

"When do you go home on leave again?"

"Don't know really. In a month or two. Sometime in June I imagine."

"Will you tell your parents about me?"

"I already have, in letters of course."

Heidi stopped.

"*Ach Du Schreck*! Whatever for?" The girl seemed discomfited, ill at ease, "Are they not very disappointed to learn you go out with a German girl?"

"No, and they're not surprised either. They'd be more surprised if I did not write about German girls. They'd think then I'd got something to hide. They trust me like your Mom and Dad trust you. And I don't see that you need to tell parents everything when you're nearly twenty–three. Just think, in a few days time, I shall have caught you up. It is sometimes quite nice to go out with an older woman."

Heidi frowned, looking puzzled.

"Yes, that 'older woman' bit was just a joke. Come on, smile."

Heidi did so and giggled.

"That's better. By the way, have you always been a waitress since you left school?"

"No. I trained first as a seamstress but things didn't work out so then I trained as a waitress. But I still like sewing very much and making dresses. I'm always altering something or other for Mom."

"Any good at mending soldiers' socks?"

"Maybe. But I haven't yet had the opportunity."

She smiled, a hint of challenge now in those large grey eyes.

"Just how do soldiers get their socks repaired?"

"Oh, we are issued with what is called a *Hausfrau...*"

"Now you my leg again pull."

"Not altogether. What we are given is called a housewife a sort of little wallet. It contains needles, cotton, bits of wool, a few buttons."

"So, you can sew on buttons?"

"Of course."

"Now tell me what you did before you obtained a *Hausfrau*?"

Heidi giggled again. She was catching on.

"I worked in an office as a clerk."

"Will you go back there?"

"Possibly. I expect to hear from my old employer soon. But there's a chance I might go to university."

"University!"

Heidi seemed impressed.

"You must be clever."

"Well, I easily decided you were the pick of the bunch of four."

Heidi laughed.

"Time might tell."

Again there was much to think about as they walked slowly back to the Kaffeekanne.

## Chapter Eight

# Conversations

"Geroff, geroff!"

Jim's voice was thick, his words slurred. In a low, growling mutter he continued, "Pack it in, you twerp. I've told you already I don't want to buy one of your bloody battleships – not even the blasted pocket size."

In his dazed, less than half awake state, Jim's thoughts dreamily surfaced from Nissen hut memories of a prankster about to dip Jim's wrist in a bucket of ice-cold water.

His comment on the repeated and vigorous shoulder shaking was markedly crisper.

"Sod off!"

He turned over on the camp bed to face the wall. It was no good, the shaking continued.

"Sarge, Sarge! Wake up, there's a couple of Fräuleins here, right crisp crackling they are."

Drowsily awake now, Jim answered irritably, "Well, you see to 'em. You're supposed to be the Don Juan of HQ Company!"

Lance Corporal Enfield smirked at the compliment.

"Well, normally I'd be glad to, Sarge. But they're both asking for you by name."

"Cripes!"

Jim sat bolt upright and swivelled rapidly around to sit on the edge of the bed. He sniffed trouble. After smoothing out the rumples in his uniform and running a comb through his hair, he stumped, in hob-nailed boots from his sheltering alcove into the guardroom proper. In the open doorway stood Frau Freda and Fräulein Heidi, both smiling warmly.

"*Guten Abend*, Sergeant Jim," they chorused cheerily.

"*Um Himmelswillen,* what are you doing here at this time of night?"

He looked, sounded and felt cross.

Unruffled, Freda continued to smile an impudent, defiant smile. Heidi looked at the ground, her smile replaced by a look of flustered anxiety. Jim thought, 'Well, I suppose Heidi won't have a clue that she's not supposed to be here. Still, she's got to learn. Off duty is one thing and on duty quite another. Freda will know well enough that she might be leading her friend into trouble – and me into the bargain. She's a scheming cat – mischief and no mistake. Yes, she's trouble, big trouble.'

"We've not long finished work... and as you might suppose, Heidi has missed your sunny smile at the club. She wanted to see what a British Army guardroom looked like and she also wondered..."

Here, Freda hesitated, not on account of Heidi's frantic warning glances and agitated finger movements but simply to calculate how far she dare go. '*Zum Teufel*' she seemed to say to herself. She was speaking German rapidly so it was odds on that only Jim among the Tommies present might understand.

"Yes, Heidi wondered if we might find you asleep and we had a little bet about whether you snored."

Heidi's downcast eyes seemed hypnotised by the grimy grey concrete floor but her cheeks flushed deep pink at Freda's mischievous revelation.

Jim pretended not to have understood.

"You must both go and go quickly. If an officer finds you here, I shall be in real trouble. Go on, quickly now, go."

"Jim, you're a real old crosspatch tonight. Sweet dreams though – of you know what and you know who."

Jim flushed with anger. He wasn't going to let this saucy, worldly wench get the better of him. Damn her attractive, roguish black eyes, her challenging, beguiling smile. He would not let her be the possible cause of his being taken down a stripe or two. Quite apart from pride, manly and martial, a post-war gratuity related partly to rank was not to be sniffed at, certainly not if he was to become an undergraduate on a student's grant.

"Corporal Enfield, escort these young women to the main gate!"

"You bet, Sarge."

*

"Jim."

"Hmm."

"You're very quiet. You're not still angry with me about my visit to the guardroom?"

"No, not really."

He squeezed Heidi's hand reassuringly.

"I sometimes have a short temper. But I usually calm down pretty quickly."

"Well, tell me what is troubling you so – please."

Jim reflected as he strolled with Heidi through the drab, down at heel shopping centre. They mingled unselfconsciously with German civilians, mostly middle-aged women and elderly men, with a few soldiers here and there.

"I had a nasty shock the day before yesterday and another one yesterday."

"Not bad news from home, I hope?"

Heidi looked concerned.

"No, nothing like that."

"Do tell me, please. Close friends should share sadness as well as joy – isn't that right?"

"Yes, of course – but."

"*Aber*? Come on now, I am grown up."

Still Jim hesitated. He didn't want to hurt this gentle, sensitive, good hearted girl. He struggled to find the right words. But he accepted that Heidi and every single German should know, should be made to know, about such things.

"Two days ago we were ordered to attend a special film show at that *Kino* near the railway station. Many Germans had to go as well. It was horrible, frightening."

"What was?"

"What we were shown. Films of the German concentration camps. I never thought human beings could be so cruel to one another and the cruel ones were the Germans."

Heidi visibly shivered. Her grey eyes clouded with tears. For a moment or two she stayed silent and then looked imploringly into Jim's eyes.

"Jim, you do believe me, don't you, when I say that I knew nothing of such terrible, terrible things? Neither did my parents or families like ours."

"I do believe you."

And in truth he did. Except for the 'accident' of being born German, he could make no connection in his mind between the temperament, character and fine, natural human decency of the girl beside him and the sadistic monsters responsible for Belsen, Auschwitz, and Dachau.

"With Hitler and the Nazis in control, there were many bad things ordinary people in villages like ours did not know about. Even at home we had to be careful not to say the wrong thing. A few neighbours were out and out Nazis. It was difficult to know who to trust at times. One of my uncles was sent to prison for making a joke, in a pub as you call it, about Hitler. One of the neighbours, a party official, reported him to the authorities." Jim was tempted to ask what the joke had been but knew this wasn't the occasion to do so.

"It must have been frightening at times."

"Yes, more frightening in a way than air raids because you weren't sure who to trust."

"Was your village bombed?"

"Luckily, no. Many bombers passed near on their way to the Ruhr so we had to shelter quite often in a very big concrete bunker in the main street. It was hot, smelly and uncomfortable. Ugh!"

"Was it British troops who captured Beckmühle?"

"No, it was the Americans. First of all, we were shelled. That was very frightening. Our flat was badly damaged and we had to move out. Then the American tanks came and for the first time in my life I saw black men. It was strange."

"There are no soldiers in Beckmühle now?"

Heidi smiled – that shy, slightly enigmatic smile of the eternally baffling female.

"Perhaps there could be one."

"Oh."

"Yes, if you came to see me there one day."

Before Jim could say anything, Heidi hurriedly continued, "But tell me, Jim, what was it that made you feel sad yesterday?"

"A letter from the headmaster of my old school. He wrote to thank me for a payment I had made to a fund to be used to honour the memory of old boys from the school killed in the war. My two closest friends from my last year at school were both killed. We had shared some wonderful times together especially during 1939 and 1940 when we had been evacuated from the city to the countryside."

Yes, the letter had been warm and friendly yet a touch schoolmasterly in tone.

'My dear Norton' – 'Crikey!' Jim had thought, 'but for the courtesy greetings, I could be back in the Sixth Form.' Still, the dog-collared head had gone on to describe Jim's contribution (five pounds) as 'splendid'. Perhaps, in relation to his pay, it was but it seemed trivial, irrelevant even, to the sense of great loss. Doug and Syd had been such great pals. How many more from that group of fewer than twenty lively lads had gone West he wondered. A lump rose in his throat.

A soft voice disturbed his brooding.

"Jim," Heidi's face showed concern.

"Yes, *Schätzlein*."

"Hitler was a really evil man, I know that."

"One of the most evil men, perhaps the most evil man, who has ever lived."

"But you won't judge all Germans by him?"

"No, of course not. I haven't done that so far and I don't intend to start now."

"*Gott sei Dank*."

"Come on now – we mustn't let that sort of thing damage our... our... our... *was soll ich sagen?*"

"*Freundschaft?*"

"That, of course and..." Jim hummed a snatch of song "*Es ist die Liebe, Die dumme Liebe...*"

"Well, I'm not so sure."

"Nonsense. Do shut up."

Jim kissed her warmly, in the secluded doorway of a boarded up shop.

\*

"You don't really like me very much do you?" The question, bold and direct from the questioner, man-eater Freda, put Jim doubly on his guard.

"What makes you say that?"

"I can tell."

"Really?"

"Yes, from your attitude and from your behaviour in the guardroom the other night."

"You were in the wrong. You knew it yet you still encouraged Heidi to join in such *Dummheiten*."

Freda bit her full lower lip in vexation. This wasn't at all the conversation she had planned.

"All history now and I wanted to talk to you about something else."

"What?"

"Some photographs."

Jim raised his tufty blonde-brown eyebrows but said nothing.

"No, nothing like that – not naughty postcards of naked ladies – and some gentlemen."

"So?"

Fun loving Freda, sitting opposite Jim, lent forward in a confidential manner, showing her full bosom and black, sparkling eyes to best advantage. She placed one warm hand just above Jim's left knee.

"Heaven's above!"

"What do you mean?"

"Just that – Heaven's above!"

Freda looked puzzled, frowned and then flung her head back to release peal after peal of melodious, merry laughter. She sat back on her chair, giggling and with a playful wave removed her hand from Jim's thigh.

"I see what you mean. You wouldn't have said that to Heidi."

"No, of course I wouldn't. Compared to you, an experienced woman of the world, Heidi is an innocent babe."

"So, let's get back to the photographs."

"Yes, lets."

"I have a German officer friend."

"That doesn't surprise me."

"Please try not to interrupt. I really am trying to tell you something that might interest you."

"Go ahead."

"This officer was on duty when the British bombers attacked the Möhne and Eder dams. He wasn't supposed to, of course, but he took a number of photographs of hits made on the dam and of the damage that was done. While he's not prepared to let you have the photographs, he is willing to lend you the negatives so that you can have photographs made. He will pass the negatives to me. What do you think?"

"Naturally, I am very interested but what does your friend want in return?"

"Two things only. Some cigarettes – and the promise that you will return the negatives."

"He can certainly have my promise but as to cigarettes..."

The haggling began.

A day or two later, Jim began to study with interest the tremendous damage caused by the heroic Dambusters to what he took to be the Möhne dam.

The photographer himself must have been a daring chap, not only for having taken such photographs when vicious tyranny still held sway as it did in 1943, but for approaching so close to the broken edge of where the dam water rushed through a jagged gap with Niagara-like ferocity. The air was thick with drifting spray but through it could be seen one of the two towers atop the dam.

Other, clearer photographs, obviously taken later, showed a steady waterfall dropping through the immense, near semi-circular gap carved out between both towers by the rushing waters.

Two 'postcards' revealed something of the aftermath of the dam's destruction. Looking, at mud level, back towards the dam at a distance of some two hundred yards, it was as though some gargantuan excavator had bitten a half moon from the centre of the dam, nearly equidistant from each tower. To left and right on the great waste of mud lay great sprawling piles of massive planks and timbers, jagged, broken and strewn about like untidy heaps of giant-sized spillikins.

In the reservoir, or what had been the reservoir, direction, stretched a mess of mud, muddied stone, muddied water – as unappealing as any reservoir must look once its plug has been forcefully pulled. And this basin of water supply for the Ruhr factories and homes had been quite a basin, several miles in length as far as Jim could remember.

For the attacked and the attackers the whole experience must have seemed apocalyptic thought Jim, something akin to an Old Testament horror story. So much energy, so much ingenuity, so much courage; all to destructive purposes. Jim, at his most philosophical thought 'God we are a barmy lot!'

*

"Jim, shall we have a cup of coffee?"

"Suits me, but where?"

"In my flat if you like. I've been meaning to invite you for some time but..." the words tumbled over one another, Heidi looking a little embarrassed. Jim did the decent thing.

"Never mind, we're not far from the Kaffeekanne at this minute which is what matters now."

"Of course, it's not really my flat. It goes with the job. Most of the things in it don't belong to me. Just clothes, some crockery and a few personal things."

She blushed slightly.

"Show me the way then."

Heidi, light of foot, nimbly climbed the broad, bare wooden but well waxed staircase to the first floor. On the small landing before her door, she turned to face Jim, her cheeks flushed, her smile warm and welcoming, her manner excited.

"*Herzlich Willkommen lieber sergea...*"

The sentence remained unfinished.

After a few minutes, Heidi wriggled free of Jim's warm embrace and panting slightly, she opened the door to the flat, which comprised a cosily furnished lounge, modest in size but not cramped – a small bedroom to one side and a cubicle of a kitchen.

At the far end of the light, high ceilinged room a large window looked onto that grim, disapproving, locked and bolted church that Jim regularly walked by. The window itself could be fully screened by day by fine meshed, net curtains and by night thick curtains of heavy material would be carefully drawn to fashion a snugly private nest.

It was not a room characterised by feminine fripperies and vanities but, as Jim had expected, everywhere appeared tidy, clean and cared for. No nub ends lay in the ashtrays. To say 'neat as a new pin' would have been an exaggeration – for chairs, an occasional table and floor coverings all showed signs of heavy wear.

Jim glanced curiously at a few small, framed photographs set on one wall.

"This your Mom and Dad?"

"Yes."

The father's face looked drawn, his features, especially his nose, sharp and his fair hair thin. But he was smiling. Probably a good natured man, Jim thought, and one born to toil. Come to think of it, not too unlike an older version of his own Uncle Les. The mother had a much rounder face, a warm smile, a good mop of dark hair and strong, even teeth – in appearance a bit like his Aunt Nell, but much tougher, he suspected, in physique and character.

"And who's this sergeant chap on the chest of drawers? He looks a bit of no good to me."

"You should know," came the amused voice from the cubicle.

"Please sit down. Coffee is nearly ready."

Heidi glanced around her, "Yes, I do like living here. It's so much nicer than having to go home at all sorts of hours and having to share what little space we have with my parents, good to me though they are." As an afterthought she added, "And there's a bathroom here as well, on the next floor, shared with the other girls of course."

"Yes, I can well understand how you enjoy the freedom and the space here – and the hot baths. We have no bathroom at home. I do have my own bedroom but three of us in the tiny living room does cause a traffic jam sometimes, and when relatives come – whew!"

"Tell me please, what is traffic jam?"

"*Eine Stau.*"

"Ah, so."

"You know, Jim, I would like to learn English properly."

"So that's why you've invited me in for coffee?"

Heidi frowned.

"No, of course not. I-I-I like you anyway – for yourself."

"Sorry, I was only joking."

"You English, you're always joking. No, please teach me and help me to understand. I do really like your language."

"That gives me a good idea."

"Oh, what?"

Heidi's voice betrayed her uncertainty.

"No need to be alarmed, *keine Angst*. But if I've got it right, Hitler's abysmal thinking in regard to women was summed up in the three Ks. *Kinder* (children), *Küche* (the kitchen) and *Kirche* (the church). Well, guess what. I've thought of three quite different Ks – much more appropriate for Heidi Braun, yes, much more." Jim grinned broadly.

"So, what are they then?" Heidi couldn't fully conceal her apprehension that a joke was about to be played on her.

"*Ruhig*, like I said '*keine Angst*'. My three Ks are *Kaffee*, *Kenntnis* (knowledge) and *Küsse*."

Heidi laughed with relief – and pleasure.

"Well, I've had the coffee, I've given you a little *Kenntnis* so it's time for…"

"K three?"

"Exactly – more if you agree."

A near silence ensued.

"Jim, that's enough."

"Just one more for luck."

Another silence.

"Just one for the road."

"One last one, then you must go."

Silence.

"My English lesson, it is over for today. Please go."

Jim moved to the door. Within seconds Heidi had called him back.

"Jim, please promise me one thing."

"If I can. What is it?"

"Please don't teach me the dirty words of your language."

"No, I won't do that. We don't use such words in my home nor do my friends, not before girls anyway, but…"

Heidi looked up anxiously at the 'but'.

"I think you should know some of them in case you hear them spoken by other people."

Heidi reflected.

"Perhaps you are right. Anyway, I can always ask you if I'm puzzled about something can't I?"

"So long as I'm here."

"Oh Jim, I shall be so sad if you have to leave."

"Cheer up, I think we'll be here another few weeks yet, so as we say, it's a jolly good English expression – 'Let's make hay while the sun shines'."

"Let's make hay while the sun shines." Heidi repeated slowly, musingly, "I suppose that could mean many things?"

"It could. Give me a kiss and think about it."

## Chapter Nine

# Personal Questions

"Good old Rams – they well and truly stuffed 'em and no mistake."

"But that's what rams are for, as the actress said to the bishop."

A chorus of laughter anticipated 'the bishop'.

"The result will certainly please Tara. He comes from Derby, doesn't he?"

"Think so."

"After this win, I'll bet he'll be well on target like Jack Stamps – with Lady Alabaster tonight."

More ribald laughter.

Six HQ sergeants, and the jolly, moon faced Dutch interpreter attached to the battalion, had been listening outdoors to the radio broadcast of the Cup Final. The weather was so relaxingly warm, so brilliantly sunny that several of the men had stripped to the waist. Jim, clad only in bathing trunks, sat, like some colonial wallah, in a cane armchair having first made sure that a piece of thick matting rested securely on the seat. He too rejoiced. Great stuff that! A London, well near enough London, team had been thumped, thraped, walloped, even if it had taken extra time. Charlton one, Derby County four.

"I wonder if it's a record?" he asked of no one in particular, "one chap scoring for both sides in a cup final, and in such a way. First, sticking the ball in your own net and then, a minute later, scoring for your own side." He mused on, "Great forward line Derby's. I wish Villa had players like Duncan, 'Raich' Carter, Doherty and Jack Stamps."

"Never mind the useless Villa. It's time you got some clobber on. Don't forget we said we'd take Mrs Müller's kids out to the park after the game."

A tall, slim, sergeant with slicked back hair and wearing glasses had interrupted the after match analysis.

"Right, Terry, be with you in a tick."

Mysterious Mrs Müller, née Frobisher, who lived just a few doors away, had married a German a year or two before the war had begun. Soon after his transfer to HQ Company, Jim and later Terry, had been tactfully approached by this well spoken lady, ostensibly because she longed for English conversation once more.

Occasionally Terry and Jim were invited to take tea and biscuits in Frau Müller's large, comfortable, well furnished home. Jim smiled, recognising how his homespun Mom would have raved and been green with envy about the real bone china on plentiful display in the handsome, spacious glass fronted cabinets – with some of it in use for careful tea sipping. Had she been there, Jim would have squirmed in embarrassment, as his Mom assumed her most refeened Mothers' Union committee member voice.

As it was, Jim supposed he must be in the home of someone from the well-heeled middle class – a German equivalent of one of his evacuation period billets in Stroud, that of the 'seedy' Captain's – no tablecloths, but lace place mats on fine, burnished wood, that sort of thing – and memsahib with her cut glass voice.

Herr Müller had gone to war but had not yet returned. Jim would have liked to ask many questions of Herr Müller's wife, but he held back because earlier attempts to discover something of Miss Frobisher's history had been politely, but deftly, parried with vague, generalised comments about life with a capital L.

Again he glanced at the lady. Yes, she could have been any one of a number of his middle aged, matronly aunts at the posher end of the family, Aunt Gertrude, for instance who lived in stately (kippers and curtains) pride in Sutton Coldfield. Well groomed and dignified in appearance, Frau Müller was assuredly no beauty in Jim's eyes – far more your Margaret Rutherford than your Margaret Lockwood he thought. This stately lady appeared to be in her early forties. She must have borne her children late; the eldest girl was about eight, the twin girls about six and the lively nipper, young Helmut, was a boy of about three. All four youngsters were well clad, kept spotlessly clean for visitors, and showed excellent manners.

How had Frau Müller coped in the late 1930s in a country so virulently anti-British? *Gott strafe* England and all that. And had she experienced agonising inner turmoil arising from the struggle between love of England and love of husband? No comment had passed her lips to suggest that she had ever entertained Nazi sympathies. But you couldn't rely on that. Only those now glowering behind barbed wire might be ready to voice, or at least not deny, their support for the Nazi cause.

What had Frau Müller felt, thought, said about the Nazi gloating over the raid on Coventry? How had she handled probable local hostility after the Dambusters' raid? After all, the *Ruhrgebiet* was only a few miles away. So many questions could be asked for which no answers would be given.

One factor in the inter-locking conundrums seemed clear, at least as a fair assumption. Miss Frobisher must have loved Herr Müller very deeply to have left her free speaking homeland to live such a different, don't step out of line, fear-haunted life in Nazi Germany.

Suddenly, it occurred to Jim that some slight parallels existed between his own developing life and that of Mrs Müller. He could now acknowledge to himself that he had fallen in love with a sweet natured, tender-hearted girl who, until about a year ago, had been 'one of the enemy'. Jim was pretty convinced that Heidi experienced similar feelings for him. Daunting complications beckoned.

He, again like Frau Müller, was not in his homeland but probably unlike her experience, he felt secure, fully at ease, living quite unthreatened as a member of an occupation force, surrounded and shielded by close military camaraderie, potential military might and the sense, in no way smug, of moral superiority stemming from the absolute rightness of the Allies' victory over a repellently evil regime. But what say, if Heidi ever paid a visit to England, how might she feel in an alien land, as a single individual of the defeated *Herrenvolk*? She would know no one except himself. No parents, no relatives, no friends, no colleagues, no neighbours or acquaintances, to provide any kind of support. It could be devastating, desolating – nasty remarks directed her way... and yet... sneers and snubs... and yet...

"James."

'Who the dickens was James? He was never called that except by his Mom and only then when she felt cross with him.'

"James," a firm, clear, but not unfriendly voice.

He looked up. Mrs Müller had seemingly asked him a question.

"I do beg your pardon. I was daydreaming. It's a habit of mine I'm afraid."

Mrs Müller gave a gracious, dismissive wave with one hand and poured him another cup of tea with the other.

*

The spell of fine warm weather continued – as was only right and proper, for it was May time, 'hey nonino' time once again. Time to strip off and plunge into the open air swimming baths just a few miles away. Getting there was no trouble as the motor pool sergeant was a member of the Tarzan gang.

So, on some sunny afternoons six or seven men became six or seven schoolboys once more, at least for an hour or two. Dick, of the pioneers, took care to remove his false teeth before leaping, with a Tarzan yell, into the refreshing water. Duffy, still inspired by the convincing win of the battalion's team over the Grenadier Guards, struck a classic boxing pose as the Great White Hope – soon to become the Great Light Brown Hope after wrestling in the sand with toothless Tarzan.

Jim knew well enough that he was no great shakes as a swimmer but he manfully thrashed about trying to improve his crawl stroke. What troubled him most was having to swim in a blur of combined myopia and chlorinated water. Was he seeing things at the edge of the pool? With a final flail, at which even Johnny Weissmuller would have marvelled, or more likely tut tutted, Jim touched concrete, side and bottom.

He gasped, rubbed his eyes free of water and tried to slow his pounding heart. With slight sobs between words he panted, "So you managed to get here after all. I'm glad."

"Yes, I came on my bicycle."

Golly, Heidi really did look a snip. Jim remembered that he had made similar evaluations of other girls in the past, most especially Mary. But that was different; this was mature, not calf love, marvellous and disturbing though that had been.

Come to think of it, before today he hadn't seen Heidi dressed for warm sunshine days. *Ohne Zweifel*, she did look a real snip. The late afternoon sun glinted in her fair hair and on the neat brooch which fastened the collar of her spotless, white blouse. Over the blouse she wore a cream coloured, short sleeved, knitted jacket – a bolero would it be? 'I'll bet she's knitted that herself,' he thought, including the complicated border design of flowers. Her skirt, of bright red plaid design, hung about her in soft, gentle folds.

Jim heaved himself out of the pool and put on his civvy street specs. Heidi came more clearly into focus. His heart raced.

"By Jiminy, you do look pretty today, Fräulein Braun."

"Why thank you, Sergeant Norton. Do you like my new shoes?" Jim went and sat by Heidi on the simple wooden bench, not snuggling close, he was still too damp for that.

"They look fine to me."

And so they did – white, light and open toed in the way of summer shoes. He didn't ask if they were comfortable. From his native experience he knew well enough that it was a dangerous folly for the male to venture any comment which implied even the slightest criticism of the female's choice of footwear. Jim thought it better to change the subject.

"Has Freda come with you, by any chance?"

Heidi looked startled.

"No, why do you ask?"

"Just thought she might have enjoyed the floor show." Heidi glanced with amusement at Tarzan and Duffy engaged in round two of their 'make up the rules as you go along' wrestling match.

"You crazy English. But I can't see Freda cycling anywhere, let alone to this playground."

"No, you are right. She'd expect at least a staff car." Jim, wary of wooden splinters, edged a little nearer to his sweetheart.

"One of these fine days, Heidi, I would like to buy you a real tartan skirt."

"Do you mean that, Jim, or are you just teasing again?"

"No, I'm serious. Well, I think I am. But it may take a while to save enough money and enough coupons. Clothing, like food is still rationed back home."

"Does that mean that *Schwarzhandlung* is very common? it is in Germany, as you know."

"No, the Black Market is nothing like as bad in England as it is here. Not for ordinary people anyway. But Mom still has to 'butter up', as we say, our butcher to make sure of fair play."

"'Butter up', what does that mean?"

"Well, it's sort of *Umgangsprache* for *schmeicheln*, flattery, a bit like Freda chats when she needs a favour from someone."

"You *Engländer* do have many interesting expressions, 'butter up', 'keep the home fires burning', 'make hay while the sun shines'." Jim edged a little nearer and gave Heidi a quick peck on her smooth, warm cheek. She giggled.

"By the way, I've not forgotten that I've promised to write you a little booklet about the English language."

"Good. But as long as you are here, I shan't need a book, shall I?"

She smiled a teasing smile.

He kissed the smiling lips.

During their conversation Heidi and Jim had become aware that the other sergeants had become aware of them. It didn't seem to matter. No one considered it necessary to show off ( except perhaps Jim, just a little) simply because an attractive young woman was in their midst. It was as though Heidi was a younger sister of them all. Jim himself thought it would be difficult to imagine the circumstances in which, nationality apart, anyone, except a real rotter, would want to be nasty to her. Hers was such a pleasant, open, good-natured, unassertive temperament. Jim detected no symptoms of meanness of spirit, or of an emergent strident nag in her make up. She wanted to please. She wanted to learn.

Yes, that was it – she was like a kid sister to his fellow sergeants. She seemed, quite artlessly, quite unconsciously, to draw out their protective qualities. After all, that's how he himself had been attracted to her, wanting to protect her charming innocence from that smooth talking threat, the stalking Limper.

So, during the next week or two, whenever they could successfully coincide their wangling of 'off duty' hours, Heidi and Jim would meet at the swimming baths. Afterwards Heidi would sometimes cycle home to her parents and at others she and Jim would catch a tram back to town.

During their last meeting at the baths, the air became menacingly still, heavy and uncomfortably sultry. Away to the west, rolling banks of dark, sullen clouds began to gather in louring tempest formation. Occasionally, distant lightning flickered to be followed, after longish intervals, by deep growls of thunder.

"Come on, this is no hay making weather – we'd better dash."

So dash they did, back to Heidi's flat.

"Do you remember Sergeant Ernie Griffiths, a big burly chap, the one who was the referee at that 'head to head' battle?"

"I didn't watch," Heidi shivered slightly, "but I do remember him. He seemed a nice man."

"I had a letter from him the other day."

"How is he getting on?"

"OK, it seems."

Jim fished out the letter from his blouse pocket.

"'Give my regards (to all) to', he names several girls from our old kitchen staff 'and Jock'."

"Does he have a job yet?"

"Yes, he doesn't exactly say what as – a butcher I suppose, like he was before he joined the Army. Anyway, he seems pleased with the hours of work and the money. 'I clear £5 4/- a week.' That means after tax has been deducted."

"Is that a good wage?"

"Well, Ernie says 'not bad' but he's looking for something better. 'We are all OK (waiting for a big event at the end of July)...'"

"*Bitte*, what does that mean?"

"That he and his wife, he's been married twelve months, are expecting a baby."

"Oh, I see. Yes, that must be a 'big event'."

The storm was now raging close to Pullenstadt.

"I do so hate storms. We get a lot during the summer but this one is early."

Heidi started at a particularly loud volley of thunder. Jim held her tight as she pressed her face against his chest. Her hair smelled clean and delicately fragrant.

"You will stay with me until the storm is over, won't you?" came Heidi's muffled voice.

Jim tenderly kissed the top of her head.

"Of course I will."

"Have you heard any more about being moved away from Pullenstadt?"

Her voice had now become an anxious murmur.

"Nothing definite. As I said before, it will probably be early next month. The rumour is growing that we shall go to somewhere in North Germany, probably in the Bremen or Hamburg area."

"Oh Jim, I am going to miss you so much, so very, very much. It will be *schrecklich* without you here!"

"And I shall miss you. Believe me I really will. But I will write and come and see you as often as I can."

"Promise?"

"Promise."

Silence, apart from the noise of the storm, prevailed for a little while.

Jim turned on his back on the lumpy old sofa and spoke, a rather serious note in his voice.

"I have been thinking about the future quite a lot recently and there are various things I could perhaps do to make matters, oh, easier for us."

Heidi turned her head to look him clearly in the eye with her own, oh so honest grey eyes. Her manner was serious, expectant.

"Please tell me."

"As my Army duties are now those of a teacher, it might be better for me, for us, and what I hope to do later in life, to transfer to what we call the Army Education Corps, the AEC, which is responsible for the education of soldiers. I would, of course, have to apply for such a transfer. But if accepted, I might be lucky and be posted nearer here than Bremen and Hamburg are."

"I think I have understood. And would it also mean that you would not have to carry a rifle or a machine gun anymore?"

Jim smiled, then kissed her. "No, just a stick of chalk."

Heidi reflected.

"I am not sure I understand all the 'ins and outs' as your expression says, but if you think that such a move is best for you – not just for me, then please try."

"Right, I will. The other thing is, and I will speak slowly, the other thing I could do is to 'sign on', as we say, for an extra six months service in the Army. The chances are that I would serve that extra time in Germany. You see, if I get a place at a university I wouldn't be able to start until October of next year, when the university year starts. So, if I carry out this plan, I will be demobbed about this time next year instead of November this year. Sorry for such a lengthy speech. What do you think?"

This time it was Jim who looked anxious.

Heidi sat up, put on her slippers and walked about the room deep in thought. The lightning flashes had lessened, the thunder rumbles had become fewer and fainter, but heavy rain lashed in violent squalls against the window, dashing onto the cobbles around that grim church and spilling from overflowing gutters.

"But Jim, if you did serve for another six months, you would be away from home, from your parents and friends for another six months. That hardly seems fair to them, or to you. And what about if you miss the chance of a good job? You've told me your former employer will have to offer you a job of some sort. It's the law."

"All of that is true, but I would be quite happy," he hesitated but only for seconds, "in fact, it's what I want, to sign on for another six months."

Heidi gave him an old-fashioned look but for a moment or two stayed silent.

"Come on now, Jim, what you really seem to be saying is that you're doing this mostly for my sake. If you hadn't met me you would have been going home in November. Isn't that the truth of the matter?"

Jim looking slightly foolish, shuffled his stockinged feet.

"Yes, I suppose so."

Heidi went to the window and lifted a corner of the heavy curtain.

"It's still, as you say, raining dogs and cats."

"Cats and dogs."

"Dogs and cats," Heidi hadn't heard.

"I think you should stay a little longer, 'sign on' as you say – for…" she gave a slight shrug of her shoulders and her voice trailed away.

She turned to smile at him, the kind of smile that down the ages, from Mark Antony to Fred Fanakapan of Oswaldtwistle has sent men loopy.

So Jim did stay, quite a lot longer.

# Chapter Ten

# Resolutions

*Good evening Pop,*
*...please thank Mother very heartily on my behalf'*
(Mother had gone to Blackpool for a holiday, address unknown to Jim) *for her letter enclosing the silks for Heidi. Heidi was very grateful for them and has given me a couple of bottles of champagne to bring back with me as a present for Mother. No doubt Mother will invite you to participate in the imbibing thereof.*
*...altho' we are definitely moving it is not to Bremen for we have to stay in a place called Billeburg until the Canadians have cleared out of the barracks where we are to be eventually stationed in Blumenhorst... then I should be coming on leave... just the job!*

Just the job. Jim paused in his scribbling of a letter home. Yes, of course he would be pleased to be back home again, in that poky, brick built, soot-begrimed, terraced house in Brum, a house with no running hot water, no bathroom and with the lav outside in the yard.

He knew he would feel confined, restricted, and restless within the tiny, shabby rooms. But at least, he would still have his three quarter size divan bed in which to sprawl and day dream of his possible, probable life with Heidi? To dream like that as the wonderful fragrance of bacon and egg frying drifted up the narrow, dog-leg staircase was bliss indeed!

In his mind, he rehearsed once more the words he might use to break the news. Still plenty of time for revision, on slow moving, clanking trains, on the leisurely sea crossing, and then on more clanking but slightly faster, and definitely more comfortable trains.

It would be great to see close relatives again. Was sporty Uncle Les really going to give up the care free life of a bird fancier and settle down? Just who was this Erdington wench who had so thrown him off balance? It would be great to see friends as well. Most of his pals were now sporting their demob suits. Dave, ex-Fleet Air Arm, would be going up or was it down to/from Cambridge – they used such odd expressions, these toffs. Bob, ex-RAF, would be entering a teacher's training college. He had heard that Jack, an old form mate at the grammar, and ex-Navy, might be settling in Canada. Once more Jim railed against fate for having robbed Doug and Syd of any chance of choice. He would certainly make a point of going to see Syd's aunt and Dad during his leave.

He glanced at the photograph of the smiling girl on his table and his thoughts went winging back to the exciting events and dizzying emotional turmoil of the past couple of weeks. Lightning, thunder and tempest rain had all gone their various ways after that night of storm and wind, but Jim had returned and stayed, whatever the weather, when circumstances allowed. He felt bucked that he had been able to give a tweak here and there to alter the state of 'circumstances' from neutral to favourable, as far as young lovers were concerned. Swapping duties for instance, slipping a packet of fags to Else, the cleaner, to let him know when the coast was clear – that sort of thing.

With a broad smile he recollected one particular 'English for Heidi' session, a lesson with far reaching consequences.

"Heidi, I was passing a book shop earlier today when this caught my eye. Here's a little present for you."

With a charming *'Dankeschön'*, and a shy smile, Heidi took the book from him. As she looked at the cover, her round cheeks reddened a little. That puzzled Jim, as did the silent enquiry that could be seen both in her eyes and general expression of pleasure.

"Go on, open it, I've written something inside." She looked and blushed faintly.

*To my darling Heidi,*
*    With the hope that you will enjoy many pleasant*
*hours in reading this book.*
*    Jim*

Nothing effusive thought Jim, sincerity doesn't need to be.

"That kind of English I like."

"As you will see, there is English and German in the book; an English poem, or part of one on one page and the German translation on the facing page. Mind you, I don't know all the English poems myself but one or two of my favourites are there, and one of my Dad's."

"What does your Dad like so much?"

"Pass me the book please. Yes, here it is, page fifty, *'Letzte Rose'*. 'Tis the last rose of summer, Left blooming alone'; that's how it starts."

"And in German?"

*"Letzte Rose, du blühst dort, So einsam, allein,"*

"It sounds sad."

"It is a bit. But how do you like this for advice? *'Dies über alles: sei dir selber treu, And daraus folgt, so wie Nacht dem Tage, Du kannst nicht falsch sein gegen irgendwen.'"*

"And please, what is the English? Very slowly please."

*"'This above all: to thine own self be true, And it must follow, as night the day, Thou canst not then be false to any man.'"*

"*Bitte*, what is 'thou'?"

"Oh, that's old fashioned English for 'you'. We don't have *Du* and *Sie* like Germans do. We used to though – words like thee and thou for *Du* but now everyone is *Sie*, you. I was once *Sie* to *Sie* but I have now long been *Du, nicht wahr?*"

"*Selbstverständlich*. But who was the clever writer of that last quotation?"

"Shakespeare, our greatest poet. In the same league as Goethe."

Jim handed back the book.

"But it's not a book to be read from cover to cover. Just dip into it."

"Sei dir selber treu," murmured Heidi, "That I like."

"I'm afraid I must dash. See you after work tonight. Like the great Scottish poet Robert Burns said, *'Einen Kuss noch, eh wir scheiden'*, one more kiss before we part."

With that, and the kiss, Jim clumped, in his on-duty hobnails down the wooden stairs singing:

*"Du bist mein ganzes Herz*

*Und wo Du bist, da muss ich sein...* "

Jim took care to stress *Du* and *Du*, in a manner Richard Tauber would have blanched at.

Much later that same day, or to be accurate, early the following morning, Jim after a longish period of silence suddenly blurted out, "Heidi, have you had a chance yet to look at the book I gave you?"

"Only at the first poem."

"So what did you think of it?"

"It seems pretty but some of the words are strange."

"Yes, it is a very old poem, but there's a bit I want to read to you."

He smiled inwardly thinking of how his Dad liked to read verses of Byron to his Mom.

"What? Now?"

Heidi's voice sounded drowsily surprised. She might well have been saying to herself, 'Ach you never know with these crazy Engländer do you?'

"Yes, now."

Jim switched on the light, put his glasses on and went to fetch the book from the coffee table in the living room. He turned to the first page and glanced down it.

> There will I make thee beds of roses
> And a thousand fragrant posies.

No, that was rather overdoing things. All right for Kit Marlowe – he was always getting into scrapes and anyway, this wasn't the poetic Elizabethan age. No, best keep it simple. The first line alone should be enough. In slow, clear tones he read,

"'Come live with me, and be my love', or, if you prefer, '*Komm, leb mit mir und liebe mich*', or better still, Heidi darling, will you marry me?"

Heidi sat bolt upright, flung her arms about him, kissed him with great tenderness and said,

"Yes I will, my dear, dear Jim."

\*

At breakfast, coffee and *Brötchen*, that morning, the lovers ate in a glow of happiness, subdued happiness to be sure, both thinking of how best to tackle 'the problems' inevitably attached to their few hours old joint commitment.

"I think it would best to wait a little while before we make our engagement generally known."

He noticed the look of disappointment that flitted across Heidi's face.

"I know girls like to show off their engagement rings but it will take me some time to save for a good ring. Besides, we have to break the news to our parents. Not that we need their permission to marry, but it seems only fair to put them, 'In the picture' as we say."

"Yes, I would like you to come and see my Mom and Dad before you leave Pullenstadt."

"Of course. It had better be soon then."

"What do you think your parents will say?"

"I can't think the news will come as any great shock. They'll be uneasy about whether I'm doing the right thing and will probably urge me to make the engagement a long one – to allow time for me to change my mind."

"You won't, will you?"

Heidi sounded anxious. Jim kissed her.

"Certainly not."

"I expect my parents will react very much like yours."

A few days later Jim was to find out.

*

Having alighted from the single-decker tram, Jim began looking curiously about him. As far as he could tell, Beckmühle seemed to be bordered by flat green fields, lines of trees, and open countryside. A quiet, pleasant, rural setting.

Walking by Heidi's side, Jim was aware of her being on edge. While he took care not to hold her hand or to touch her in any way, his uniform obviously marked him out as a Tommy, an alien, and the girl beside him as – well, who could divine what nasty, ungenerous thoughts lay behind the various, curious eyes that glanced their way. Not hostile eyes exactly, but certainly not friendly.

So, this was what one German mining village looked like. Wide straight roads, mature trees, now in full broad leaf, down either side, and broad pavements inset with brick paths. The brick built houses looked sturdy, if rather grimy, and surprisingly large. But as Heidi told him, most of the property had been designed to accommodate four families. In separate flats, two families shared the ground floor and two the first floor. A large cellar, divided into four compartments stored coal, logs and kindling wood together with carefully harvested spuds, bottled fruits and vegetables.

Rooms in the top storey, immediately beneath the sloping roof, could be haggled over in relation to the number of children in the families concerned. Heidi had told him that her own small room lay just beneath the roof. No running water at that height, let alone a toilet.

Only employees of the mine were eligible to apply for one of the flats, all of which were rented. Except for the marked differences in architectural styles, similar cramped and basic living conditions seemed present in this village as in the miners' cottages of Hamstead pit village, and, he assumed, many other such villages back home.

Jim looked up to watch flocks of pigeons wheeling their curving ways, back and forth across the bright blue sky. Now and then, one or more of the flocks would suddenly vanish from view behind the roof tops and chimneys – only to reappear, just as suddenly, from an entirely different direction.

"Your coal miners, just like ours, seem to like pigeons."

"Yes, my Dad keeps some. He is what we call a '*Taubenvater*'. He races them at weekends."

Heidi and Jim walked into a yard where lines of well scrubbed washing swayed gently in the warm breeze. The day was bright and sunny.

"*Guten Tag, Fräulein Braun.*"

"*Guten Tag, Frau Pilzowski.*"

The woman who had greeted Heidi stood pegging out miners' grey socks. A merry-eyed, buxom Hausfrau in her mid-thirties perhaps, Eva Pilzowski gave Heidi a warm smile and Jim a shyer one. Friendly curiosity marked her manner.

Jim returned the smile, gave a slight nod of the head and said, "*Guten Tag.*"

'Now for it,' he thought as he approached the half dozen or so concrete steps leading to the open door which served as the shared entrance to the two flats. Heidi paused before climbing the broad wooden staircase, well waxed and polished, to the first floor.

"That was Frau Pilzowski – she's a good sort. She comes from the Rhineland and so she enjoys a good joke and sing-song. She married a miner whose parents came from Poland. Many miners' families come from Silesia and that way."

The *Verlobten* (engaged pair) climbed the stairs and Heidi pressed the bell push of her parents' flat.

Seconds later, Jim, having passed through the small, neat kitchen, sat in the *Wohnzimmer*, the living room, on a simple wooden chair, its hardness just a little softened by some sort of cloth pad. Heidi, having made the introductions, went to sit by her mother on a couch beneath the large, spotless window which looked upon the street below. Pushed close to the couch was the dining table covered by a snowy cloth.

Given the 'tricky' nature of the 'interview' that was to follow, Jim's first impressions remained fleeting and imprecise. But later he did remember bright sunlight shining through mesh curtains and glinting on glassware displayed in a handsome, glass fronted cabinet.

To Jim's right sat Heidi's father in a simple easy chair. Speaking or silent, this man with fair, thinning hair, hunched shoulders and the blue scars of the miner about his hands and face, wheezed laboriously as he struggled for breath.

Heidi's parents looked as Jim imagined they would, having seen their photos in Heidi's flat. Above the father's head hung a colour tinted photograph of a youth, hardly a young man – the dead son, no doubt.

Mr and Mrs Braun did not look at Jim with accusation in their eyes as though he could somehow be personally responsible for their son's death. Nor did they look accusingly at him because he might be the cause of 'robbing' them of their only daughter by taking her to a far off, mist-shrouded, land. They simply looked ill at ease, uncomfortable, embarrassed. For one thing, neither of them could speak a word of English, save perhaps that word – Tommy.

Although not feeling that way, Jim assumed the jaunty, cheerful air of a self-confident twenty-three year old while remaining respectful in the presence of mid-forty year olds who looked to be in their mid-fifties due to wartime privations and their aftermath.

Slowly, the ice floe of incomprehension and wariness that lay between Heidi's parents and Jim began to thaw, the warming process being greatly helped by Heidi's own tactful comments. She had obviously told her parents quite a bit about Jim and made it absolutely plain to them that Jim was the only man for her.

Jim guessed that Mutti and Vater were already resigned to the inevitable. The father's ill at ease manner brightened and relaxed a little when Jim mentioned '*Tauben*' and brightened still more at the word '*Fussball*'. The mother remained more guarded but the moment arrived when she offered her dry-mouthed guest a cup of tea. "The English are known for being big tea drinkers, *ne?*"

"You are right, Frau Braun. And this cup tastes, er, fine."

The mother was immediately anxious, "Not too strong? I'm sorry we have no fresh milk."

"No, just fine. Thank you."

"Heidi, perhaps you could show Jim round the garden while Father and I have a little talk."

Heidi led the way past the extensive line of brick outhouses, (from some of which could be heard the throaty cooing of pigeons) then turned a corner where clucking hens, fenced off by wire mesh, were busily scratching the bare earth, to reach the garden. Opening a little wooden gate, Heidi ushered Jim into – not so much a garden as a good-sized allotment. At a glance he could tell that this plot of land was lovingly tended and highly productive. He walked slowly along the narrow brick path. After a few yards, the path turned left to bisect the full length of the garden.

Jim sauntered on, admiring the neat, well hoed rows of onions, of spuds, and of lettuce. He noticed some beetroot, radishes, carrots and a solid, sturdy wooden frame up which densely leaved, scarlet flowered runner beans had busily and luxuriantly clambered. Some vegetables he didn't recognise. Few weeds could be seen and most of those seemed to be of one type running alongside the dense, tidily clipped hawthorn hedges that bordered the garden. Heidi noticed the direction of his glance.

"We call that *französiches Unkraut*."

Jim laughed. Something unpleasant, something unauthorised? Give it a foreign name – German measles, Neapolitan boneache, French leave and now 'French weed'.

"Why do you laugh?"

"I'll explain some other time."

"Do you like gardening?"

"Well, I've not had the chance to do very much. But I've always enjoyed helping out my three uncles and Grandad who all have gardens, rather like this, but all together on a larger piece of land. We call them allotments."

"I expect we should say *Schrebergärten*."

The path ended at a little wooden bench, clumps of bright asters planted at either side. Heidi and Jim sat down.

"Jim, I'm sure you have made a good impression."

"I hope so."

"Yes, I'm sure. I know they like your cheerful smile and cheerful open manner."

"Do you really think so? I feel quite glum at times."

He pulled a face which he thought might represent glum. Heidi giggled.

"No, that's not you. But you do look stern, very stern sometimes."

"Oh heck!"

"Come on," Heidi touched his arm, "I expect Mom and Dad will have finished their chat by now."

"I'd like to use your toilet first."

"I'll fetch the key. Just wait here."

Jim sat admiring her trim figure as she walked quickly away.

\*

"Here we are then, I'll show you where it is."

They retraced their steps, past the straight rowed onions, the industrious chickens, the heard but unseen pigeons, back to the yard. Heidi handed over the key and pointed to a wooden, padlocked door.

"See you upstairs."

Seconds later Jim stepped into a narrow cubicle, made narrower near its entrance by an old miner's 'tin' bath hanging from a bare brick wall. As far as crumbly, un-whitewashed brick and hard earth could be made clean, the toilet was immaculate. In the far wall, a small square window filtered in soft, pale golden day light. Beneath the window, and wall to wall, stood the 'throne', a wooden boarded thunderbox. 'A box very similar to the one at home,' thought Jim. He looked around. No cistern! Heck he had walked into medieval times!

Still, it didn't matter that much. He had become inured to the past vagaries of Army latrines and their indelicate associations. There flashed, unbidden, into his mind, a vivid memory from his early training days.

A moving convoy of three tonners, filled with troops, some sitting, some standing, was trundling towards an expanse of heath land. Many of the squaddies, Jim excluded, had been suffering badly from the trots. This enemy bug attacked, yet again, but the truck driver was not allowed to stop. With the enterprising, make do and mend spirit of 'saucepans into Spitfires', steel helmets, in a trice, became bedpans.

Jim did what he had to do – golly, the drop did seem a long one, and then rinsed his hands at the cold water tap in the yard. Frau Pilzowski watched his movements and gave him a broad, motherly smile.

As he climbed the staircase once more, Jim thought about the warped priorities of those mysterious people who held power over ordinary folk. Here was a mining village with broad roads and fine avenues of trees – but no piped hot water in miners' homes, no bathroom and only primitive sanitation. All right, so miners had their pit head baths but what about their families and the toil and moil of washing clothes? What with the danger, the back-breaking toil, dirt, modest pay and hardly classy housing conditions, it was no wonder that miners, German, British, French and Belgian could be a bolshie lot at times.

Back in the *Wohnzimmer* after the tea break and vegetable patch tour, the atmosphere seemed much more relaxed than before. Herr Braun came quickly to the point.

"We are convinced that you love one another. We know you want to marry and you have our blessing. We ask just two things: a promise that you will look after our daughter properly..."

"I will certainly do that."

"And a promise that you will not marry too soon. We think that you should stay apart for some time before you do marry."

"That will happen anyway as Heidi may have explained to you."

"Well, we can talk about that another time. Here's my hand."

Jim shook warmly the rough, calloused hand that was held out to him.

"Now Mother, *ein Schnäpschen*."

Mother carefully filled four tiny glasses with a colourless liquid.

"To a happy future to you both."

*Mutter* took a sip and spluttered.

Heidi took a larger sip – and coughed.

Jim drank half the glass, blinked and smiled as a warm glow began to creep through his innards.

Vater had swallowed his glassful at a gulp.

"Not viski, but good, *ne*?"

"*Sehr gut*. But it's very strong. What's in it?" Herr Braun smiled, tapped his nose with his forefinger and winked.

"I make it myself. *Noch ein*?"

"Please. *Zum Wohle*."

"*Zum Wohle*."

Ten minutes later Jim was feeling very '*Wohle*' and much more at home.

With shining eyes Heidi, after glancing at her dainty wrist watch, suddenly said, "Come on, Jim. I'll walk with you to the tram stop." Once in the yard, she crooked her arm inside Jim's and beamed at Frau Pilzowski.

"Jim, I'm so happy, so very happy. That went well."

Jim, in something of a glow himself, agreed.

"But I notice some curtains twitching as we walk along."

"I don't care."

Heidi, with heightened colour, gave a defiant toss of her head – and then reflected.

"But perhaps it would be better when you come again, if you could dress as a civilian. It would make things much easier for me. Be a soldier out of uniform."

"Saucy, *Mädchen*. But I will see what I can do."

\*

Jim picked up his pen again:

> *We had our farewell dinner in the club last night and it passed off quite successfully and one or two members – out quite quietly.*
>
> *Once settled in Blumenhorst, I should be coming on leave... Just the job!*

'Oh, tender, tearful Heidi when shall we two meet again?' "Don't brood man," he said sternly to himself. "Get that seven pound tin of cocoa to that tailor and get your suit made."

## Chapter Eleven
# Powwow in Blighty

"Jim."

"Sir."

"Skip the sir for the moment. Jack here tells me that you might be interested in a trip to Pullenstadt. Is that right?" Jim looked across at an old mucker from far off Kerzenbaum days, that gin swilling for breakfast Jack, now promoted to CSM of A company. What had this Cockney fly boy gone and told Tara?

"It's all right, lad, you've no need to feel embarrassed." Tara's eyes twinkled with great good humour.

"We're taking a jeep to Pullenstadt next weekend. If you'd like to come, you'll be welcome."

"Thank you, that would be really great."

"Right then. Make sure you're ready straight after breakfast on the Friday. We shan't hang about."

"OK, and thank you again. Thanks, Jack." Jack winked.

Bully for the magnetism of Lady Alabaster, and her perfectly splendid milk white orbs that so held Tara in thrall.

As he left the mess, Tara turned and winked.

"I take it you've got somewhere to stay?"

"You bet, sir."

The days dragged on and that weekend sped past.

*

Back in charmless, lustreless, Heidi-less Billeburg, Jim was making ready for a dreary evening in the sergeants' mess. As he knotted his khaki tie he softly whistled a highly popular wartime song, reflecting on recent events as he did so.

"That certain night... there was magic abroad in the air." Magic maybe but as for 'angels dining at the Ritz', that surely was a cynical contradiction in terms. (Fallen angels perhaps) And besides, the nearest he, Jim, had ever approached the life style of the Ritz had been a poached egg on toast in a *Kardomah*. Blimey, it was a daft song in some ways when you thought about it. What nightingale worth its trill, would stay in war torn London – barmy.

So Jim switched to humming a different melody. All right, so there had been no 'ride in a taxi when midnight had flown', but it was enough that the jeep had delivered its passengers safely to Alabaster Palace. But this particular song never did sound right when sung by a feller, least of all by raucous Harry Roy in what seemed to be a mocking, urine-extracting manner.

> Your kit to be packed, a train to be caught,
> Sorry I cried but I just felt that way.

What feller, who was a feller, would warble and snivel in that way?

Still, fair dos, part of the lyric was – spot on, both for 'him' and for 'her'.

> Those two days of heaven you helped me to spend.

Attaboy! And for that matter: Attagirl!

*

"I just hope you know what you're doing, that's all." From the majesty of her shabby, winged armchair Mrs Sally Norton addressed her only chick, a mixture of asperity, concern and bewilderment evident in her voice.

"I won't say any more."

She pursed her lips both to express disapproval and to emphasise her determination to remain silent.

'Fat chance of that,' thought Jim. He was right.

"I can't understand why you want to marry a foreigner and a German at that!"

"Steady, mother," said Wilf Norton frowning.

"I don't suppose they're all tarred with the same brush. Think of old Uncle Hans who married my sister Clara. You couldn't wish to meet a more inoffensive man and he was born of German parents. I know he blew up one or two garden sheds with his potty experiments but never with the intention of harming anyone." Wilf chuckled at his memories of the great, wildly eccentric, amateur inventor in the family.

Sal promptly switched to a different tack.

"Is she a good cook?"

"I don't honestly know, but Heidi is an expert needlewoman and always appears neat and tidy."

"Well, if she can iron your shirts as well as I do, that's something to be said for her."

"German housewives are noted for their home making skills." Wilf sagely nodded his head in agreement. Sal sniffed her disdain.

"But why couldn't you have found and married a nice English girl?"

"Things don't work out like that do they? I simply happened to fall in love with a girl who happened to be a German. I didn't set out to marry a German."

Jim added what he sensed could be a shrewd jab to the moral midriff.

"Look, Mom, I don't suppose that when you were young, say like me, you imagined that one day you would marry a widower quite a bit older than yourself, who already had four grown children. Everyone agrees that you were a marvellous stepmother, especially to Ted and May."

Sal smiled with pleasure, but still had to make a tart remark.

"Yes, and look what good it's done me – stuck with that old donkey there," she glanced across the faded hearth rug at her husband, "for the rest of my life!"

The old donkey, quite unruffled, gave a broad, complacent grin.

"Oh, come on now, you get on well enough. You might not like Dad's poetry readings from Byron but you do enjoy the tit-bits of scandal and obituaries he reads to you from the *Mail*."

Silence prevailed for a while. Jim looked around the familiar living room – everything seemed much the same as it had in 1938 when, as a bitterly resentful schoolboy, he had first set foot in the 'dump', now affectionately tolerated instead of heartily loathed. This small living room remained cramped, clean certainly, but shabby and cluttered with the same old sticks of furniture in their accustomed places. A few unfamiliar knickknacks could be spotted – some brassware, bits of cheap souvenir pottery from Blackpool and from Weston-Super-Mare. That bulky, oak roll-topped desk remained firmly anchored in its familiar mooring. On its narrow top Jim noticed that first photograph of himself in khaki battle dress. Golly, didn't he look young, just nineteen and looking what, just sixteen? Perhaps he flattered himself; he wasn't sure and didn't much care.

"What's her English like, this Heidi of yours?"

"She's picked up quite a bit from working with British troops. She's very keen to learn and I've been giving her lessons. Given time and encouragement I'm sure she will make good progress. Heidi is a very conscientious girl."

"If she's so attractive and capable, why isn't she already married?"

"She's quite choosy. And perhaps she was waiting for me to come along." Jim grinned.

"Conceited young pup!"

Jim neatly dodged the ball of knitting wool his mother had thrown at his head.

"So when are you thinking of actually getting married?"

"Not for quite some time. As I explained earlier, much will depend on when I leave the Army and whether I can get into a university and..."

"I hope you're not thinking of going to Cambridge like Dave."

"As a matter of fact..."

Again Sal Norton cut in sharply. "Just you think, young man, by the time you're demobbed, you will have been away from home for over five years. It's high time you stayed here for a while – married or unmarried. In any case, at Cambridge or anywhere else for that matter, Heidi would be very lonely especially with you with your nose in a book all the bloomin' time."

Jim reflected. His Mom had made a good point. For him Cambridge represented academic glamour and prestige as well as Dave's company. For Heidi it might come to represent a form of dismal, lonely exile.

"Do I take it then that we could live here?"

"Of course. Until you get established. I'm not going to turn my only son out after five years away from home. Besides what else could you do? if Heidi's as nice a girl as you say she is, I'm sure we'll get along."

"Thanks, Mom, thanks, Pop."

"Now your Mother's had her say, perhaps I could get a word in."

Wilf gave a serious, not mock serious, frown in his wife's direction. Sal pursed her lips again but said nothing.

"Are you really sure, son, that your heart is not ruling your head?"

"I've asked myself that question many times, but I'm quite sure I'm doing the right thing. This is the first time I have ever felt I wanted to marry someone."

"It's a big step for anyone and in this case I expect there'll be lots of red tape involved."

"I expect so, but I haven't really looked into that side of things yet."

Sal just had to chip in.

"And weddings and wedding receptions don't come cheap. Have you thought about that?"

"No, not in detail. But I can't imagine we would want a big splash. Most likely no one from Heidi's side will be able to come."

Sal's voice became gentle.

"Heidi must love you very much, Jim."

"Yes. I'm lucky."

"But who would give her away?"

"Steady, Sal, don't start rushing your fences. Plenty of time yet to get things properly sorted out. Does she have any savings, Jim?"

"I haven't asked her."

"Well, your mother says you've only got a few bob in your savings account and even if you do get a job or a grant, it will be tough going."

"There's nothing new about that."

The conversation lapsed as mother, father and son each thought about the hard times of the thirties, war time shortages, and now, post-war shortages. Would rationing, first by the purse and then by coupons and the purse, ever end?

"Just put the kettle on, son, will you?"

It pleased Jim to hear such a familiar and reassuring request from his Mom. He went into the tiny kitchen and filled the kettle from the single tap over the chipped and scarred old sink. Everything seemed much as it had been back in '38 – the ancient gas cooker, the roller towel against the door, the cast iron mangle opposite, the gloss painted walls. 'That's something that will have to change,' he thought, 'once I'm living back here again. I'll buy a hot water geyser to go over this blasted sink.'

As he dipped his nose towards his steaming tea, Wilf spoke.

"Tell you what, son, we'll have some mouse trap and crackers this evening and open one of the bottles of bubbly you've brought. Then we'll drink to Heidi and to you. What do you say, Sal?"

"Just so long as you don't get tiddly, you old donkey." Sal frowned with mock severity at her husband. "And no spouting of Byron!"

Matters were back on an even keel again.

"Right ho, Mrs Caudle."

*

Feeling much lighter in spirit with the air now cleared and the bubbly drunk, Jim went to bed and re-read Heidi's letter. She had written in German. The words were clear enough and knowing that she was not effusive by nature, he remained secure in his belief that her feelings for him remained both deep and genuine. Sighing, he wrote the figure one on the envelope, drew a circle round the one and fell to musing.

He felt glad now that he had not broached another of his ideas, either with Heidi or his own parents. For a time he had wondered whether it might be the best thing to stay on in the Army and make a career of military service. If he did join the AEC, he would probably become, in time, the equivalent of a Tara, a Warrant Officer, First Class. And then? He'd probably stay stuck, he thought, for holding a university degree would presumably be necessary for entry to commissioned rank.

More importantly though, he shrank from the idea of life in married quarters. From what he'd heard and read, all sorts of messy emotional and social problems could arise from living in such inward looking 'colonies'. British wives, well, some of them, could apparently be so bitchy with one another and one or two might well pick on Heidi, simply because of her German birth and upbringing. As such a nice-natured girl herself, Heidi would find it very difficult to cope with nasty remarks, British or for that matter German. Sarcasm, let alone direct insult, was foreign to her mode of expression. No, best dismiss altogether the notion of an Army career.

He yawned and reached across for the April copy of *The Stagbearer,* and started another browse through the 'Official Organ of Birchfield Harriers', founded 1877. Bob Reid, that fine Scottish runner, had done well again. The old Alexander ground had been reopened at the end of April. Jim idly wondered whether he would ever pull on the black vest of the 'Fleet and Free' again. Somehow he didn't think so, but it was early days yet and still difficult to know what threads of pre-Army life could be, or should be picked up again.

He wouldn't bother to go to church again, that much was certain, except for the formalities of relevant, hatches, matches and despatches. Not that he had become anti-church. Religion just left him cold. Man surely had made God in his own image. He acknowledged now that as a Sunday School attender, and then regular churchgoer, he had really been an agnostic and a pretty bored one very often. Certainly, he had enjoyed the friendship, the good fellowship, the fun associated with Social Centre activities. But the heady atmosphere made up of unspoken youthful desires, 'Midnight in Paris', 'California Poppy', the physical glow and warmth, the excitement of the Saturday night hop, wailing sirens and crashing bombs, could not be recaptured. Wonderful tingling memories of people, quicksteps and waltzes, table tennis, laughter and good natured chaff, a goodnight kiss and a scamper home in the blackout. All were gone now like the blackout itself, such events, such emotions could never be re-experienced.

Some friends from those days remained, Dave in particular, Bob and Ken as well. But some were moving from Brum, if only temporarily, for educational reasons. A few had married. Odd how newly married wives commonly appeared to resent what they seemed to regard as the baleful influence of bachelor friends on their freshly acquired husbands. 'Rum that,' thought Jim, 'but I can't think I'll have that problem with Heidi, or will I?'

Yes, many things considered, it would be a queer business settling back into civvy street. So disturbingly different from the certainties of service life.

He nodded off, soon to be immersed in an agitating dream. He struggled to put his left leg in a blue trouser and his right leg in a grey. Then with blue trousers on he slipped into a grey jacket. A twist of a button and he found himself clad in grey trousers and blue jacket. His agitation grew. He knew he had to be in either all blue or all grey attire. He had once sported a swish, splendidly natty, navy blue suit for Sunday best, at fashion conscious age of fourteen. But he didn't have a grey suit. 'Oh, yes you do,' said some inner voice. 'That Pullenstadt tailor has done you proud for that tin of cocoa.' With an immense sense of relief Jim rushed, trouserless, into a shallow sea and leapt lithely onto the back of a golden stag, with the date 1877 stamped on its rump.

*

"Mother, I'd like to see my savings book please."

Sal sensed the edge in her son's voice and made no demur except to say, "I hope you're not thinking of taking out any money just yet. You'll need every penny, you know."

"I just want to do a few rough sums, that's all."

Since 1940, when he had started work, Jim, with encouraging help from his mother, had been saving in the Co-operative Permanent Building Society. (The old values still held – 'vote Labour, shop at the Co-op and support the Villa') The latest entry showed a payment in of £20 in February '46 giving a grandish total of £156 14/7. Hardly a fortune but it would be enough to marry on. Using Ernie Griffiths's net weekly wage of £5 4/- say just over half a year's pay. His post war gratuity should also help quite a bit.

"Do you think Ted could help me to get an engagement ring?" Ted was Jim's half-brother who worked in the jewellery trade and who enjoyed useful 'contacts'.

"I'm sure he will help. He's a very warm-hearted chap, and like you, a bit of a romantic. But don't go for anything too fancy. As I keep reminding you, you'll need every copper you can lay your hands on."

Later that Saturday morning, Jim strolled to the local Working Men's Club set at the edge of its wide sweep of allotments. The Club's crown green bowling rink still looked in good nick but the tennis court languished in a state of sad disrepair. He walked on to inspect the four plots cultivated by the three brother uncles. Gassed veteran of World War I, Uncle Sam, now kept Grandad's allotment going as well as his own.   Uncle Harold's plot still displayed a magnificent, mixed flower border, flanked by a line of rustic poles supporting vigorous climbing roses.   American Pillar would soon be flaunting massed profusions of single, deep pink flowers, white at their centres with long yellow stamens.   A real beaut of a rose.   A riotous burst of golden colour, like an exploding, showering firework, marked off Les's plot from those of his neighbours – a lightly swaying, magnificent broom at the edge of the path.

Jim tried to visualise Heidi in these surroundings.   He knew these uncles would make a fuss of her – especially Les.   Harold had recently married a rosy-cheeked, jolly, sparkling eyed widder woman who kept a small confectioner's shop.   Poll seemed a generous sensible woman, and always good for a laugh.   She seemed to accept that she could only ever play second fiddle to Harold's first love – gardening.   Harold would be loquaciously ready to answer Heidi's questions about plants that were new to her.   For good measure he would give her their Latin names as well.

Sam   was   far   less   talkative   but   remained   essentially   a golden-hearted and staunch family man.   Heidi wouldn't always understand his quiet, artful leg-pulling but no matter – that 'peculiar' aspect of British culture could be slowly absorbed.

And then there was Les, Jim's favourite uncle.   Jim, now having met Peggy, could well see why Les had fallen for her, but Jim remained confident that this sporty uncle would continue with his long-standing, basic bachelor pursuits of cards, dominoes, snooker, darts, bowls, fishing, canary and budgie breeding, gardening but not since he had now met Peggy, 'playing the field' as the saying went; but even Peg would just have to fit in with bowls and the rest.   Jim also had a good idea of what Les would do as soon as he saw Heidi for the first time.   'Guy Squint, you're a darling!' and fling his arms around her.

Jim slowly returned home to start packing.

*

"I shouldn't bother to unpack completely.   You're being posted."
"Oh, where to?"
"Corps HQ, of all places."
"So where do these brasshats hang out?"

"A place called Blanktal – same region roughly as Kerzenbaum but it's a decent sized town.  Here have a look."

Jim studied the map pushed across to him – and began to calculate. How many miles to Heidi?

## Chapter Twelve

# On the Move

"So, Jim, what did your parents have to say?"

"Oh, they said I looked well, that Army life must suit me and they grumbled about the government."

Heidi frowned, and then her face brightened.

"You're teasing me again, aren't you? What did they say about us?"

Jim's manner became more serious. He spoke slowly, clearly, earnestly.

"Much as expected. They won't try to talk me out of marrying you but they don't want us to be in a hurry to get married. Maybe, like your parents, they're secretly hoping that we'll grow tired of separation and lose interest in one another."

"Please say that won't happen, Jim."

Jim kissed her long and tenderly.

"No, I'm sure it won't."

He kissed her again for extra good luck.

"My mother wanted to know if you are a good cook. Are you?"

"Yes, I think so. I certainly hope so. We were well trained at school and my mother, who doesn't praise anyone lightly, says I'm quite good."

"I suppose, if I'd had any sense, I should have asked you before. But there you are, that's how it is, the heart too often rules the head. We have an old saying that the way to a man's heart is through his stomach. Do you understand?"

"I think so. If I feed you well, you won't leave me?"

"If you're as good a cook as my Mom, I'll be yours for keeps."

Smiling, Heidi went to make coffee. Jim turned on his back and watched a small spider slowly edging its way round the ceiling. He thought about his first experience of hitch hiking from Blanktal to

Pullenstadt. How far had it been? About fifty miles he guessed, by what might be called the country route via Menden, Wickede, Werl and the *Autobahn*.

The spider had changed course. Should I do the same, wondered Jim. Go back through part of the shattered Ruhr area, through Bochum and Hagen – the battered route so to speak. It might be five or ten miles shorter that way and there was almost certain to be more military traffic through these rubble bordered roads on a Sunday, than on the country route. It was worth thinking about. So much depended on the assigned destination of the first of his good Samaritans, alias drivers Tom, Dick and Harry.

Heidi re-entered the lounge bearing large cups of steaming black coffee. She set them down on a small circular table and then went to snuggle against Jim on the couch. With an affectionate smile she ran her fingers through his tousled brown hair. The long net curtains stirred gently as the warm summer breeze moved softly through the partly open window. A broad band of dusty sunlight edged across a pale, striped rug.

"So, tell me, what did you do on your leave?"

"Apart from telling everyone what a nice girl you are, not a great deal, really. I put some of my friends in the picture about us."

"And what did they say?"

"They were surprised, naturally, but they seem to have accepted the situation well enough. No one said anything unkind, or unpleasant. All of them said it could be tough going for us but wished us luck."

Heidi sighed.

"You must have nice friends."

"Yes, I'm sure Dave, for instance, would be happy to be best man."

"But what did you do besides talk?"

Jim carefully disengaged one arm from around Heidi's shoulder and took a sip of coffee.

"I played tennis with Dave and Bob in our local park. Once or twice I went rowing on the park pool by myself, something I've always liked doing. We also went swimming in the public baths. I don't remember much about that though – we'd had a few too many beers earlier on."

"Pfui! Pfui!"

Jim took that to mean 'Tut! Tut!'

"Actually, it wasn't all that bad. The other swimmers had a good laugh at our expense."

"And did you go and see any of your old girlfriends?" Jim was genuinely taken by surprise. Was it a trait of women world wide to be always on the watch for possible rivals?

"Pfui! Pfui! yourself. Of course not. It never occurred to me to do so. Most of the girls I knew from church and social centre days are married any way. But I did go and see one most attractive lady and..."

"And what?"

Heidi didn't seem sure whether to show anxiety or just casual interest, feigned or real.

"And she was not a bit like Lady Alabaster. For one thing she had red hair and for another, my Mom and Dad and several hundred other people were with me at the same time. Jeanette Macdonald, a famous American film star, gave a concert in our town hall. She is a most beautiful singer. She sang a mixture of songs – English, Scottish, Italian, French. She must have been dry at the end of it all – like me. May I have another cup of coffee please."

"With pleasure, *Liebling*."

"So, to change the subject, what do you think of my suit?"

"I'd like to see you in it first, before I pass any opinion."

Jim knew the material itself wasn't much cop, being poor quality stuff of rough, coarse weave. The overall impression was one of light grey sackcloth flecked with soot grey, suety grey and off-white. Still all things considered it was no bad exchange for seven pounds of buckshee cocoa. The trousers and jacket had been well enough tailored, forming an obviously made to measure suit. But even Jim, with negligible ironing experience to his credit, could see that it would never be possible to maintain a knife edge crease in the trousers for any length of time. A couple of days wear and the bags would sag, limp, shapeless, and, well, baggy.

In short, it was a suit in which Jim would not stand out in a crowd – or even a small knot of people. *Desto besser*. So much the better. Just the job, in fact. This was a prime civilian camouflage outfit in which to court a German sweetheart in the land of her birth.

"It fits you very well, Jim. And it's so nice to see you in civilian clothes. But please turn round."

Jim did as he was politely bid and waited, just a little fidgety, as Heidi smoothed down the collar and the back of the jacket, tugging its edge into a better line. She moved to stand in front of him, head slightly to one side, and gave him an appraising look. She stepped forward, patted his shoulders, and gave him a warm kiss.

"You'll do," she whispered.

"I'd like you to keep this suit here, if you don't mind, Heidi. I won't be able to get lifts from British drivers if I'm dressed as a civilian."

"No, I see that. I'll be pleased to take good care of your clothes."

With the flat of one hand she stroked the trousers, almost carressingly, as they lay on the seat of a chair.

"I do hope you are not taking too many risks by hitch-hiking. You're not in any danger are you?"

"No, I don't think so. Women drivers are few and far between. And anyway, they're usually driving for some brass hat or other." Heidi looked puzzled about the reference to women drivers. 'Someday she'll understand the joke,' thought Jim. 'That really is one of the German failings, at least in my experience. They do take everything so literally. And dear Heidi, she is so anxious not to say the wrong thing, to cause hurt or give offence. I really must try not to tease her so much.'

"During the coming weeks, months maybe, I should gain a lot of hitch-hiking experience. There's a good chance I shall be with you most weekends because I shan't have any regimental duties like guard duties. I think it will be next week when I am officially transferred to the Education Corps. But I will have to go on a training course shortly to Göttingen, at the College of the Rhine Army."

"For how long?"

"About three weeks, I think. No hitch-hiking from there, I'm afraid."

"No, I suppose not. It's good of you to travel what, 150 kilometres here and back to Blanktal. I do appreciate it very much, Jim."

"I know, *Schätzlein*." He kissed her.

"But how do you get permission? You must need a pass surely? Don't you have to give the address of where you are staying?"

"From what I can make out, weekend passes are easy to come by and for this visit I have given the address of the CIC, you know, the

Civilian Internment Camp where I was sometimes on guard duty. We have to give an official army address, but I can't think anyone will check up on my whereabouts. Besides, it's worth running a risk to spend time in my very own internment camp alone with my pretty guard, Heidi Braun."

Jim promptly embraced his wardress.

"Oh Jim, do please be careful. I wouldn't want you to get into trouble on my account."

"No, I know. But now I must get back into uniform. See you next week."

'No, know and now – bit hard that for any foreigner,' he thought, as he clumped down the familiar wooden stairs. Shortly he was on the tram, making his way towards the *Autobahn*, and the battered route.

*

The battalion's company clerk had been right. Blanktal did seem 'a fair-sized town', set among low, conifer-clad hills. Yet Jim saw little of it. Corps HQ barracks, modern, light and airy buildings, were located just outside the town. Jim spent most of his off-duty hours in the spacious, well appointed sergeants' mess. He soon set about seeking to recover his badly neglected table-tennis skills. The mess membership, consisting mostly of technical experts of one sort or another, struck Jim as being far more sophisticated, more crossword conscious, more aloof, than the members of an infantry sergeants' mess, not so earthily matey, say, as Ernie, Jock and Jack.

As for his on-duty hours, these were principally spent in the working company of four other AEC sergeants, an ATS typist and a male clerk – a private.

Laurie, he outwardly tolerated but inwardly despised for being a man obsessed with dreams of grandeur, a passion for promotion – and the temperament of the toady. An oft repeated moan followed each daily consultation of the notice board – a gripe that he had not yet been elevated to WO II rank. What a crawler, a bloke who among the lower ranks would be curtly tagged 'the CO's bum boy'.

Cool, blasé Geoff, tall and slim, with his khaki uniform immaculately pressed, had spent a year at university before joining up and so, tended to give himself airs as he smoked with languid grace. Alan stood equally tall but broader, a man of calm and genial disposition. Just as well he is, thought Jim, for the typist clung to him, in and out of working hours, with puma-like ferocity. Of South American origin, Conchita was plainly not pretty but what she lacked in looks was more than compensated by Latin passion. Alan seemed positively washed out at times.

And so to Derek, a gifted, easy going art teacher from somewhere called Yorkshire. Possessed of a thick moustache, modelled to match a good sense of humour, Jim found Derek's company far more congenial than that of his other colleagues.

But congenial was not the word for 'Crowbar'. This tall fresh-faced, sandy-haired Scot had the outlook of an embittered ancient of some deeply depressing Calvinistic sect. Young Crowbar soon made it threateningly clear that he held the deepest detestation of anything and everything German – whether alive or dead. Differentiation between shades of good and evil appeared impossible in his cold, unforgiving creed. 'Poppycock mon!' Jim sensed that trouble might come from this merciless Mac – a serious potential threat to his 'sinful' weekends. Jim resolved to be very much on his guard where Crowbar was concerned. Och aye.

Jim's duties were light, he was put in charge of educational stores, their receipt and distribution, mostly brand new books, stationery, and bolts of dressmaking material for the ATS. It was a job that made more demands on his muscles than his brains and he soon found out that Crowbar was somehow always too busy with urgent clerical duties to lend Jim a hand. It seemed a bit risky to order that self-righteous prig to hump parcels of books about. Crowbar might well scotch Jim's weekend plans by a wink here, a nod there, for Crowbar understood the authority structure and where viewpoints, sympathetic to his own bigotry, could be found, and cunningly informed of fraternisation 'crimes'. Jim's CIC cover could so easily be blown.

'Steady lad,' said Jim to himself, 'rein in the imagination a little. It will soon be weekend again.' And soon it was. On the road once more, past the attractive half-timbered houses of Wickede, the grey, grim prison at Werl to the welcome sight of the concrete *Autobahn* running east and west to the south of Hamm. Relatively plain sailing now. Five different truck drivers had taken part in 'Operation Thumb up' – *Hin*, this time. Fortunately, Jim didn't have to wait long between lifts, but what would things be like, '*Zurück*', and, for that matter in the bleak mid-winter?

Drivers were usually on their own and glad of a bit of company. For all they cared, a passenger could be on privilege, compassionate or straight passionate leave, and making his way to or from some place and person of interest. For all the freemasonry of the open road, Jim always tried, by one dodge or another, to steer talk away from plump-thighed birds. Not that he had any rooted objection to lewd remarks, witty or witless; he just didn't want what he had come to regard as a fine relationship, to be even indirectly sullied by coarse comments, language or anecdotes of sexual prowess and adventure. One ploy was to light a cigarette and pass it to a garrulous driver dwelling excessively on last night's conquest.

\*

"By the way, Heidi, I had a letter from my old employer a couple of days ago. Perhaps you'd like to have a go at reading it." Heidi carefully unfolded the typed letter and began to study it. After a few moments of perplexed concentration, she sighed and handed back the letter.

"No, I'm sorry, Jim, it's just too hard for me. But I see there are numbers in it. Would those be about your pay?"

"Yes."

The letter had been written in circumspect but friendly terms:

> *The position with regard to reinstatement, as you already know, is that each member of the Forces who returns to us will be placed in the position that he would be occupying if he had not left us for National Service. You know, of course, that the salary is governed by a scale, and in your case the commencing rate will be £5 3/6.*

"What does that mean, Jim?"

"It means that I would get about five pounds a week."

"Is five pounds a good wage?"

"Many people marry on less."

"And what about the future?"

"'...we do feel that you younger men who have had the advantage of wider experience whilst serving in the Forces should receive first consideration for promotion.' It seems that ex-servicemen will be well placed for promotion."

"What do you think, then? I don't fully understand but it all sounds good." She looked at him with wide eyes, her manner anxious, eager for reassurance.

"Well, it is a fair offer and it is tempting. It reminds me of another of our old sayings, 'a bird in the hand is worth two in the bush'. That sort of means take a safe and sure opportunity when it comes along because if you are too ambitious, or greedy, you may end up with nothing."

"So what will you do?"

"I'll think it well over."

"Jim, darling, there's something I've been wanting to tell you for some time. I have hesitated so long because I have felt so ashamed."

Heidi looked like a miserable little girl who has been badly but unjustly scolded.

Bewildered and apprehensive, Jim put a comforting arm around her slim shoulders as she turned her unhappy face imploringly towards him.

"Please don't be cross, Jim, please."

"I've no reason to be as far as I know."

The partly rehearsed words came spilling out.

"I don't think I can bring any money to our marriage."

A moment or two passed before Jim replied.

"Well, it's not something I've given much thought to – the cost of setting up a home that is. But I'm not altogether surprised at what you've just told me. But can you tell me why?" He quickly added, "You don't have to if you don't want to."

"No, I must tell you, I really must. The news came as a great shock to me. When I asked my Mom and Dad about my savings account, at first they didn't want to tell me what had happened. When I insisted they tell me, I finally got it out of my mother that all the money, all my savings, had been used to buy food for the family on the black market during the last years of the war when things were very bad. This means I can't help you with money in any way for the wedding or the start of our married life. I feel so badly let down by my own parents. I had trusted them so, and now..." Heidi's grey eyes, those so honest eyes, filled with tears and she began to sob, quietly.

"Oh, Heidi, Heidi, please don't, please don't. The money isn't that important."

Jim dabbed her eyes with a khaki handkerchief.

"*C'est la vie*, as the French say – that's life. Just so long as you iron my shirts OK then..."

"Please don't joke, Jim." Heidi sobbed, "this is a serious matter and I never had the slightest idea of what my parents were doing with my hard earned savings."

Heidi began to cry again, and she reached for Jim's handkerchief.

"I suppose they did what they thought was best for everyone. And if they had asked you for the money, I can't imagine you would have refused them knowing what it was for?"

"No, I suppose not. But they should have asked me."

"I agree. But then, they couldn't know, and neither could you, that someone like me would come along to complicate your lives."

"But they should have asked me."

Heidi had stopped crying and Jim tenderly kissed her red-rimmed eyes. She kissed him on the lips.

"Thank you, Jim."

"What for?"

"For being Jim."

"We have an old saying."

"What another one?" Heidi gave a wan smile.

"Yes, it goes 'it's no good crying over spilled milk'!"

"It's no good crying over spilled milk. Oh, yes, I see." Heidi gave a brighter smile.

"I feel a bit better now I've told you. But you will understand why I was so interested in that letter you showed me from your old employer."

"Naturally, but deep down I know I would still like to go to university if I can. I shall always feel cheated unless I try seriously for a place. Once I was stopped because I had not studied Latin – and besides, the war was on as well. But now, chances, especially for ex-servicemen, seem much brighter."

"Jim, although I don't understand as much as I would like to about such things, I'll *drücke beide Daumen für Dich.*"

"And I'll keep my fingers crossed for you too *Schätzlein.*"

Heidi gave a sparkling smile.

"I've just remembered another of your funny English sayings." She glanced merrily at the bright afternoon sunlight streaming into the room.

"Oh, and what might that be?"

"Let's make hay while the sun shines."

\*

Bowling along the *Autobahn*, roughly in the direction of Blanktal, Jim thought not only about Heidi but about how much better 'things' had been handled after the Second World War than after the First. At the end of the Great War, large numbers of ex-servicemen had been dumped on the labour market in an impoverished land fit for heroes. Virtually no planning had taken place and scant consideration had been shown for the men's plight. Now, men and women were being released back into the labour market in a fair and phased manner and with a statutory right, in many instances, to re-employment with their former employers.

This time no thin, haggard men, shabbily dressed and hollow-eyed, should appear on the streets, trying, with forced cheerful grins, to sell matches and boot laces from their trays to people often little better off than themselves.

No, this time, training, vocational and educational opportunities were extensively available even before entering the labour market. Such opportunities were well resourced. Not least the College of the Rhine Army, as Jim was soon to discover.

## Chapter Thirteen

# Back and Forth

With mild curiosity Jim picked up the bright blue covered prospectus of the College of the Rhine Army and skimmed through a number of its pages.

> The town of GÖTTINGEN is set in most attractive country, on the edge of the HARZ mountains... day-trips are run most Sundays; on these trips students are taken in TCVs (troop carrying vehicles), dropped off at some appropriate point, allowed to walk on a well defined trail, and then picked up at the other end of the 'hike'.

'I'll certainly have a bash at that,' thought Jim, and did. The Harz scenery, if on a grander scale, seemed very similar to that around dear old Kerzenbaum – hilly, well wooded and with pleasant green valleys. But the beauty had a curious sinister edge to it. On the well trodden path, an occasional mid-distance glimpse could be gained of towers jutting above their nearby trees – grim Russian watchtowers ceaselessly on the lookout for enemies of Uncle Joe – hm, more likely desperate, displaced persons risking life and limb to seek sanctuary in the West.

That ramble, his encounter with a German spiv, fine old buildings, together with the attractive Goose Girl and her gaggle, formed Jim's most pleasing and abiding impressions of the quiet, old university town. The training course itself was OK. Beta plus possibly, but rating a straight Alpha for confirming his belief that if he ever became a talk and chalk wallah, he would stand before well-motivated adults and never, most decidedly never, bolshie school kids.

Jim made a reasonable fist of the required translations from English to German, wrote a short essay in German about his recent leave, including a brief account of that tipsy swim in the public baths (Pfui!  Pfui!) but evaluated the recommended structure for sixty minute lessons as a bit too regimental.  'Look sharp you 'orrible little lot – on parade for five minutes declensions drill!' But, 'fair play is an *Edelstein*', as his old *Vater* might have said, the diagrams setting out the careful build up (on a blackboard) of explanations of grammatical points, showed good imagination.  A good tip that, as well – use different coloured chalks for *der, die, das.* (Such guidance gave Jim useful ideas about how to compose his 'English for Heidi', whenever he could get round to it.)  That, in turn, prompted another thought – the required text on the course was 'German from Scratch'.

'*Englisch von Kratzen*'?  No, couldn't possibly be right.  *Kratzen* did mean to scratch – the nose, the back – wherever the tiresome itch arose.  He'd have to check.  Interesting point this, but how much to read into it?  Anglo-Saxon tall buildings scraped the sky but the German translation took them a lesser distance as cloud scratchers – *Wolkenkratzer*.

Lesson XXI
Purpose: To teach separable and inseparable verbs.

Hell, he'd been 'separable' from his 'inseparable' Heidi for far too long – nearly a whole fortnight now!

Lesson XXIII – weak and strong verbs and tenses.

Now there – in Section Four could be found a golden nugget of a word '*Plusquamperfekt*'.  Stand back and marvel at its solidity, such dignity.  Would Heidi regard plus something perfect, as a compliment?  No, of course not.  She would look delightfully baffled, those trusting grey eyes open wide, a slight frown of concentration on her face.

Jim was well aware that his formal knowledge of German grammar was superior to Heidi's or Trudi's or Freda's and most certainly hearty Helga's.  He held it to be right that the structure of a language should be clearly understood.  But the snag was, as he ruefully acknowledged to himself, that he fretted too much about the accuracy of his declensions, his word order and the like.  This fretting impaired the fluency of his everyday speech.  Many Germans didn't seem that fussy about grammatical niceties.  More than once he had noticed a German say *'besser wie'* instead of *'besser als'* – better than.

But turn things the other way round. Take that German spiv he had been chatting with a few days ago. Now his English, spoken with a strong American accent, was easily understood but, from an English viewpoint, still much influenced by German word order.

"Not thinking of kidnapping her, are you?"

Jim nodded in the direction of the comely Goose Girl.

"This week, *nicht*."

Max sniggered.

"But if her geese real had been, they would long ago in the pot disappeared have."

The two young men discussed comparative economics, agreeing that coffee prices and more particularly the price of cigarettes, was probably the most important indicator of local economic and living conditions. A fag standard so to speak. For the same number of fags, twice as many marks would be paid in Pullenstadt as in Kerzenbaum, and more than three times the 'K rate' in war damaged Bochum. (Jim while gently trying to persuade Heidi to give up smoking altogether, gladly gave her most of his cigarette ration to use as she chose. For one thing, good stockings were always hard to come by.)

Max may have been boasting in order to impress, Jim wasn't sure, but the German spiv maintained that for 3,000 marks a customer could get someone bumped off, whereas 4,000 were needed to buy a car tyre.

Certainly, the black market, with its hard, cynical values permeated every day life – just take a gander around any sizeable railway station if evidence were needed. Without question, millions of people had been brutalised by the war. Great numbers of refugees and displaced persons lived in degrading conditions. Continuing harsh deprivation might well drive hitherto law abiding citizens, of any or no country, to desperate measures – a few no doubt to murder, many more to amateurish prostitution and many more still to *'klauen'* – stealing.

Jim retained his admiration for a young lance corporal driver, back in A Company days, who had refused a piteous invitation to nip behind some bushes and have his soldier's way in return for some scraps of fuel. This Tommy Atkins allowed a few lumps of coal to fall off the back of his truck leaving the young mother no doubt wondering at the ways of 'the English'.

*Ach Mensch*, it was all very well reflecting in this way, but he had a lesson to prepare. Jim touched his cap to the pretty Goose Girl, a finely modelled statue in the open air, and sauntered back to his billet. But, even so, he mused on – yes, that was a major element in his love for Heidi – she was a naturally good and considerate human being, setting a quiet, unselfconscious example of basic human decency amid much that was rotten.

\*

"Oh, I'm so glad you're back, Jim. I have missed you so." Jim squeezed Heidi's hand.

The young lovers stood close together on a slope of the Dortmund racecourse. For six consecutive evenings ('gates open 1900 hours') the British Army was presenting a tattoo to British personnel and German civilians alike. '*Buntes Nachtspiel Millionen Lichter*' – blimey, ten German syllables for the British two! Presumably 'tattoo' meant nothing to Germans, whereas 'a colourful display by night with a million lights' might well draw the crowds long starved of bright, mass entertainment.

Jim considered the tattoo to be wonderfully stirring, spectacular and patriotic. While as a schoolboy and youth, he had always enjoyed watching (the infinite variety of knobbly knees notwithstanding) the annual Scouts Rally in Handsworth Park, this present military display could be placed in a different league altogether – adult, smart, efficient, spirited. To himself he acknowledged feeling a tinge of disappointment that Heidi seemed unable to share his own obvious enthusiasm. It wasn't as though the various displays contained any element of triumphal crowing over the defeat of Germany.

The informing spirit of the tattoo was surely that military displays could be designed and presented with no aggressive intent, free of association with political bombast and propaganda, but with musical, open-hearted delight in colourful pageantry. The whole concept and its execution was a healthy world away from the obscene, jackboot strutting, of the hysterical Nuremburg rallies.

"Look, they're going to play one of our favourites '*Caprifischer*'."

"Oh, good. That is a nice melody."

The song sheet provided for community singing contained both German songs (printed in German) and English. There was nothing on the sheet to cause offence to either nation. No songs relating to the recent war – won and lost, except one, the shared Lilli Marlene. Apart from the 'Fishermen of Capri', the German songs were traditional folk songs. And as for the British tunes, they derived principally from the old music halls – good old singsong melodies; 'Daisy', 'Swanee River', 'Lily of Laguna', ('Dad would like that,' thought Jim) 'Two lovely black eyes', 'After the Ball', 'I love a lassie', 'She was a dear little Dicky Bird'. Even the one First World War song, 'Pack up your troubles' was a cheer 'em up favourite, not a jingoistic bray.

Dark steadily deepened into night, a rich black, velvety night. Suddenly all lights went out, leaving only cigarette tips to glow and move in the blackness. Seconds later, a single spotlight lit with intense brilliance, a kilted piper, as he entered the arena to the eerie strains of the bagpipes. 'Highly effective and dramatic,' thought Jim 'just the stuff to make your hair curl.'

And so, back to Blanktal and the resumption of 'Operation Thumb up'.

'The short hours we were together were so lovely and now I'm looking forward to next weekend with you. I'm so pleased your return journey worked out so well,' ('Funny that,' thought Jim, 'the German phrase could be translated as 'without a hitch', yet successful hitches were essential to the whole business, ah well!') 'But now that it's getting dark so early, it will be better that you don't leave here so late – even though I love you to be with me.' As always, Heidi was being a considerate girl, bless her. Jim now faced the eternal torturing dilemma, even for the experienced hitchhiker – when to start back? How long to stay?

'Who won then at table tennis? I believe Jim that your thoughts were still in Pullenstadt... or?' Well, the little tease. 'I can't believe that you lost.' The little flatterer. 'Things are much the same here, no prospect of work yet.'

Damn! With the process of demobilisation well under way, the Hammer On Club had closed. How long could Heidi keep her flat above the shop? 'All my love, Heidi.' No uncertainty there. Heidi would share her company with others, but not her love. Of that, Jim was certain.  Letter number thirty was carefully replaced in its envelope.

Jim quite fancied his chances at table tennis but was forced by results to acknowledge that he was by no means the best player in the mess.  That piqued him rather.  So, he couldn't entirely repress a touch of *Schadenfreude*, in his reaction to the best player's own defeat, by none other than the visiting Hungarian, G.V. Barna, world champion, or was it Bergmann?  Either way, this international wizard of the pimpled paddle walloped the best of British.  He went on to enhance, without any trace of 'showing off', his distance above the mess standard, by challenging anyone to beat him, while he himself played from a sitting position on an ordinary wooden chair.  He remained easily undefeated.  Such speed of reflexes, such wonderful anticipation, such power, such dexterity.  Jim among the crowd of cheering spectators, stood goggle eyed in admiration.

*

"Jim."

Jim looked across his desk towards Derek.  "Yes, oh Grand Lama of the dung hills."

"Salaam, oh wise one of the imperial yak stall.  Isn't the CIC in Pullenstadt the place where you spend your weekends?"  Derek gave a broad wink.

Jim winked back.

"Sure.  Why do you ask?"

"Bit about it in a paper here.  Better not let Crowbar see it.  He'll go spare if he does!"

Derek passed across a raggedly torn newspaper cutting.

'British feed them well because of their infamy' an eye catching headline.  Despite 'fearful' handicaps placed in his way, the 'fearless' reporter gained access to this camp for Germans 'in the "automatic" arrest class...  Each of them now gets a 'basic' ration of 1,800 calories a day compared with the 1,050 of the non-Nazis outside... breakfast consisted of one-seventh of a loaf of good brown bread that tastes exactly like pre-war Hovis, three ounces of sausage, three quarters of an ounce of butter, a pint of black coffee per man, and eight herrings among each ten men...'

"What do you make of it, Jim?"

"Don't know, really. I only had to guard the blighters not dish out their rations. A number of them had obviously lost their beer and sausage bellies since being in the camp. You could easily tell from the folds in their flab. I imagine this reporter has his facts right about the calories and menus, but I suspect his selection of quotes from the guards is a bit biased – in the Crowbar direction."

Jim folded the cutting and placed it in his wallet. After a few minutes, he spoke again.

"As these Nazis have to go for trial, I imagine it makes good sense not to have 'em appearing in the dock looking half-starved. If that happened, fearless reporters would accuse us of being just as bad as the Nazis."

"You might have something there," murmured Derek, "but whatever the number of herrings involved, I expect you hope the camp won't close down before next summer."

"Oh Grand Lama of the dung hills, you're dead right."

*

So the weeks drifted by in a steady, repeated rhythm of five days of relative routine followed by 'that lovely weekend'! 'The ride in a three tonner that you couldn't share...' The parody of the popular war time song was never completed. Doing what he was paid to do caused Jim few problems, except when man-handling heavy parcels of books from truck to storeroom. Truth to tell, during parts of many days, time dragged.

And so Jim was glad, mighty glad when an old heartthrob re-entered his life. He grudgingly accepted that she was not his alone and that in the pecking order of suitors, he must be near the end of a long, long line, way way behind Colonel Egham, Kurt von Kalbsfleisch, von Knückelduster, Guttlinger, Schmallpanz, Havanutha, Wishiwashi – tough competition.

'Beachcomber' of the *Daily Express*, imaginative creator of such splendid comic characters as Captain Foulenough, Charles Suet, Mr Justice Cocklecarrot, Dr Strabismus and Mrs McGurgle was really responsible for the return to Jim's life of that Mata Hari of Tibet, one ravishing Dingi-Poos.

Derek and Jim had opened a file, on scrap paper let it be noted, on the development of relationships between various members of the

Education Section and intrigues in Tibet, much concerned with rancid butter, tea, brick and yakkery, widespread. The two contributors sought to out-do one another in facetiousness. Drawn up by the joint head Lamas of the monastery of The Swinging Icicle, 'Yak Standing Orders' were promulgated and an exchange of silly memoranda began.

> The time has come to squash the perfidious rumours relating to Dingi-Poos' ancestry. Neither NANKI nor WINNIE (The) are any relation to our Blossom of the Dung Hills. Dlngis' ancestors can be smelled back to the lst YAK Dynasty, and then some.

Turning over that half page of scrap, Jim read something of the 'life is real, life is earnest' school of thinking.

> 5. Should the soldier be found unsatisfactory from a military standard or should the GERMAN firm make any justifiable complaint about him, he will be returned to his unit forthwith.
> 6. The soldier will be attached to a military unit in the town for accommodation, rations and discipline and that unit is being requested to send an officer or NCO periodically to visit the soldier at his work.
> 7. The scheme is experimental and should it be found undesirable or unsatisfactory because of language or other difficulties it will be discontinued. As, however, thc fitting of soldiers for their return to civilian life is considered of paramount importance, it is hoped to give the scheme a good trial.

Crikey, that was a bold imaginative scheme and no mistake. Just think of it, getting some Jerry firms to give vocational, 'on the job' training to some British Tommies who were hoping to work as tradesmen in civvy street. And were there deeper motives involved in 'bridge-building' and reparation seeking? It was a risky business, though, for the squaddies concerned – one 'unfortunate' remark on the shop floor about squareheads, sauerkraut, 'hot stuff' Fräuleins – and, Boom! *Alles kaputt*! RTU'D – returned to unit.

Had 'other difficulties' besides language put paid to the scheme, or was it still operational? The amount of this scrap paper did not encourage optimism.

"Heidi."

"Hmm?"

"Have you ever had to fill out a form like this one?"

"Show me, please."

Jim passed an official document to her headed, 'Military Government of Germany – *Fragebogen.*' (Questionnaire) – 'CCG' (Control Commission Germany) 'Public Safety (Special Branch)'.

She studied the document, printed partly in English but mostly in German, then quietly answered, "No," and shivered.

"What's the matter?"

"Just some bad memories, some about the few fanatical Nazis in our village, including one of our schoolteachers." She hunched her shoulders, a mixture of disgust and fear crossing her face.

"Want to tell me about them?"

Heidi reflected, hesitated.

"No, if you don't mind, I'd rather not. Except..." She paused, "to say that once I started work, that horrible schoolmaster began making eyes at me, to... how you say, chat me up, whenever he met me in the street. Ugh! He was horrible. As he was an official in the party, you could never know what he might be saying about you or what harm he might do you or your family. Ugh! A vile man." She shivered again.

Jim squeezed her hand reassuringly.

"Never mind, it's all in the past and I expect we've got the *Schweinhund* under lock and key by now."

"But why are you showing me this form? It looks so... so official and it's so long."

"Yes it is. But even once I am out of the Army, and we fix the date of our marriage, for, say in a year's time, or a bit longer, I expect you will still have to fill out lots of forms before you are allowed to come to England."

"Oh dear. Why do things have to be so complicated. Why can't two grown up people like ourselves, who love one another, simply go and get married. It's not fair that other people should make life so difficult for us."

Jim was silent for a moment or two. At the level of what might be called 'decent human values', Heidi's case was unanswerable. But the nettle of unpleasant facts had to be grasped.

"Maybe not. But we can't make the rules and remember, we have both promised our parents to stay apart for a while. And, as I've said, we don't make the official rules for people in our position."

"No, I suppose you are right. But it makes me so unhappy when I think that we shall be so far apart from one another for maybe quite a long time."

Jim kissed her, tenderly.

"Come on now, please just glance down this list of German organisations and tell me if you've ever been a member of any of them. I know there are more than fifty there but it won't take you a minute to check."

"No, it won't. I've not been a member of anything."

"Not even the girls' section of the Hitler Youth Movement. No. 46. HJ. *einschliesslich* BdM?"

"No, not even that. You must have realised by now that I am not fond of uniforms. With one exception, of course."

"Of course."

They kissed.

Jim pressed Heidi no further, at least, not in connection with the questionnaire, but when she went to brew a pot of tea, he glanced at some of the remaining questions of the twelve page *Fragebogen*.

> 115.    Have you ever been imprisoned, or, have restrictions of movement, residence or freedom to practice your trade or profession been imposed on you for racial or religious reasons or because of active or passive resistance to the Nazis?
>
> 116.    If you have answered "yes" to any of the questions from 110 to 115 (evidence of anti-Nazism) give particulars and the names and addresses of two persons who can confirm the truth of your statements.

Ye Gods, what a test! Just suppose your two 'referees' had vanished, into a concentration camp or a gas chamber!

Not for the first time, Jim thanked his lucky stars that he had not been born and raised in Nazi Germany. For all its imperfections,

Britain remained essentially a country of wonderful and well guarded
freedoms when compared to that Nazi Hell hole. He wondered how
Heidi would react to unaccustomed liberties of speech, travel, thought
and belief; to the right to stick your tongue out, within reason, at
starchy authority; to being able to live in an atmosphere free of the
poison of neighbour blabbing on neighbour to the dreaded authorities.
No knock on the door, of that terrifyingly sinister kind, in the night,
in Brum.

Heidi returned with the teapot.

"And now Heidi, I've got one bit of good news for you." She
looked at him eagerly, so trustingly.

"And what might that be?"

"My application to stay on in the Army for an extra six months has
been approved."

"*Gott sei Dank*, that's wonderful. That means you won't be out of
the Army – until when?"

"Oh, about the end of next May, I should think."

"Are you likely to be moved somewhere else?"

"It's always possible. But I think there's a good chance that I shall
stay in Germany."

"*Gott sei Dank* – and now I've a bit of encouraging news for you."

"Fire away."

"It now seems quite possible that I shall get another job working
for the British."

"Good show. But what as and where?"

"My usual work as a waitress; this time in the officers' mess at
Ruhr Coal District head offices."

"And where might that be?"

"At one of the mines just south of Pullenstadt, a bit nearer your
*Autobahn*. *Komm'* I'll show you on the map."

"Does that mean you'll have to leave this flat?" They both
glanced with affection at all the familiar objects in the room – the
round coffee table, the long, heavy '*Donner und Blitzen*' night
curtains, the couch.

Heidi's eyes sparkled.

"Well..." She smiled, a hint of mischief in her expression.

"Well, what?"

"Well, why do you ask?"

"Come on, don't keep me in suspenders."

Heidi smiled that smile.

"No," she whispered softly, "I can still stay here, you too if you are good."

"*Gott sei Dank.*"

*

A mere fifty miles from romance to fantasy.

*Outer Yakland*
*2nd Wax 3rd Moon*

*Dear Jim,*

> *I have just returned from... after some good scouting round the mountains. In... I met Colonel Egham who was bird watching and 'dear' stalking. Near the summit of... I met a shaggy beast who said it was related to 'Orace (Corps HQ Yak). Further it informed me that it ate rancid butter with its porridge...*

Good old Derek, actually enjoying, so he said, a leave on the isle of Arran in late November.

Soon it would be Jim's turn for leave. The first time at home for Christmas since 1941. Home which meant 'real bacon and egg' as only his mother could cook it. Wonderful. And yet he knew his thoughts would be echoing Marlowe's plea, or rather its translation - *'Komm' leb mit mir und liebe mich.'*

## Chapter Fourteen
# Go to Gaol

"Well, aren't you going to open it?"

Jim detected the edgy note of irritation in his mother's voice, and smiled inwardly.

"Well, aren't you?"

Sal's son chewed on, savouring every luscious bite of the superbly crisp bacon. He swallowed, then paused.

"What's the hurry? Bacon and egg soon grow cold, especially in this weather. A love letter will keep warm enough for long enough – at least until the next letter."

"You saucy young devil. You'd never have talked to me like that before you joined that nasty Army."

Jim saw no reason to comment, and spread marmalade, thickly across a slice of buttered toast.

"Any way, why all this fuss now? You could easily have given me the letter last night. Why didn't you?"

Seldom at a loss for a reply of some sort or other, Sal Norton retorted, "You looked so tired after your long journey and so I thought it best to wait 'til this morning."

Jim stayed quiet but again smiled inwardly, this time at the 'I thought'. Mothers, bless 'em, invariably seemed to know what was 'best' for their sons, especially only sons.

Jim carefully slit the envelope with his penknife and began to read Heidi's letter.

"What does she say?"

Wilf Norton lowered his newspaper and looked sternly over his glasses at his wife.

"For goodness sake, Mother, give the lad a chance. Just remember, German isn't his native language."

"Sorry, I forgot," mumbled Sal peevishly.

She waited a few minutes longer and then, "Can you tell us anything yet, Jim?"

"She writes much as you would expect one sweetheart to write to another. She misses me greatly but realises that you in particular, Mother, will be pleased to have me home again." Jim read on, then chuckled.

"I wonder what on earth she means by that – 'don't cause your Mother any worries'. As if I would. It's very cold over there, especially when travelling to work. It's so cold that she's taken to wearing trousers – says that in long boots, bobble hat and trousers, she looks like a little Eskimo. She sends her best wishes and greetings to you both."

Sal Norton visibly relaxed, her pursed lips changing to a soft smile.

"She seems a kind and considerate girl."

"She most certainly is. She wrote this letter knowing it would be waiting for me when I got home."

"A nice thought. May I look at her handwriting please, Jim?" Jim passed the letter to his Mother.

"It's nice clear handwriting – I can see 'England' written here. What is she referring to?"

"She is simply saying, 'this is my first letter to England'."

First to England but number fifty-two in the series that had begun with Jim's departure from Pullenstadt. He wondered what number the letter might be that signalled, 'I'm on my way, Love Heidi'. Drying the breakfast crockery in the tiny kitchen, Jim tapped his Mother on her plump shoulder.

"Do you think you'll be able to share your kitchen with another woman, Ma?"

"Don't call me Ma! Yes, I think so. The poor girl will need quite a lot of help, being so far from home. You say she's not the argumentative type?"

"I've not heard her raise her voice, not even to some of her colleagues when, to my mind, they've obviously been clowning on her at work. Mind you, I think she'll stick to her guns on things that really matter to her, but in a quiet unaggressive way. But remember, in England, she'll be struggling all the time, to improve her English."

"Jim, when you think about it, you're both taking something on. Do you still want to go ahead with your wedding plans? Tell me the truth now."

"We both want to go ahead. We are both convinced we can make a go of things."

Jim gave a memory evoking pull at the wooden handle of the large cast iron mangle standing stolidly opposite the gas stove.

"You'll be pleased to know that I have more or less decided now to apply for a place at Birmingham University. I think it would be better in every way."

"Well, I'm really glad about that. It will make things so much easier for Heidi living with us rather than with total strangers, especially as she is starting married life in a foreign country."

"Yes, you are right. By the way, has Ted been able to rustle up an engagement ring that I can take back with me for Heidi?"

"I believe he has, but it's been difficult for him, everything is still so short."

Jim put the last dried plate back in the rack above the gas stove.

"The Germans have a different custom from us concerning engagement rings."

"Is that so?"

"Yes, one gold ring serves as both an engagement ring and a wedding ring. During the engagement, the ring is worn on the left hand and then transferred to the right at the wedding ceremony."

"Well, that is interesting. Talking of weddings, your Uncle Les is planning to get married to Peggy next year. I'm almost sure he's going to ask you to be best man if you're demobbed in time."

"Crikey! What does a best man have to do?"

"There'll be time enough to talk about that later. What are your plans for today?"

"I'm going to see the Whitleys this afternoon. It's almost a year since Syd was killed." Jim paused, swallowed hard, and went on, "Then Dave and I are going to the flicks this evening."

"He's not got a steady girlfriend yet, then?"

"No, as Fred Astaire warbled: 'he's still fancy free and free for anything fancy'!"

"Time that flighty young man settled down."

"Why don't you tell him so?"

"I will." And she would.

Jim chuckled and walked to the cubicle that separated the roaring, open coal-fired living room from the ice box front room, picked up his scarf and raincoat from the clothes rack on the wall, and made ready to meet the wintery blast.

"So where are you going now?"

"Oh, just for a walk round the park. There's a lot to think about."

Gosh, Brummagem and the British homeland generally did seem drab and drear. People appeared tired, fed-up with rationing, with shortages of every kind. The sparkle of pre-war Christmases had not reappeared. 'Perhaps it's just me,' thought Jim, 'growing older.' Whatever the muddle of reasons for the lack of unforced jollity, he knew he would not feel sad when his leave came to an end. It would be bloody cold back on the *Autobahn* though!

*

Once more, the train shuddered, juddered and clanked to a halt.

"Bloody 'ell not again," muttered one of Jim's fellow passengers. "If things carry on like this, it'll be a damn sight quicker to get out and walk."

Jerked fully out of a doze by the sudden stop, Jim poked his head out of the carriage window and looked up and down the track. To the rear of the train, and near the adjoining track, a few men stood waving their arms. A tall burly WO II strode purposefully past the carriages.

"Right, I need some help from a senior NCO."

He caught sight of Jim's three stripes.

"Follow me, sergeant."

"What on earth for?" muttered Jim as he scrambled down onto the stone chippings.

As he approached the group of men, he could make out someone lying on his back at right angles to and across the adjacent railway lines.

'Someone drunk?' he wondered.

The two khaki clad legs stretching away from the lines looked ordinary enough. Then, suddenly, Jim's stomach gave a violent, convulsive heave. From the groin area upwards lay the mangled remains of flesh and bone, exposed entrails mashed together with blood soaked khaki cloth, some jaggedly smashed ribs, a bloody, pulped mess that had once been a face, a badly crushed skull. One eye had remained in its broken socket, the other had been sprung loose to land a couple of feet away, its unharmed iris and pupil looking blankly at the grey winter sky.

"See if you can get his AB 64, sergeant – and his identity discs."

Gritting his teeth, Jim made a slow, cautious start to open the left-hand pocket of the shattered corpse's battle dress blouse. That pocket was far less damaged and bloodied than the right. Hopefully this poor sod, like Jim himself, kept his Army papers in the pocket nearer the heart. Jim was lucky. He gingerly withdrew the scarcely dented, dark red-brown covered 'Soldier's Service and Pay Book'.

Inwardly, Jim jibbed at raising the badly fractured, bloody and splintered skull with his bare hands, in order to slip the cord 'necklace' of two discs from around the pulped and bloody neck, and up over what remained of the 'head'. Thank God, and Sheffield, that from even quite early days as a schoolboy, he had always carried a good penknife. Carefully Jim cut through the cord and handed over discs and AB 64 to the 'CSM'.

The body having been carefully covered with a ragged tarpaulin from the guard's van, the train slowly resumed its journey.

Within the packed carriages of men returning from leave, speculation ran rife as to how a bloke had come to be run over by a train. In Jim's compartment, the verdict of 'foul play' was unanimous – well almost so. Jim himself wasn't too sure. If the poor devil had fallen or been pushed from an earlier train, on to either track, would he have landed in quite that particular way? There would be lots of questions for the Redcaps to consider. But Jim's main concern remained – to suppress, as far as he could, the grisly memory of that pathetic, and detached single eye staring so weirdly lifeless at the heavens.

*

"Colonel wants to see you."

A malicious smirk accompanied Crowbar's openly insincere 'welcome back'.

"Any idea what for?"

As soon as he had noticed that tell-tale smirk, Jim had immediately assumed his well-practised, Buster Keaton, old Stoneface, expression.

Damn it, he wouldn't, if he could possibly help it, give Crowbar the satisfaction of gloating over any expressions of anxiety, misgiving, alarm that might flit across his face.

"Not really sure. Maybe something to do with that CIC you're so fond of visiting, or, it might be a posting."

With his 'holier than thou' expression of disdain on his features, Crowbar stalked off to rejoice in the 'good riddance' of that 'Jerry lover'.

His thoughts running rapidly on possible lines of defence, Jim argued to himself that his outright lie about where he spent his weekends was unlikely to be the matter to be discussed with His Nibs. Typically, Crowbar had been trying to rattle him. Many officers, their wives still in Britain, did not chose to remain celibate. Lady Alabasters remained unrationed. Besides, officers in the Education Corps seemed a pretty enlightened bunch. No, it was more likely a posting that the Colonel wished to see him about.

Jim was right, a posting to Weberfeld, to the glasshouse sited there! Hell and damnation – on both counts!

First move, look at the map. After a few minutes study, Jim estimated the distance between Pullenstadt and Weberfeld to be about seventy-five miles – quite a jaunt in this mind-numbing, freezing winter weather.

> The snow is snowing, the wind is blowing,
> [...]
> What do I care if icicles form,
> I've got my love to keep me warm.

A catchy and pertinent song – no doubt composed by some sleek tunesmith in front of a blazing log fire.

'Stick to the point lad,' he thought. 'If the prison is on the south side of the town, then I should be well placed for the *Autobahn* which should be pretty busy, running as it does, from Hannover to the Ruhr District. But against that, daylight hours are few and I probably won't be able to get away from chokey until Saturday morning. Then I'll probably have to leave Heidi about midday on Sunday. Hell! But maybe there's a train service between Pullenstadt and Weberfeld? From the map, Weberfeld seems to be a pretty big town.' His mood brightened. Plenty then to discuss with Heidi during this coming weekend, the last to be enjoyed from the base camp at the Monastery of the Swinging Icicle.

"So, if anyone asks me where you are, if I'm honest, I shall have to, say 'in prison'."

Heidi didn't seem sure whether to giggle or look terribly serious.

"You can go on to tell them, if you wish, that I shall be one of a team trying to help naughty soldiers become better soldiers or useful civilians. What I'm actually supposed to do, on a day to day basis, I shan't know until after the prison gates have shut behind me."

He gave a mock shudder.

Heidi gave a real shiver.

"Come on, I'm sure it isn't that bad. It might turn out to be quite interesting in a way. But tell me, how have you been getting on? Do the officers at the mine treat you all right?"

"Yes, they are nice and polite. There are three of them a Frenchman, a Belgian and an Englishman. The Wing Commander is old enough to be my father, almost my grandfather, he's in his early sixties, I should think. The Belgian major is certainly middle-aged. Both these men are married and have German, er, lady friends."

"And how about the Frenchman?"

"Oh, he's quite a bit younger, but he's no trouble." Jim frowned and Heidi quickly added, "No he isn't, really. I promise you."

"Well, just watch your step with Frenchmen. They're so conceited where girls are concerned. This feller might have charming manners but that doesn't mean his intentions are good. Just you be careful."

"Very good, Sergeant Jim."

Heidi gave him an Army salute. He grinned. "And how are your parents?"

"Very well, thank you, but they don't like this terribly cold weather. My Dad was pleased I was able to give him a bottle of cognac for Christmas and yet I nearly lost it."

"How was that?"

"Well, I was being driven home late at night from the mine, when the car, a little Volkswagen, skidded on the icy road and we finished up in a ditch." Heidi swiftly anticipated Jim's question. "No. I wasn't hurt, just a bit shaken that's all. But I did manage to keep the bottle safe. That present did mean so much to Dad with his bad chest."

"Talking of cold weather, what do you think of my new boots?"

"Yes, I've been wondering about those, but I didn't like to ask how you had come by them."

In a previous life the mid-brown, square-toed footwear, clearly modelled on skiing boots, had been a regulation issue leather jerkin. Thanks to a cobbler's skill and some packets of fags, a wonderfully comforting conversion had taken place. Swords into ploughshares – Army jerkin into civvy boots – it was an honourable tradition.

"And now, young Heidi, I've got a couple of presents for you." Heidi said nothing but her eyes revealed affection and a kind of little girl expectancy, that reminded Jim strongly of the excited, round-eyed children sitting at that simple table in Kerzenbaum, eagerly awaiting the arrival of Saint Nicholas, and his boisterous buddy, Ruprecht.

Blushing slightly, Heidi graciously took the cube-shaped box, wrapped in tissue paper, that was held out to her. She had already guessed what it might contain.

Jim looked and sounded uncomfortable. He struggled clumsily in a mixture of German and English, to express complicated thoughts and feelings.

"It's not as posh a ring as I would like to buy you, but things are difficult at home. My brother Ted had quite a job getting it. One day, I'll buy you something better, much better, I promise. Really I will. Anyway, I hope it will fit. I've never given a ring to a girl before and I hope..."

Heidi stopped his yammering with a long, warm kiss. "You don't have to make excuses," she whispered. "It's a present from you and I know you are sincere. That's what really matters."

She kissed him again, then raised the lid of the box, to reveal a slim, silver coloured ring clasping a single stone, pale blue in colour. Heidi slipped the ring on her 'engagement' ring finger, and stretched out her left arm twisting the hand this way and that to view the effect from all angles.

"It's very pretty, very pretty. *Dankeschön vielmals, lieber* Jim. Now we really are engaged."

She beamed with genuine delight.

Jim wondered once more why girls, women, ladies, even old gels, much older than his Mom, set such store by jewellery. He wouldn't wear a ring himself, no fear, not for any price, not even for Heidi, no, not even for her.

"Now with your birthday coming up later this month, here is your other present."

As Heidi stripped off the wrapping paper she gave a low gasp of surprise and pleasure. Her cheeks reddened slightly.

"Well, I hadn't expected anything at all like this, or is it these?"

"I'm not too sure myself. But anyway, not knowing your size, I had to make a guess. They may be on the big side, but they'll help to keep you warm these cold Winter nights."

"Jim they're lovely – and you're lovely."

Heidi gave him an ardent kiss.

"They're such good quality too. So nice to the touch. But didn't your Mother say anything?"

"No, she just sniffed. And Dad just winked."

Heidi held the garments close to her.

"I take it they're men's pyjamas?"

"Yes, the blue and black stripes are more suitable for a man than a woman – and anyway, you can tell by the trousers." Heidi frowned and then laughed.

"I'm afraid they're more my size than yours but you can perhaps turn up the legs and sleeves."

As he said this, Jim was thinking not only of Heidi but of delectable Claudette Colbert, star of *It Happened One Night*. OK, so he, Jim Norton, wasn't a bit like Clark Gable but it mattered not. In all probability, Heidi had never even heard of that he-man heart throb.

"So, *Liebling* Heidi, as your song says *'Zum Abschied reiche ich dir die Hände'*, I must go soon. I don't know when I can see you next. I'll have to find out how things are in Weberfeld. But you know I'll try very hard to 'escape' – and I'll write to you in any case."

Heidi, her eyes moist, voice subdued, but hugging Jim oh so tightly, cautioned him not to take any undue risks, of any kind, to wrap up warm and, "Please to take this little bottle of brandy with you."

And so, the last *Zurück* hitch back to Blanktal. Pack the kit bag yet again, thread the metal bar through the eye holes, close the handle, click the lock to, and wonder what was in store for you in jug, stir, chokey, clink; specifically Number X Military Prison and Detention Barracks – but a glasshouse by any other name is still a glasshouse.

## Chapter Fifteen
# Crime and Punishment

While he had ignored 'Keep off the Grass' signs on occasion, crudely carved his initials on a wooden park bench, and cycled the wrong way down a one way street, Jim had never seriously fallen foul of the law. Of that much he was sure. All right, so he'd 'fiddled' a bit in the Army – that tin of cocoa, for instance, now a suit and the 'spare' jerkin recently transmuted to a pair of boots. But he regarded such transgressions as being basically in the interests of self-preservation in a predatory post-war world. Such 'crimes' remained chicken feed compared to some of the rackets that went on.

Leaving the CIC out of account, the nearest he had previously been to a prison, was simply as a passenger on the good old number 11 bus, the outer-circle, as it trundled past the forbiddingly high wall and massive gates of Winson Green Prison, Birmingham.

'Glasshouse' he knew to be Army slang, a term thought to derive from an early, glass-roofed military prison in Aldershot. No glass roof was visible at Weberfeld, but something like eight, three or four storied, tile roofed modern buildings grouped symmetrically in pairs around a massive parade ground. Between that 'square bashing' arena and the cell blocks ran a broad road, a wide pavement to either side. Small trees, spaced at regular intervals, edged the inner pavement. Everything looked very orderly, even under a light coating of snow.

Jim noted with joy that 'the authorities' had shown the great good sense to locate the prison, in its probable former existence as a purpose built barracks, to the south side of the town, relatively near to the one *Autobahn* that mattered so much to the Heidi bound hitch hiker.

'Who was that poet chap who said April is the cruellest month? Off his rocker, completely off his chump! Nothing could be worse than this January of '47.'

Jim vigorously stamped his feet, now beginning to chill in his square toed, jerkin re-cycled boots, as he walked a few paces along the side of Route 240, and then turned and stumped back on the hardened snow. It was a bit like sentry go, except that there was no sturdy sentry box to provide protection from the piercingly bitter, savage Siberian type wind. What a desolate wasteland of white and grey; spindrift whirling about, the skeletal trees shuddering dismally before the keenest of biting blasts. No houses in sight, no trucks visible.

Thank heavens for that balaclava helmet so lovingly knitted by 'good old Ma' – thank heavens for the cognac so warm-heartedly given to him by his own little Heidi. Gosh, she would be in a tiz thinking of him hitch hiking in such numbingly freezing conditions.

'That's it, a bit of bawdy, and a nip of cognac helps cheer up a chap at a time like this. Let's have the old classic.' Jim set off on another sentry beat, reciting to himself.

> "As cold as a frog by an ice bound pool.
> As cold as the knob of an Eskimo's tool.
> As cold as the hairs on a polar bear's bum.
> As cold as your love for a whore when you've cum.
> As cold as charity and that's pretty chilly,
> But not so cold as our little Willy.
> He's dead – poor bastard."

"Hey, Sarge – want a lift?"
"You bet – ta muchly."
"Hop in then."
"Bloody parky."
"Dead right."
"Real brass monkey weather."
"And no mistake."

\*

"My dearest Jim, would you like a hot bath, to thaw out?"
"That would be great."

And indeed it was. Splashing vigorously about, Jim suddenly remembered an entry in his 1940 diary, written as a schoolboy evacuee in Stroud which said:

'Had bath and sang well in it...' or something like that. Then, as now, a 'lovely hot bath' had been such a treat.

Si, si, si, sing a love song for a penny,
Si, si, si, just a penny serenade.

Heidi liked that song. Pity he didn't have much of a singing voice. But boyish, boisterous enthusiasm sometimes made up for a lack of class.

Later, snuggled warmly together, Heidi began to ask Jim questions about prison life.

"So you see, I'm one of five 'schoolies' as we are called, whose job it is to try and help the prisoners to reform their ways, to give them training and instruction, to help them make a better life for themselves. Rehabilitation is the posh, long word for it. Harry, for instance, takes regular classes for some soldiers who can hardly read or write."

"And what do you actually do?"

"As before, I take some classes in German. Of course, the soldiers aren't forced to 'go to school' but conditions are often better in the classrooms than elsewhere in the prison – warmer and more comfortable. Then I teach English to Polish soldiers."

"Polish?"

"Yes, refugees who joined the British Army and later, when the war was over, they simply wanted to get back to Poland as quickly as possible, so they deserted. They are the hardest lot of all to do anything with."

"Why's that? They don't look as though they're going to hit you, do they?" Heidi sounded anxious. Jim chuckled.

"No, nothing like that. If they misbehaved, they know they would not be able to continue sitting in a warm classroom. No, it's more subtle and difficult than that – and, in a way, I really feel sorry for these chaps. They simply want to get home, highly dangerous though their journeys might be.

"Many of these chaps have a reasonable command of English, or rather we're pretty sure they have. Their leader, a big, beefy, round-faced chap, is obviously highly intelligent and well educated, speaking excellent English when he chooses to do so. Usually he keeps his squad almost silent – so they sit there, surly, resentful and I can't make any real headway with them. It's as though they use the classes, partly to keep warm, and partly to make a sullen, silent protest against their situation."

Heidi sighed. "Poor Jim."

"Oh, you get used to it and there is a brighter side. This experience and some of the things I learned at Göttingen and Ghent have given me some good ideas about 'English for Heidi'. On my next visit, I'll bring with me what I've written so far."

"Oh good, I shall look forward to that."

"I also run sessions on current affairs; and quizzes as well sometimes."

"*Bitte*, what are quizzes?"

"Whoever is in charge asks questions on, say geography, sport, history and the like and the 'students' shout out the answers if they know them. Played by two competing teams, it can be good fun. I get a lot of help from a British magazine called *John Bull* in drawing up the questions. It's an easy and interesting way of improving a person's knowledge. For example, I might ask: 'When is the next General Election?'"

"And the answer?"

"1950. And you'll be able to vote, young lady. And you'll be Mrs Norton."

"Mrs Norton. It does sound strange – but nice."

"And I hope you'll vote for the Labour Party. The other lot are a waste of time."

"Is the Labour Party the *Arbeiter Partei*?"

"Yes."

"Well, I'm all for the workers, like my Dad."

"That's the stuff."

Jim gave her a congratulatory kiss.

"There's one curious thing about the prisoners we teach – and the ones we don't."

"Oh, what's that?"

"They are not known as prisoners but SUS."

"SUS?"

"Yes, it stands for soldiers under sentence. I don't really know why. Maybe it's something to do with morale. Sounds better than – prisoner, or convict. I don't know."

"And how about the men who carry the keys, the guards?"

"Oh, they're an interesting bunch and no mistake."

"Why do you say that?"

"For one thing, they all hold at least the rank of sergeant and I suspect that some, maybe many of them, would never have been promoted to sergeant if they had not been in the prison service. Some of the staff seem just as rough and tough as the men they lock up – the thieves, deserters, black marketeers."

Jim's face grew thoughtful. "It's a strange business."

"What is?"

"Crime and punishment. People have puzzled about it for centuries."

"I am sure that is so, but what matters to me, young Jim, is that you look after yourself in the here and now."

"I will. Promise. But is my woolly hat dry? We call it a balaclava helmet." (No need for a short history lesson now, thought Jim.)

"I expect so, I'll fetch it for you."

*

"Congratulations, Jim."

"What for? Having a short back and sides in this heat wave?"

"No, you twerp! You presumably haven't been told officially yet. You've been promoted to WO II. So get those stripes off lad." Ron was right. Promotion to warrant rank wef (with effect from) 1 Feb. Although not greatly surprised, Jim felt very gratified at the step up. After all, he hadn't put in for promotion or hinted that he expected it. He wouldn't have been greatly disappointed if he had been overlooked. He had simply worked conscientiously as a sergeant on ten shillings and sixpence a day (all found) and had been duly rewarded. He had become schoolie number two now in the pecking order. Not that it mattered.

But one tricky decision had to be made, one that touched his vanity. Should he have cloth or metal for his new badge of rank, the laurels encircling a crown? Cloth would need to be stitched. 'Brass' would need to be regularly 'brassoed' entailing the use of the old, well worn button stick.

Jim breathed hard on his specs, then polished the lenses with care and vigour. His own hornrims had long been substituted for the regulation wire framed 'goggles'. Having taken careful measurements of distance from each side of both sleeves, and from the bottom of each sleeve, Jim began, in slow laborious fashion, to stitch the crown and laurels into place. Don't forget the greatcoat, he reminded himself.

"Ron, I've been meaning to ask you for some time, but have kept forgetting. Who's that chap who's exercised on his own on the square, when no one else is about? I've noticed there's one staff in front of him and one behind, all the time he's out there."

"Oh that poor devil. I don't know his name but he's under a death sentence and due for the drop in a few day's time."

Jim stopped stitching – a daft, trivial business in view of what he had just heard. "What was his crime?"

"I don't know exactly. Murder and rape I believe. Anyway, Pierrepoint, you know, the official hangman, is expected to be coming over in a few days time to do the job. Not here, but in Hannover I believe. But all the same, there might be ructions from our SUS."

Happily, no ructions ensued. On that fateful day, the SUS were assembled and seated in the prison chapel and adjoining areas. The staff, expressionless, backs to the walls, stood near one another, a tight human ring around those penned in. The atmosphere remained calm, sombre, and reflective. Schoolie number four had volunteered to give a talk on 'The Development of the Jet Engine'. He gave an excellent presentation in Jim's estimation. But how could one tell how much had been absorbed by this particular captive audience? A silly question to raise, really – the intention had been to provide a distraction before a man's neck was officially broken.

The lecture finished, everyone waited tensely and in silence for the fatal moment. Each man seemed largely impervious to his neighbour's presence. A short prayer was mumbled and the SUS filed quietly back to their cells.

It seldom occurred that Jim had occasion to visit the cell blocks, but whenever he did, he was always vastly impressed by the spotless conditions of the cells and corridors. He had never, ever seen anywhere cleaner – a quite immaculate standard of hygiene was set – and achieved in glistening, sparkling fashion.

Then there was the condition of the kit to marvel at. Jim himself had been involved in quite a few kit inspections in his time, but the rigid neatness of the folded blankets and clothes; the perfect displays of equipment, in these cells, beggared belief.

On one particular morning while still admiring these shining results of a spit and polish regime, he suddenly stopped in his walk. On hands and knees, crawling towards him along the corridor, came three men, line abreast, energetically scrubbing an already clean floor. Heads down, scrubbing as if their next meal depended on their swift, sure, well practised motions, they ignored Jim.

Jim approached the line and addressed the man in the centre.

"What the devil are you doing here?"

The ex-fellow sergeant from Jim's battalion days, looked up briefly, still scrubbing.

"Well, that's a bloody tomfool question if ever I heard one."

"Sorry, I meant what are you in for?"

With his eyes again following the arc of his moving brush, 'Tosher' hissed, "For floggin' too many effin' Army blankets on the black market. Now piss off, Jim, else I'll be in bigger lumber still." Jim walked on, pondering.

He hadn't seen Tosher as a criminal type. 'Suppose he grew greedy and paid the penalty.' Jim wondered whether he might be able to 'swing' things a bit for an old mucker and land him a cushier job. He put out feelers to that end and was sharply rebuffed.

Still, it couldn't be denied, black marketeering was a thorny problem. Only the other day, he'd come across an article about it in an old copy of the fortnightly *British Zone Review* – 'Fighting The Black Market'. In September for instance, railways police had seized 279 young pigs, most of them drugged, for removal out of the British Zone. ('To the gourmet French, I'll bet,' thought Jim.)

> With a view to reducing this traffic to a minimum, every train has been checked before entering the French Zone.

'I knew it!' Jim gave a chortle of satisfaction at this confirmation of his suspicion of the untrustworthy French.

> Reports indicate an increase in so-called compensation business between firms and merchants, whereby large quantities of goods such as furniture, textiles, etc., are exchanged against coal and other raw materials. As a result of a recent vehicle check it was found that a hardware firm was engaged in bartering

hardware against cheese for the population of Wuppertal.

('Blimey, quite a slice of cheese!')

Thefts and forgeries of ration cards of all types continue on the same scale.

Those were the blighters to crack down on – the forgers, the big fish, the profiteers who grew fat on others' misery – not the ordinary folk who bartered to raise their living standards from just above starvation to just above subsistence levels. Jim's thoughts went winging once more to the polite, shabbily clad, wide-eyed and hungry children in and about Kerzenbaum.

Still, the courts, Military Government and German, had been quite busy. Three thousand plus convictions between them for the month of September.

'Ah me,' he thought, 'crime and punishment. Inevitably, it became a major pre-occupation when you worked in a glasshouse. What am I to do,' thought Jim, 'about young Private Conway. Is he shooting me a line, a genuinely pathetic case, hard done by, or is he simply an untrustworthy, crafty young sod? Well perhaps the least, or even most I can do, is help him write his plea for another chance – but essentially in his own style and entirely in his own handwriting.'

> *To the Welfare Officer,*
> *Sir,*
>
> *I wish to submit this my petition against the sentence I received of discharged with ignominy. My reasons for this appeal are these.*
>
> *It is my considered opinion that I have not been given a fair chance in life.*
>
> *I was in an approved school, from the age of nine until I reached the age of eighteen, simply because my parents could not control me.*
>
> *Since the age of nine my parents have refused to have anything to do with me, and on leaving the school and having no home to which to return, I volunteered for the Army.*

*I realise that I have not proved myself to be a good soldier, but if I am discharged from the Army, I not only have no home to go back to, but in addition have little prospect of obtaining a worthwhile job.*

*I would therefore like the chance to make the Army my career and if given the opportunity, I am quite sure that I could be a good soldier. All I ask is to be given the chance of making a fresh start.*

*Trusting this application will meet with your kind approval,*

*I am sir...*

Jim never knew the outcome of this moving plea for 'one more chance': an artful try-on, cynical manipulation? Which was it? Conway had the language pat and was certainly *au fait* with how to trade on the concept of 'benefit of the doubt'.

Yes, life in prison could make you cynical. That was why a few hours in charming Heidi's innocent, guileless company was so appealing, such a refreshing reminder of decent human values.

Some tales of prison life she wouldn't want to hear – and Jim wouldn't tell her. Anyway, he didn't know the German for padded cell, or strait jacket. And he couldn't tell her why a certain few of the SUS chose to attend his own and others' classes. These lusty students may have had some thirst for knowledge – but that masked a greater longing.

At the back of one of the classrooms ran a row of toilets. The toilets had tiny windows. Through a window a glimpse could be gained of part of a road outside the prison. Occasionally, along the snow covered road, a woman might walk, in thick winter clothes certainly, but still, visibly a woman.

At first Jim wondered why a certain few husky fellows had such weak bladders and spent so long having a Jimmy Riddle, but a fellow schoolie tipped him off.

"We don't check on them. They don't all go at once. That wouldn't be on any way, any more than it was at school. We let 'em go – and they let go. Some of them haven't been with a woman for ages, and there's more than one Mafeking to be relieved."

"Message understood."

Of course, prison was also home for a few great lovers who had 'loved not wisely but too well', and had caught a 'dose' or 'packet'. Just occasionally, Jim would act as escort on the pox wagon that took the VD sufferers for treatment. The back chat in the back of the truck was not 'pretty', or witty and might well not have amused Jane Austen, assuming she could have understood it.

So, no matter the continuing Siberian weather, and the repeated recitation, incantation almost, of the 'frozen frog', it was a blessed relief to get away from chokey at the weekends.

But now danger began to threaten the continuance of the 'hitch hiker's romance', not in the form of another Crowbar, but an archetypal martinet, straight from the pages of a pre-war *Wizard*, *Hotspur* or *Adventure*. A new sergeant, with special responsibilities for discipline, was appointed. Among those responsibilities was the checking and handing out of passes.

'Bullshine' was an anti-frat fanatic. He proudly and quickly made that plain, robustly expletively plain.

And he quickly made it clear to Jim, not explicitly, but by muttered asides that he didn't believe a word of Jim's claim that he stayed at the CIC in Pullenstadt. He began to put probing questions to Jim, who, fortunately, was not caught off guard, for two reasons.

By a piece of good fortune, he had recently read an article about Civilian Internment Camps; quite a lengthy, well informed and balanced article at that. Pullenstadt was even mentioned by name as having 'a well equipped hospital within the camp perimeter and an outside hospital at Schloss...' That was new and worth knowing. The CCG had taken on overall responsibility for the camps but British troops, from the local units concerned, still ran them on a day-to-day basis.

And so, Jim was able to parry Bullshine's thrusts, both men knowing that Jim had no intention of staying at the mess of the resident guard.

Bullshine would then switch tactics to implied insults and indirect sneers, thereby hoping to goad Jim into making indiscreet or belligerent remarks. Jim was ready for that ploy too. During his first few weeks in the Army, at an infantry Training Centre, he had learned a valuable lesson – and not just that the town's main street was called rowboat alley because it had whores down both sides.

Among his fellow raw recruits in number three platoon was a real awkward Johnny, not from conscious choice, but from the way nature had fashioned him. Peter simply couldn't keep in step, for more than a few paces, with the rest of the squad – or even look soldierly.

"Straighten up, lad. Chin up, chest out, thumbs in line with the seam of yer trousers. Chest out, lad, out, out! Stop drooping like a lily that's been pissed on from a great height!"

Slowly Jim began to realise that Peter was being picked on not only for his lack of co-ordination and indifference to correct military bearing, but for some other reason as well.

Then the shekel dropped. Of course, Peter was a Jew! He should have guessed from the small, tight curls and the Semitic nose.

Jim had never before encountered anti-Semitism. Jokes against and about Jews yes, lots of 'em – but outright nastiness, no. Jim didn't like the sergeant's approach and chummed up with Peter, an intelligent and likeable lad. He grew to admire the way Peter handled the provocative abuse volleyed his way. His mouth would assume a slight smile, a very special kind of smile, a subtle mix of – how best to describe it? A mix of condescension, latent superiority and slightly patronising absolution of the sinner.

When Bullshine deliberately flung the precious pale buff coloured pass onto the floor – in earlier days it might have been a gauntlet – Jim remained impassive for a few seconds. Then with that Peter Weinberg special smile, he retrieved the pass, quietly said, "Thank you," and made for the prison lodge. No trouble there, so, 'Heigh Ho, Heigh Ho – for two hundred and forty we go!'

## Chapter Sixteen

# Icicles and Red Tape

"*Mensch, ach Mensch*, what terrible *Wetter!*"

Heidi nodded in sympathetic agreement but giggled nonetheless.

"Sorry, Jim, but you do have such a *rote Nase!*" She flicked away the few remaining snowflakes from Jim's 'spare' leather jerkin, and Army greatcoat, before hanging them up to dry.

"Is the weather as bad in England?"

"Worse, I think. There seems to be more snow at home than here. And it's been freezing hard for weeks. Electricity power cuts have hit many parts of the country: millions of people can't work. Many are without coal. It's rotten bad luck for the Labour Government. Nearly all our newspapers are anti-Labour and will try to make out that everything that goes wrong is Labour's fault. And to cap it all, the Government had to reduce the meat ration last month. The bread ration might well be cut as well. It's such a blasted shame when we now have a much fairer-minded government in office."

"Goodness, Jim, you are upset."

Jim did not answer but remained looking thoughtful. Yes, every Jack Frost nipped letter he had received in recent weeks, had included a grim and gloomy weather report – even one from Bexhill on Sea. Ah, Bexhill on Sea in the soft, sunny south where, with other NCOs, he had once struggled, with limited success, to convert slovenly, deeply resentful ack ack gunners into alert, well-trained, infantrymen ready for the battles raging in France. During this period of dispiriting, uphill work, away from his own battalion, a Bexhill family had brightened some of his off-duty hours with their warm-hearted hospitality. But now...

*You are right, Jim. The sunny south has felt the cold shoulder this winter and no mistake... we haven't been*

*able to work on the land for over a month now... owing*
*to lack of fuel for heating the school, and water pipes*
*frozen, children haven't been at school much these past*
*few weeks. Even our De la Warr Pavilion has no heat*
*nor the cinemas. What a to do!*

What a to do indeed! Even plump faced Anne-Marie, ex-dancing partner from Ghent, in her last long letter, neatly typed in French, had commiserated with him about England's dire plight. She had commented on *le froid intense*, counselled him to keep well wrapped up and confided to him that she had given up *le Polon*. And why? Because she had met a former schoolboy she had once adored as a younger schoolgirl. Now, she and François were an engaged couple.

Jim was pleased for this intelligent, introspective chatterbox, but remained thankful that Heidi was no prattler – she couldn't yet be in English, but she didn't seem to be in German either, so Jim felt himself reasonably safe for a tranquil future – on one dimension at least.

"Lost in thought again?"

Jim blinked. "Sorry."

Heidi smiled indulgently.

"I suppose it's one of your funny little ways I'll have to get used to..."

"My Mother's never quite managed it. But I think you'll be more patient."

"How are your Mother and Father in this terrible weather?"

"Oh, they'll cope. We've got good neighbours and two of my Mother's brothers live less than ten minutes walk away. I know Dad will get very irritable because he can't walk about as he would like. His stiff leg makes it dangerous for him to go out when the roads and pavements are so slippery. But that's enough about this rotten weather.

"Your letter gave Mom and Dad a great deal of pleasure, Heidi. Naturally they knew that I helped you with it, but the expressions are yours – and you as you, can be read between the lines, as we say."

Heidi's first letter to England, in English had been composed with great care and genuine concern to please.

"Yes, they especially liked 'Dear Momma and Poppa'."

It was Heidi herself who had insisted on that mode of address. Respect for an older generation lay deeply ingrained in her nature but in the clear, simple statements that followed, it was the deep, but not effusive, love for Jim that shone through.

*

"By the way, you'll be pleased to know, Heidi, that my old colonel in Blanktal was kind enough to write a letter supporting my application for a place at Birmingham University. I've filled out and returned the necessary forms. But where the devil are my socks?"

"That is *gut*, that is very good," came a sleep-heavy reply "Your socks?" The voice was now clearer, sharply clearer. "Why do you want your socks?"

Jim suppressed an urge to be 'humorously' sarcastic. "Because I must get ready to go. Just look at the time. The train won't wait for me."

Heidi was now sitting up, fine spun fair hair disarranged but so soft and pretty in the dim light of a shaded table lamp. With her cheeks deeply flushed, her grey eyes round with alarm and moist with held back tears, Heidi looked so endearingly vulnerable, especially in those over sized striped pyjamas which hung so enchantingly rumpled yet revealing about her youthful figure.

"Please, please, Jim, don't go yet. Please catch the later train. Do please."

'Well, I'm for it now,' thought Jim. 'Will it be my heart or my head that wins out?'

"But why do you want me to run this unnecessary risk of being late back for duty?"

"I don't know Jim, I truly don't."

Heidi gave a half stifled sob.

"I can't explain it. We women have such funny feelings sometimes. Sometimes I'm afraid I might never see you again. Please stay, Jim, just a little longer. And hug me tight, please."

"Well, just help me to get my things together so I can get away quickly, now – or later."

Heidi swung her legs round and placed her feet on the rug. She stood up and began to shuffle awkwardly towards the door reminding Jim yet again of curvy Claudette Colbert in OS nightware, (Gable,

Clark for the issue of). As one over long trouser caught in its twin over long trouser, Heidi stumbled. Jim quickly caught her in his arms and whispered, huskily, "Right, I'll stay."

The later train arrived in Weberfeld on time and Jim, with luck on his side, continued his career on the outside of the cells.

> *Dear Mother and Dad,*
>
> *Yesterday I felt particularly pleased with life, for I received a letter from Heidi and your magnificent parcel, Mother. I felt exactly like a small boy eagerly untying his birthday present, altho' in my case I simply cut the string.*

'...simply cut the string.'

Jim gave a slight shudder as an image flashed before his eyes of a mangled, bloody neck, a railway, a cord, and his penknife. He shuddered again and turned to the parcel.

How many parcels from his 'good old Ma' did that make, he wondered. Quite a few, over the years, given, what, three parts of a year as an evacuee and now nearly five years in the Army. A lot of brown paper and string, of tasty, nutritious goodies and unquantifiable sacrifice and love. Good old Ma. Come to think of it, she was only in her mid-fifties. Never mind, she was still 'good old Ma'.

> *You will see from the papers that Weberfeld is featured as one of the centres of the hunger strikes. Here they have been orderly and there is no serious trouble, save from the acute bread shortage. What is required is an all out drive against the black marketeers and a resident minister of the government here in Germany, on the spot, not waffling complacently in the House... crocuses and snowdrops are popping up everywhere... You must have read in the papers about the abolition of the glasshouse. As from tomorrow we become a 'military corrective establishment'. Ours will still be one of the 'tougher' types for first stagers where discipline is tough and there are few privileges. This won't affect me personally but naturally I have to display an interest in these changes.*

*The next time I write, on Wednesday, I should have Heidi with me. We shall be going to the theatre... I have bought tickets for the German version of "The Taming of the Shrew". It will help me with my German, give Heidi some idea of Shakespeare and perhaps impress her that 'nagging' in a wife doesn't always pay. I can pull her leg about it, anyhow.*

Jim's jaunty predictions proved to be very curate eggish in character. Heidi did arrive – and that was fine. Her uncomplicated German remained of far more help, than the heard at too great a distance spouting by actors, of a German version of rich, complex, Elizabethan poetry. What Heidi made of Shakespeare, and of badinage he wasn't really sure. On reflection, it seemed best to keep off the topic of 'nagging'. So far, Heidi seemed to be one of that rare, and greatly to be cherished, breed of non-naggers. So why go looking for trouble?

Heidi's visit, by train, had come about through the generosity of Bill Bentley and Mrs Bill – sweet-faced, dark-haired Margery. Bill, one of the more humane and intelligent of the warders, lived with his wife and their two young boys in married quarters, a good-sized German house, outside but close to the prison.

"You can have our spare room – and welcome!" chorused Bill and Marge, "Whenever Heidi is free to visit."

How thrilling that the first visit should coincide with Jim's twenty-fourth birthday; the winter snows all gone and with 'even the trees... at long last showing signs of budding'.

A few days later and Jim had hitched back to Heidi for a celebratory feast at that swish restaurant (a few miles from Heidi's home) the historic *Mühlenrad* which dated, so it proclaimed, from 1230 AD. Set in pleasant, gently undulating countryside of fields and woodland, the sprucely maintained black and white timbered building, with a stream running alongside, and over a now stationary mill wheel, gave out an air of quiet, well heeled, well mannered, but faded, charm.

The menu was pitifully, 1947 AD meagre. Jim kept the small sheet of coarse paper on which the lunch time dishes had been typed – in German. Perhaps any grandchildren they might have, would be interested to see it in, say, fifty years time.

Everything was regulated by rationing – even the customers seemed in very short supply. Heidi and Jim were free to take their pick of the best seats by one of the windows which looked across a fine, stone slabbed terrace to the clear, sparkling mill stream.

Jim had no food coupons but Heidi had carefully saved enough for both of them to dine off 'this' or 'that' according to the coupons available.

| Ration Book Coupons | | Dish | Price |
|---|---|---|---|
| Amount | Type | | Marks |
| | | 1 cup clear broth | 0.30 |
| 50 grams | Meat | Slices of liver or black pudding | |
| 50 grams bread | | sausages, or mixture | 0.80 |
| 50 grams | Bread | A portion of radishes with | |
| 5 grams | Fat | bread and butter | 0.50 |
| 25 grams | Flour | Dish of noodle soup | 0.60 |
| 50 grams | Flour | Fried semolina cakes garnished | |
| 10 grams | Fat | with vegetables | |
| | | Julienne soup | 1.50 |
| | | Julienne soup | |
| 50 grams | Meat | Fried sausage, sauerkraut and | |
| 5 grams | Fat | potato puree | 1.50 |
| 1 | Potato | | |

"I wonder what Brussels is really like?" Heidi looked puzzled.

"Why do you ask?"

"Why do you think?"

Heidi took a sip of wine and reflected.

"Is that where Anne-Marie lives, your Belgian girlfriend?"

"No, that's Ghent. And she was never a girlfriend like you might mean it. For one thing, she doesn't dance as well as you. She's much heavier on her feet, and besides..."

"Poor Jim, you don't seem to have much luck with your dancing partners."

Was it a statement or a question? The little minx was being arch.

"Oh, I don't know, you're the first dancer, the first girl even, who's ever treated me to radishes. But about Brussels."

"Ah, yes – Brussels."

"That's where I'm supposed to be now, on leave. Somehow, I lost my way. After all that training on map reading I had in the infantry! Just shows how a girl can upset a chap's sense of direction and send his compass spinning madly." Jim chuckled.

Heidi was less interested in his 'wit' than his well being.

"You're not going to get... in any trouble are you? Not with old Bull something or other, as you call him."

"I doubt it very much. I shall stay in 'Brussels' again for my last leave just before, before... I go home."

He squeezed Heidi's hand as he saw her face become grave and thoughtful.

"We'll say no more about it now. *Prosit.*"

They clinked glasses.

"Good health, *Liebling*. Safe journey."

*

"Blow me! it's just like one of those thirties gangster movies – but in full, glorious, Natalie Kalmus Technicolor."

Jim had been roused from dream filled slumber by the harsh, strident wailing of sirens, and by the blinding glare of searchlights probing nearby streets and parkland. He slipped his greatcoat over his pyjamas and hurried to the front door of his billet. Sirens continued to howl and yowl. Hurrying, scurrying figures darted about in shifting pools of darkness and light; curses and agitated orders could be heard but the words were indistinct.

"What's up, Bill?"

The running figure paused, panted, then gave a half chuckle. "More like, what's over. Some of the Poles have gone over the wall."

Bill dashed off to join his colleagues.

Truck engines spluttered into life, revved up, and with gears crashing, roared off in pursuit of the desperate gaol breakers/homeseekers.

Jim never found out how many Poles were recaptured or how many had broken out in the first place. Staff naturally tended to be tight-lipped about such matters. 'English for Poles' was temporarily suspended, with no regrets on Jim's part. In any case, he had more closely personal things to think about than those poor devils seeking to make their dangerous way eastwards.

Towards the end of April, Jim's favourite prison visitor came to keep him company. As a diversion from the 'shades of the prison house', the lovers again visited the *Stadttheater*. A mortifying mistake for flesh and spirit. It was so damnably cramped in 'the gods'. Even Jim, with his relatively short (but stocky) legs couldn't sit comfortably in one position for more than a few minutes together. Furthermore, the theatre was packed, the spring weather very mild, making the resulting atmosphere stickily and abominably sweaty.

And what a performance! *If* he could really believe that opera lovers generally, truthfully enjoyed grand opera then he, Jim, would switch his allegiance from Aston Villa to Birmingham City. (Something he never did.) But he did have the good grace to admit that some, just some, of the operatic singing was a trifle better (louder certainly) than that he fondly remembered from his old grammar school's ebullient productions of *The Mikado* and *The Pirates of Penzance*. And those operas had jolly, catchy tunes and plenty of humour as well.

As for *Cavalleria Rusticana,* the music contained one good bit admittedly, but as for the rest of the opera, Jim felt it was all extravagant posturing and prancing – the taxing, boring tedium of theatrical repetition – 'farcical tragedy' that pushed a chap of any sense towards irreverent laughter.

Part of the so-called 'grandness' of grand opera surely lay in its inflated language. Puncture it – call the opera 'Rustic Chivalry' – and see what happens. Giuseppe Verdi of Busseto: genius operatic composer; Joe Green, Brixton, master plumber.

Worse was to follow – the one Act *Lisu,* a quite unknown quantity. Again a bewitchingly attractive maiden (fifteen stone?) wrought havoc and tragedy, this time amongst artless, Finnish woodcutters. This sturdy, spirited damsel strangled, with her bare hands, the odious villain and became unwitting cause of the death of one of her two hero suitors, 'and in her arms he peacefully breathes his last'. It took quite a while for the lad to expire but perhaps the cushioning Valkyric bosom had something to do with it.

Jim resolved to stick to his earlier schoolboy policy of listening only to the 'best bits' from operas, operettas, shows whatever – like smashing Deanna Durbin singing in her bell clear voice *Les filles de Cadiz*.

*

"Heidi, I've heard from the University again. They are prepared to let me start in October. All I need now is confirmation that I will be paid a grant by our Ministry of Education. I'm hoping to receive that before I leave Germany."

"Well, that is good news, Jim. I'm so pleased for you."

She gave him a quick peck on the cheek as they walked away from grand opera.

"And I've also found out a few things about arrangements for your trip to England. I'll show you the letters later."

Later they pored over the documents together especially the one headed 'Entry to the United Kingdom of foreign women for marriage to men of British Nationality'.

"I have to be able to support you and provide you with somewhere to live – and must marry you within two months of arrival. Well, that part's all right.

"(d) The woman must be of good character.

"I could tease you about that, but not now.

"It seems that first of all I have to write you a letter inviting you to England and saying that I will marry you within two months... de dum, de dum... then I have to write to Berlin asking for an entry visa for you... I also have to attach a letter 'from a responsible person, such as a bank manager, lawyer or clergyman, guaranteeing' that I can support you and am free to marry.

"I dare say my old headmaster would do that for me... de dum, de dum... then the Passport Control Officer will write to you Heidi, saying what you have to do to get a 'Military Exit Permit to leave Germany'. Apparently, you have to go to your local *Landrat* or *Oberbürgermeister* for a start and you have to show these authorities four things:

"a) the letter from Passport Control Office, Berlin

"b) my offer of marriage

"c) some evidence that you are free to marry

"d) a medical certificate that you are free from infections and mental diseases.

"I'll write all this down for you later. But what a business. It's enough to drive you *verrückt*, barmy, potty and daft even when you haven't got 'mental diseases'!" Jim leaned back, sighed and snorted, "Bloomin' red tape."

Heidi remained silent, slowly trying to make sense, clear sense of what Jim had been explaining.

Jim returned to the 'procedure'.

"Half a tick, there's a footnote,

"Paragraph 2 (a) makes it clear that service personnel cannot submit an application for a visa for a woman under these regulations until they have returned to the United Kingdom for permanent residence..."

He read out the words once more.

"Does that mean you can't do much until you are living with your parents again?"

"That's right. There are some other bits and pieces as well. If the correct procedure is followed, it will take about six weeks from your making an application, Heidi, to being given a visa. Oh, and there's a bit more – you can bring with you to England no more than forty marks and up to eighty kilograms of luggage. And don't attempt any smuggling." He smiled.

Heidi smiled.

"No, I'm serious, Heidi. There's too much at stake to take any risks. I know it's in your nature to give presents but, please, please, 'play it by the book' as we say, stick exactly to the rules in this case."

"I promise, Jim – but it does look as though we are going to be apart for quite a long time, much longer than I wanted."

"I agree – but before I come to Pullenstadt again, perhaps you could have a word with your parents. Find out, if you can, how long they want you to stay unmarried. They're not putting any pressure on you are they to break off our engagement?"

Heidi answered hurriedly, "Oh no, nothing at all like that. They know full well my heart is set on joining you in England."

"Attagirl!"

They embraced and then went for a walk through the near by woodlands – back to that mossy, dead leaf strewn bank where the violets were in hesitant flower.

All too soon Heidi had to catch her train back to Pullenstadt.
"*Auf wiedersehen.*"
"See you soon in Brussels."

## Chapter Seventeen
# Last Hitch to Pullenstadt

With an abstracted air, Jim slowly began to separate a scattered array of papers and documents into two piles, mentally noted as, 'Keep' and, 'Chuck Away'.

Yes, he'd keep the notes he'd scribbled at Ghent and at Göttingen – some of the *John Bull* quizzes and answers, the last letters from friends and relatives, a few of the ABCA pamphlets including, most definitely, *Germany in Eclipse* by one Lindley Fraser. This was a thoughtful and thought provoking document from the Army Bureau of Current Affairs, designed for group discussion, on 'What to do about Germany?'

Jim was sensitively aware that once he was back home, he could well be drawn into discussions, heated arguments even, about the 'problem of Germany'. He would never, for one moment, defend or attempt to mitigate Nazi atrocities or their perpetrators but, by golly, he would battle hard to protect his Heidi from any verbal sniping based simply on the fact that she was born German. He was ready, now, to counter any comments such as: 'Well, what else can you expect, she's German,' when the 'fault' would have gone unremarked if made by a Briton.

Of course, 'simple solution' bigots would remain deaf to rational arguments but as far as he knew, no glowering Crowbars, no manic Bullshines, lurked within his extensive family or circle of friends. No, he expected to experience greater emotional discomfort from 'breaking the news' to those who might feel hurt and bewildered by his decision to marry a German – the father and aunt of Syd being the chief examples. They would remain polite, he believed, and friendly, not holding Heidi directly responsible for Syd's death – they were far too understanding to make such a crass connection, but they would not feel or express the joy that would genuinely have been theirs, had he chosen an English rose for his bride.

He glanced at the pamphlet.

> 1. How can we make sure that Germany cannot start another war?
>> (a) By killing all Germans?

Obviously a non-starter on a number of grounds, moral and practical.

>> (b) By leaving them to starve?
>> Already in the British zone they are living very near starvation level and are only being kept alive by supplies we are paying for. Why should we send them any food at all? Would we really be prepared to sit by and watch them die like flies? What would be the effect on British soldiers in Germany?

'A good question chum,' thought Jim, 'a very good question.' It was one that had exercised his own mind, and very much his feelings since he had first arrived in Germany and months before he had fallen in love with a German girl. He still treasured that little wooden star from Kerzenbaum days, that simple, dignified present from a waif-like young mother.

>> Can we even be content to see German rations remain at their present low level (less than half of ours)? Malnutrition means disease; if epidemics result, will they be confined to Germany?
>> (c) By destroying German war industry or preventing it from being used by the Germans?
>> (d) By any other means?

For example, dividing the country into small states?

> 2. How can we teach the Germans not to want to start another war?

Tricky one that, especially after 'twelve years of concentrated propaganda, particularly the effects on the young'.

Jim recalled that Heidi had been ten years of age when Hitler had bludgeoned his way to absolute power.

> The great mass of the German people were and are today decent, foolish, parochial individuals who in private life would never be deliberately cruel or ruthless, but who have been brought up to believe that cruelty and ruthlessness is "all right" when practised by a state (or rather, is all right when practised by the German state, in the name of the greater power and prestige of Germany).

A great deal of the guilt for creating and maintaining a vicious military dictatorship must attach itself to the Nazis and their doctrines. How to cleanse a society of such pernicious evil? No pat answers here either.

> How, for instance, is a Nazi to be defined? Some Germans joined the Nazi Party simply because it was the only way of keeping their jobs: on the other hand there were thousands of enthusiastic Nazis who never became party members at all. Is it possible to devise a system of classification which will not result in substantial injustice? Or if no hard and fast lines are drawn, can favouritism and corruption be avoided?
> Then there is the problem of former Nazis holding key posts in local administration and in industry. If they are dismissed, there will be no one competent to take their place; if they are retained in office, genuine anti-Nazis will feel aggrieved. Is it surprising that the harassed Military Government officer in Germany often views the matter rather differently from the enthusiastic democrat hundreds of miles away in Britain or America?

"Well said, that man, and tactfully too!" muttered Jim, as he placed the ABCA pamphlet on the growing pile of 'Keep' material.

Within this welter of complexities, relatively humdrum, everyday life needed to go on. He went to collect his leave pass for 'Brussels'. He noted with some amusement that the rubber stamp industry had not yet caught up with the glasshouse reform movement, his pass being clearly stamped 'No. X Military Prison'. Just three clear days with

Heidi, before a separation of...? He could only guess, and his mind jibbed at guessing – but he guessed nonetheless that it could well be a sentence of at least twelve months. Hell and Damnation!

\*

What was it that podgy warbler Dick Tauber burbled about? (A good tenor voice for all that) Ah, that was it:

'Springtime, lovetime, May.'

In prose terms and for the benefit of his parents, Jim Norton wrote:

> *The weather has been splendid this weekend and while we spent most of yesterday at Heidi's home, we did go for a walk in the cool of the evening.*

"That seems to be it then, Heidi. We are likely to be apart for at least a year."

Heidi sighed deeply.

"Yes, I'm afraid so. It's so much longer than I would really like, but I feel I owe it to my parents to respect their wishes. They miss my brother terribly, especially Mutti and..."

"And now one of the ex-enemy comes to carry off their only daughter. Yes, I can understand something of what they must feel. But they don't dislike me personally do they?"

"No, not at all. They think you'll be a good son-in-law. But they won't always understand your English sense of humour. Neither will I for that matter."

She sighed.

"Don't worry, understanding will improve with practice. And here, at long last, is something that may help a little. I have finally finished *English for Heidi* – and here it is, with my love."

Jim handed to Heidi some thirty small, lined pages torn from an Army issue exercise book, punched and held together with a length of knotted, wine red wool.

"Just glance at it now while we sit on this bench."

NOUNS

...but a special girl might want a capital, R, R and H.

Red Riding Hood (*Rotkäppchen*) or even C for Cinderella (*Aschenbrödel*)

...If a word ends in 'y' this usually becomes 'ies' e.g. penny pennies – but journey (*nach Pullenstadt*) journeys

...Now the Verb is very important, for it describes/*beschreibt*, what you do or feel.

e.g. to walk, to run, to write, to kiss, to love

[...]

We come now to the PRONOUN

[...]

You kiss the sergeant major.  You kiss me (What a smasher!)

I love the girl          I love her (Lucky isn't she?)

[...]

The ADVERB usually tells us in one of four ways more about the VERB

| die Zeit | time | now |
|---|---|---|
| die Art und Weise | manner | quickly, slowly |
| der Ort | place | inside, on the left |
| der Grad | degree | a little, enough |

Quickly I run upstairs, where I find Heidi noisily eating an apple.

...The boy and the girl go for a walk (Stadtpark?)
Would you like a Capstan or a Player's?
Since Friday I have had no letters (Bad show!)
[...]
*Es ist fast sieben Uhr und ich muss die Nachrichten und Fussball Resultate am Radio zuhören.*

Heidi laughed.

"Just like a man, you break off to listen to the news and football results.  I expect it will be like that when I join you, won't it?"

"But of course. But look, I do go on to say *'bis gleich,* darling'. And you know, lovers must have a tea break, a very British tea break."

Heidi laughed and punched Jim affectionately in the ribs.

"Still, the last part is nice."

*"Es könnte viel schöner sein, wenn ich persönlich bei Dir wäre, Dir Unterricht zu geben. Aber das kommt, ohne Zweifel, in der Zukunft. Bis Freitag, darling."*

(It would be much nicer if I were with you in person to give you lessons. But that will come about no doubt, in the future. Until Friday, darling).

"Talking of teaching and learning, Mother has now sent on to me, a letter from our Ministry of Education about a student's grant."

"So what do these people say?"

"Under what is called a 'Further Education and Training Scheme' I am to be given a grant of one hundred and sixty-three pounds a year – say about three pounds a week. The money will be paid from the beginning of the Autumn term this year and will go on until the Summer of 1950 – providing my work and exam results are thought to be good enough." Heidi squeezed his hand.

"They will be. But can we live on three pounds a week? Perhaps once I am settled, I could get a job?"

"From what I understand, ex-servicemen students have been treated quite generously, so three pounds is probably pretty good as far as students generally are concerned." Jim paused before continuing, "I wouldn't want you working in any old cafe. It would have to be somewhere like the Mühlenrad. I am sorry to have to say it, but in Britain we don't seem to value catering and waiting at table as highly as Continentals do. It's a shame, but there it is. But you have tip-top experience, and people will soon discover that you are a jolly hard worker, so we might get you fixed up in one of the better places in the town centre."

They walked on silently for a while, hand in hand. Jim in his 'grey market' suit, looking every inch quite an ordinary civilian, Heidi in a pale blue dress and white, neatly knitted bolero jacket.

"So, young Jim, in October you will be a student. Will you have to wear a uniform?"

Jim laughed.

"No, nothing like that. The fashion seems to be corduroy trousers – what you call 'Manchester *Hosen*' and sports jacket. I think I gave you a photo of me wearing such a jacket."

"You did and I still have it."

Heidi tucked her arm into his as they walked into a lane leading past a farmhouse.

"It will be a very different life for you having to learn instead of teaching – sitting still and listening instead of bossing people about as a sergeant major."

Jim laughed. "You are quite right, you saucy *Fräulein*. My Mother has told me off more than once for 'rapping out my orders' as she calls it, in a loud voice. I hope I don't do that when I am best man at Uncle Les's wedding in the summer."

They strolled past the farmhouse and entered onto a field path.

"Seriously though, I shall have to work jolly hard. After all, I left school in 1940, nearly seven years ago, and many of my fellow students will be starting straight from school at eighteen or nineteen years of age. They'll be well used to writing essays, translations and taking exams."

"I'm sure you'll manage all right. You won't be the only ex-soldier at what you call lectures and we call *Vorlesungen*."

"No, that's certainly true, there'll be many men, some women too, in the same boat as myself. It will be a strange business though, going back to school. I'll have to work like a beaver – is *Biber* the word?"

"Yes, *Biber*."

Jim's face took on a thoughtful expression. Heidi glanced at him now and again as they crossed another field. She smiled but said nothing.

Eventually, Jim broke the silence;

"I've been trying to put two and two together, as we say. Your parents would like you stay with them for at least another year. I expect I shall have to take exams in June next year. Passing those will be most important if I am to complete the three year course and get a degree. While a June wedding would be great, it would probably be better, for everyone, if we married in July. We would then be quite free to take a nice long honeymoon, a whole week, even ten days perhaps, by the seaside. I'm sure you'd love the seaside. What do you say?"

Heidi didn't reply straight away. Jim looked at her anxiously.

Her face appeared serious, but he couldn't tell whether or not she was disappointed.

"It seems such a long time – and I shall miss you so."

She looked at him with pleading eyes. Jim put a comforting arm across her shoulders.

"I know, I know, but having thought very hard about it, I do really think July will be best."

Heidi sighed.

"I have to admit I can see the sense of it – but July next year – that seems such a long time to wait. And I still feel so bad that I cannot help with money in any way."

"As I've said before, that's not your fault. And, as things have turned out, you can only bring forty marks with you anyway. So, remember what I've told you, positively no smuggling. Snuggling, *ja* – smuggling *nein*."

Heidi smiled but Jim wasn't sure whether she had fully understood. It didn't matter that much. They were together for the moment. They strolled on.

"Jim, *ich werde* – a little tired. Let's sit down for a few minutes."

"OK – but where?"

"Over there, on that bank that slopes down to the stream near where the *Schlüsselblumen* grow."

(*Schlüsselblumen* – ah, yes – cowslips.)

'I know a bank where the wild thyme grows...'

'Springtime, lovetime, May.'

\*

*Dear Mother and Dad,*

*Here it is then my last letter from Pullenstadt and possibly my last from Germany, as a soldier... D Day, or whatever we may like to call the day of separation, is fast approaching, but we're just enjoying the minutes as they slip past. Thoughts of the immediate future are kept in the background.*

*To-day, Heidi and I took a short trip on the train into the country, where we spent our time at the side of some very big lakes, on which there was plenty of canoeing and sailing, swimming too. The surrounding countryside*

*was attractive, the sun was bright and warm and we
thoroughly enjoyed our picnic.*

Soon came plenty of photos to bear black and white truth to Jim's
descriptions – a blanket spread on the soft grass before some graceful
birch trees, a bare-footed Heidi shyly smiling, broadly smiling, always
lovingly smiling – all treasures for any future family album that might
be kept – to convey something of the fleeting, but memory enduring
enjoyment of 'the minutes as they slip past'.

No duck pâté, no lobster, no rich cheeses, no bubbly at this
miner's daughter's picnic, but wholesome sausage, bread and home
grown radishes. Jim's letter to his parents continued:

> *One of the outstanding features of Heidi's character
> is that she is so happy with the simplest pleasures and
> never makes a claim on me for anything of an elaborate
> or expensive nature. It's a pity that more of the modern
> girls don't possess such old world qualities.*
>
> *Heidi has just come out of the bath and when the
> water has run in, it will be my turn... Heidi can write a
> few lines in my absence.*

She did.

> *Dear Momma and Poppa,*
>
> *Thank you so much for your kind letter... Yes,
> Momma don't worry I definitely will be a brave girl and
> will always be happy with Jim, like I am now.*
>
> *These last days we spent together were very nice, I
> could not think of anything better to do on these lovely
> days than to go out in the country.*
>
> *I'll say cheerio now and my love,*
> *Heidi.*

Jim, all aglow, what with the heat of the bath and ardent affection,
added a few more lines.

> *Tuesday morning I'll be hitching back to Weberfeld,
> and Wednesday evening I'll be on my way to Münster...*

Brace yourself, Jim – whatever you do, don't look back. Steel
yourself. Resist the temptation to look once more into those grey,

tear-filled eyes – at the brave, but tremulous forced smile. Gosh, it was scary sometimes, to feel yourself the object of so much love. He hoped and hoped he could remain worthy of such loyal devotion.

*

## Date: Wednesday 14th May 1947
## Place: Gaol

Outside the walls of the glasshouse, Jim was given a rousing send-off, principally by his fellow schoolies – but a few off-duty screws joined in as well. 'Mighty Mo', the blonde, genial giant *APTC* (Army Physical Training Corps*)* sergeant also graced the occasion. A man of splendid physique, he made Charles Atlas, in those 'don't be a 7 stone weakling' magazine adverts, look positively flabby. By popular demand, Mo repeated one of his parlour tricks.

Seizing Jim, at the back of his battle dress blouse, with one great hand, Mo placed the other beneath Jim's upper thighs and swung Jim, now horizontal, effortlessly into the air and held him aloft at stretched arms' length. From this position, Jim was lightly tossed into a large blanket held and stretched taut at fire drill height by his laughing muckers. Tossed repeatedly in the air by men possessed of the vigour of manic pancake makers, Jim was eventually released to terra only fairly firma. Handshakes and good luck calls were exchanged all round and then Jim was away, his Army Book X801, *Soldier's Release Book Class A* safely buttoned about his person.

First stop the transit camp at Münster. It was here that Jim experienced his first encounter with oysters. He didn't enquire how or why the mess there had acquired such grotesque looking food. The trick was to swallow 'em whole and let nature take its course. Hm – of a definitely slithery, jelly like texture as they slid down and very definitely extremely salty. Meant for the toffs really, like some opera fans, chappies who usually took champers with their miserable molluscs. And toffs, with their effete life-style would understandably need a kick-start to remind them of their duty to England, Home and Beauty.

And so, Jim progressed eventually to York, to the Military Dispersal Unit where a whole way of life was radically transformed within what seemed but minutes. 'Blimey,' thought Jim, 'you walk in one door, as a soldier, secure in your uniform, rank, massive supporting organisation and camaraderie – and shortly afterwards you're out at another door, wearing a demob suit, on your tod, wondering what the dickens life has in store for you. *Sic transit gloria militaria,* would that be it?'

## Chapter Eighteen

# Civvy Street

With a smooth, practised sweep of his right hand, Jim pulled the Gillette safety razor down his lathered cheeks, leaning slightly forward across the shallow kitchen sink, as he did so. He peered intently at his reflection in the small rectangular mirror, hanging slightly askew from the catch of the sash window.

As he scraped away at the stubble, he sang to himself,

"Oh, there's a lull in my life,
It's just a void, an empty place,
When you are not in my embrace.

Oh, there's a lull in my life,
The moment that you go away,
There is no night, there is no day..."

Great song that, for the yearning, separated lover.

He rinsed his lightly tanned cheeks, and then the razor under the cold tap and dried himself off on the knobbly roller towel hung against the back door. 'Watch it lad,' he thought, 'careful now with the razor, don't get cutting the towel else Ma will get mad, mad as a wet hen.'

He glanced critically around the drab, tiny kitchen, especially at the sink area. Yes, something would have to be done – and soon. For the moment, he was pretty flush with money, having recently received his war service 'divvy', to wit, the 'Payment of War Gratuity and post-war Credits'. His War Gratuity amounted to fifty-two months at 14/- a month, i.e. £36 8/- and post-war credits for the period 16 April 1942 to 30 June 1946 (when the scheme ended) at 6d per day totalled £38 8/6 making a grand, really grand total of £74 16/6 now nestling snugly in the Post Office Savings Bank. Yippee!

But how much did weddings and wedding receptions cost in that odd category, where the bridegroom had to foot the entire bill? Not that he felt resentful about that ( if anyone was to blame it was that pig dog Hitler) but facts had to be faced and some estimate would have to be made. First off though, tackle this Dickensian kitchen/scullery – for his parents' sake, for Heidi's and for a more comfortable shave.

He knew well enough that his parents couldn't chip in with much. After all, what steady income did they have? Pop's old age pension and... and... well, that was about it, really. True, Pop received a small pension for John, his son killed during World War I, but that wasn't allowed, by Jim's Dad, to count towards family income. Against that however, the gammy legged, often stiff-necked old man (he would be 70 when Jim married) looked for and sometimes did work as a night watchman. Wilf also held bright hopes of becoming a part-time salesman for a producer of coal blocks.

Sal Norton had no income in her own right. No pension for a while either. She'd only be fifty-five later this year and her regular source of funds had dried up. The one bachelor brother, Harold, for whom she had kept house and been paid for doing so, had married last year and now the other, Les, was to marry shortly.

Both brothers would undoubtedly remain kind to 'our Sal', as would brother allotment holder Sam, and a ready supply of spuds and greens at knockdown or waived prices, would come Sal's way, into colander and saucepans. Maybe an occasional florin as well, a half-dollar even, of the 'treat yourself to a glass of stout, our kid' variety. Generous men, all three.

So, it's largely up to you, young fellow me lad. And remember, come next spring, young Jim, you'll have to write a letter to Berlin testifying that you can support and accommodate a wife. So get on with it.

> If it were done, when 'tis done, then 'twere well
> It were done quickly

Quite so.

Give the job then to the local professionals.

Kitchen 'renovation' £35 13/3 including 'To extra for square vitreous gas boiler £2 19/-. To extra for Ascot sink Heater £2. Aluminium Draining Board, Reduced from 29/6 to £1 6/6'.

Each time Jim turned on the Ascot, he felt a thrill of satisfaction and of joy to come as the gas ignited and let rip with its gentle roar, blue flames slightly a quiver. Golly! Hot water 'on tap' at long last – the first time since they had moved into 'the dump' in 1938. How many years still to wait for a bathroom, for an indoor toilet?

"Think we'll be able to winkle any money out of the landlord, vinegar puss Priestley, for decorating?"

"No bloomin' fear. Regular sheeny he is. Sticks to his money like glue that one," snorted Wilf.

("In other words, like shit to an Army blanket, eh" muttered Jim inwardly.)

"No, he won't help, dear," said Sal. "He's always going on about the cost of essential repairs and wallpapering is not essential."

"A miserable skinflint, eh?"

Jim's parents nodded their agreement.

So, another bill arrived, paid on the day it was presented – Jim's mother held a deep dread of debt.

'For papering and distempering ceilings and papering walls, etc., to two bedrooms, back and front sitting rooms, as per estimate twenty pounds. Settled with thanks.'

So now there was something more to tell Heidi, though he wouldn't bother her with the money side of things. A steady flow of letters, in both directions across the North Sea, had now been established. The lovers wrote, as presumably most lovers do, without a thought for posterity or the least suspicion that their letters might be read by a third party. So, reassurance, morale boosting, ringing statements of affection and snippets of news and views, formed the staple ingredients, mixed in varying amounts, of their correspondence.

"Think I should tell Heidi about the 'New Look', Ma?"

"Don't call me Ma. Since when have you become a fashion expert?"

"I'm not, just reading what it says here."

"Well, it looks very smart, I must say – such a nice change from austerity clothing, but you need a slim waist to set it off properly."

Sal gave a deep sigh of regret at the generous expansion of her own girth.

Wilf coughed,

"I remember when some girls had real wasp waists and hour glass figures – now the Gibson Girls were really something to look at."

Sal sniffed, ignoring the comment and answered her son's question.

"No, I don't think I should trouble Heidi with details like that. You can bet your bottom dollar there'll be a different fashion for next year. And anyway, I expect a lot of coupons are needed for this New Look."

"It says here, about fourteen."

"There you are then."

And where was he? 'In jaded, tired, austerity-plagued Britain,' thought Jim. 'British soldiers being shot or blown to pieces in Palestine, trouble over Indian independence, an "export or die" campaign at home, a Marshall Plan to get Britain and other impoverished countries out of economic hock. Cuts of every sort to the tinned meat ration, the meat ration, the size of newspapers.' ("Doesn't bother me that the tripe ration is being cut," chuckled Wilf.)

But a few bright events shone through the gloom – the sweet ration went up from four to five ounces a week. Princess Elizabeth became engaged to some chap called Philip Mountbatten, a lieutenant in the Greek Navy.

"They look a lovely couple," murmured Sal. "I wonder what sort of queen she will make. It will be nice to have a woman on the throne one day. That reminds me, Jim, have you got your speech ready for Uncle Les's wedding?"

"Yes, I've made a few notes."

"And don't forget, it's your job to propose the toast to the bridesmaids. Have you remembered their names?"

Jim frowned in mock perplexity.

"I know they're two of many sisters. Gert and Daisy isn't it?"

Sal frowned in genuine puzzlement. Then her face cleared. "Why, you young devil – that's the Waters sisters on the radio."

"My mistake – Joan and Betty of course."

Sal's knitting needles resumed their placidly busy, rhythmic clicking.

"I think you should wear that grey suit you had made in Germany. It's a much better fit than your blue demob suit."

"Now there I have to agree with you."

It was Jim's first wedding, in any capacity. He still didn't feel completely at home in civilian company, even when those present included a fair sprinkling of ex-matelots, erks and squaddies from one or both World Wars. When informed, at the reception, that the 'ham and salad', was ready on the table in the next room, he soon tired of the polite ways of informing the chattering starling guests that – 'grub was up,' so to speak.

So, in best parade ground style he bawled, "QUIET! You 'orrible lot!"

This had the desired effect. Startled silence – a clear and clearly audible announcement, followed by hearty laughter and a resumption of animated gossip as the guests filed towards the 'spread'.

Yes, it was a rum business adapting to Civvy Street. While it was good to be free of the petty restrictions imposed by Army life, he missed the generous daily dollop (off the ration) of leg-pulling, the shared duties and annoyances, the evening mateiness of the mess. To himself, he acknowledged that he needed a new and stable rhythm to his life. Doubtless that would start when he became an undergraduate in the Autumn, and be vastly reinforced when he had a wife to support.

He smiled. 'A wife to support' – he would have been scornful of such a phrase applying to himself, just a few short years ago. And now look what had happened. Uncle Harold spliced to be followed by the liveliest bachelor of them all, Uncle Les. Other young relatives were about to stoop and allow the ball and chain to be shackled to their ankles. 'Twas ever thus. He would bear his loss of 'freedom' manfully. But oh, how a pair of bright eyes could change one's world. Nature was dashed clever.

In the meanwhile, Jim greatly enjoyed renewing established bachelor friendships – playing well-matched but light-hearted games of tennis with Bob in the park – going 'up' to Cambridge with Bob, to stay a few days with Dave – Queens College best man to be. What wonderful architecture to admire in those historic colleges, what bloody draughty corridors and stairways to endure. And when Dave came 'down' from Cambridge, Jim looked forward to a happy resumption of chatting, laughing, walking, discussion of 'life' duologues, similar to those shared at fifteen when they had pondered hard on the greatest of mysteries – girls. Nowadays, they would use longer words like 'duologue', and more complicated sentences – but the intellectual and emotional puzzles remained no nearer solution.

A few old Army pals continued to write, warm-hearted, adventurous Ted for one. Ted, ex-paratrooper, now married and settled with his beloved Emma near Nottingham – and soon to be a father. Ted, himself a romantic, greatly looked forward to meeting Heidi. Derek, fellow Grand Lama of The Swinging Icicle Monastery days wrote: 'May the sun forever shine on your rancid butter'. That sun certainly hadn't shone warmly on Derek – he had missed six months of an essential teaching course 'with appendix trouble... send my best wishes to Heidi (my affair seems to be over)...' He didn't hint at why, probably some unimaginative wench who couldn't, or wouldn't, understand yak culture and its shaggy Tibetan ways.

'Do you remember Tattoo 1946? I think it was much better than 1947.'

What a charming way of saying she missed him. At least, that was how Jim smugly interpreted the note Heidi had scribbled inside the Tattoo programme, a much more sophisticated document than last years. It featured a map of the Dortmund arena and gave an explanation, in German, of the origin of the word Tattoo, something Jim studied with interest. Apparently, the word derived from the practice of the *Trommler* (the drummer) calling troops back to quarters by 'TAP TO BILLETS' which, in typically sensible, British soldierly fashion, was shortened to 'TAP TO' and then to 'TATTOO'.

A brief history, again in German, was given of each of the regiments taking part in the Tap-To – including the York and Lancaster. Jim recalled that he had once been attached to that 'mob', formed in 1758 apparently. Quite a nice arm flash – as he remembered. A black square on which was set a Tudor rose, one half red, t'other half white. But for all the needles and thread, and strands of grey wool in his old 'hussif', he couldn't remember which colour was on the left – white probably as York preceded Lancaster. Not that it mattered much to an out and out Brummie, who wasn't much fussed about the sensitivities of Northerners or Southerners for that matter.

Soon Jim himself was back in camp again, under canvas too, one of many volunteers up and down the country helping to gather in the precious harvest. 'Posted' to deepest Rutland, somewhere near Oakham, he 'enjoyed' a dense dust producing, parching thirst promoting variety of jobs on and around an ancient, vibrating threshing machine attached to a juddering, smoke belching, steam engine. Perhaps not a bad analogy for University studies – sorting the grain from the chaff. Look what Denis Compton had done by picking the right ball to whack to the boundary – phew, mop the brow, 3816 runs amassed in the season including 18 centuries, two records.

\*

'Hello, that's strange.' Jim picked up the envelope bearing its dark green 50 *pfennig* stamp, from the door mat. The familiar handwriting quickened the pace of his heart. But now, to delight, was added anxiety, for along one of the short sides of the envelope had been pasted that ominous strip of white paper – 'Opened by Examiner'. And near the address – that purple circular stamp mark 'British Censorship Germany'.

Rapidly Jim slit open the letter with his penknife. Two sheets of paper – nothing cut out, nothing crossed out. Phew, that was a relief. But when you thought about it, and Jim did, what a bloody bureaucratic intrusion into private lives – with the war now more than two years over.

Hm – the Boss had had his wings clipped. Mrs Boss had now joined her husband at the pit head, and elsewhere. Heidi had been invited to 'tea and bickies' with the matriarch. The letter lapsed into daydreaming, *"Illusionen,"* as Heidi said, a way of revealing the yearnings fuelled by five months of separation.

> *We both love nature, the fresh air and sunshine – so what shall we do today in this lovely weather, darling?*
>
> *Today is your first day as a student – I do hope the great amount of work you will have to do will bring you pleasure – next year you will have an additional duty when you have to give private lessons to your girl student...*
>
> *When I see young people strolling about today in this lovely weather, I am overcome with Sehnsucht – so then I look for work to do which takes my whole attention...*
>
> *Does your Mother have a good shopping bag? I can get hold of a nice one – don't tell your Mother, you can tell me what you think...*
>
> *HAB MICH LIEB, SO WIE ICH DICH, Heidi.*

So, what did you make of that Mister Nosey Parker censor? Did Mr Snoop give a cynical snigger or an indulgent, sympathetic smile?

And what had Snoop been expecting to find – sensitive gen about Ruhr coal production, seditious political or military comment, something salacious in the wood shed? And what had he found? A loving, well timed morale boost for a rusty mature student, now clad in his deep rust coloured corduroy trousers.

Pity then, that morale and calorie intake were being attacked, mercilessly attacked, by further ration cuts – a bacon ration of one ounce a week – it was hardly credible and the rasher barely visible, let alone edible; and spuds rationed to three pounds per person per week. Enough to make an 'old sweat' hallucinate sitting in cold, cheerless, hard wooden seated lecture theatres – to hallucinate about the delights of sergeants' mess grub, even including the spinach.

In 1940 Jim had undergone his Higher School Cert. French oral exams, in Edmund Street, (along with close pals Doug and Syd, now both tragically dead, facts still hard to accept) so the Gothic horror of the Arts Faculty Building did not come as a totally unexpected shock to him. But crikey, it was a gloomy, draughty, cheerless assemblage of teaching rooms, corridors, and stairs, with a shabby, down at heel, slopped cups refectory in the basement.

In these glum surroundings, Jim often thought, not just of Heidi, but of the frenzied Rutland thresher and what it represented. Sort the grain from the chaff. That notion held good for lectures – and for books. He sensed his notes were far too copious – but then, academics, scholars, learned critics, were so bloomin' wordy, often verbose if they were PhDs.

Many and many a long dark autumn evening and many and many a longer, darker winter evening were passed in the vast, sepulchral, high ceilinged cavern of the public Central Library, at assiduous scribbling – Eng. Lit., German Lit., French Lit. Good job he had found room in his demob kit bag for quite a tolerable supply of blank exercise books – Atkins, Tommy – for the use of. And to think, this time last year, instead of the elegant, polished diction of Dryden, he had been enjoying the highly colourful vernacular of Army truck drivers as he hitch hiked back and forth to Pullenstadt. Some of those coarse grained, good hearted travellers, if not pilgrims, could have stepped straight from the pages of a latter day Chaucer.

As a senior schoolboy, Jim had greatly enjoyed *Hamlet*, *Twelfth Night* and *Julius Caesar*. In fact, he found he could still remember many lines from these particular plays, especially from *Hamlet*. And this year he had actually been, for the first time ever, to Stratford, and by golly, to the Shakespeare Memorial Theatre. A top class performance of *Romeo and Juliet*. He hadn't known anything of the principal actors but they had performed splendidly – Juliet: Daphne Slater; Romeo: Laurence Payne; Paris: Donald Sinden; Mercutio: Paul Scofield.

Such wonderful poetry to thrill the senses – but a right barmy plot. Still, the whole experience vividly underlined the fact that Will had first and foremost written plays which were to be acted, and not as source material for theses without number. But, fair dos, critics could do highly perceptive work. Jim recalled being held spellbound by the Eng. Lit. prof. who skilfully dissected, appraised and re-assembled the elements of that deservedly famous passage from *Macbeth* beginning,

> She should have died hereafter

Jim's fellow students, at least those he knew from attending the same lectures, seminars, tutorials, were, for the most part, young, bright and jolly – stirred perhaps by Shakespeare's language, but not long to be depressed by Macbeth's notion that:

> Life's but a walking shadow, a poor player
> That struts and frets his hour upon the stage,
> And then is heard no more.

Not being in their 'sear and yellow' years, picking the side for the next game of hockey and wondering who, of amorous interest and intent, they might meet at Saturday's hop, were rightly matters of more 'pith and moment' to them. Yeth sir.

*

## Letter 105: 21 December 1947, uncensored

Jim made a first quick reading and rough translation.

*Unpleasant weather – I'm too comfortable at home to want to go to the cinema – and anyway you won't be coming... I won't disturb you when you're studying... you're more likely to disturb me when I'm doing housework, ne? How did the exams go? So, you're taking on paid work during the holidays. I am marrying an industrious man! ...Your last letter took only six days to arrive prima... you ask me to pump up your bicycle tires...* (some gentle teasing followed)

*Soon 1948 will be here. Summer will come more quickly than we think, and I do so look forward to the time when we do not have to write to one another, because we can talk instead... My new overcoat is finished, I'm so pleased with it – you can hardly tell that it was once a blanket. It wasn't too dear; anyway, as I'm not yet married, I don't have to ask you! So there! ...Please come and read me a story, I have some new magazines... I'm keeping my fingers crossed that the gas mantle you have sent arrives here undamaged so that we have better light than at the moment.*

*All my love darling,*
*Heidi.*

## Chapter Nineteen

# The Great Paper Chase

Towards the end of March 1948, Jim set in sluggish motion the gummy red tape wheels that hopefully, some day, would realise Heidi's wish to replace letters with conversation. A good three months and more to the end of July. Surely to Pumpernickel and roast beef, British and German sluggard bureaucracies could work out something between them, well before that time. In buoyant, optimistic mood, Jim booked a whole two weeks holiday, last week in July, first in August, at a guest house in Newquay, Cornwall well known and strongly recommended to him by the Campbell sisters, old pals from his rambling days with the 'good old gang' from church.

However, before that booking had been made, Jim had endured an uncomfortable, near humiliating interview with his former headmaster, the Rev. H.R. Gordon.

"So, Norton, you want to marry a German girl."

Smooth skinned, rosy faced 'Holy Joe' smiled benignly, the tips of his fingers touching one another in a manner much favoured by scholarly gentlemen.

"You'll be taking something on you know, both of you."

"That is true, but we have thought things over very carefully and that is why we agreed on a year's separation. We are still both of the same mind. We wish to marry."

The sober suited, dog collared head reflected.

"Well, that's good. It's sensible. But you must not think, you know, that what goes on in the bedroom forms the bedrock of marriage. Don't let yourself be carried away by – erm, erm passion."

Jim's face flamed with anger, 'You holier than thou, cheeky old sod,' he thought. 'I wonder what goes on in your bloomin' bedroom. Is there a worn strip of carpet between two single beds?'

Jim said nothing but smiled bleakly. He needed this well meaning man's help. And, after all, Joe was an ordained preacher. Once a preacher, always a preacher – once a teacher always a teacher. This upright man was both, a kind of double barrelled morality shot gun.

"German women are reputed to make very good housewives."

"So I believe."

"Well, I'll back your application, as you request. The best of luck to you both."

Head and former sixth former shook hands. Jim silently acknowledged that Joe was no Crowbar, no Bullshine – he was simply, by nature, training and experience – pontifical.

Holy Joe was as good as his word and wrote to Berlin on 24th March. On the same day, Jim Norton wrote to the same passport office undertaking to marry one Heidi Braun within two months of her arrival in the UK.

On April the 12th Heidi moved a step nearer to 'clear for take off' status; a stamped declaration testifying that she was free from infectious diseases and that she had no criminal record. On the following day, another official and stamped declaration was completed – the same Heidi Braun owed no taxes, was solvent, of the Protestant faith and of good character.

After such official, busy-body evaluations, it was refreshing to hear from the girl herself.

## Letter 171

> *I have missed you so much today, in this lovely weather when Paul (a cousin) and I went for a cycle ride... Today is Mother's Day – I bought red and yellow tulips for Mutti... and I baked a currant cake for her – you'd be quite welcome to try it if you are passing by... Dad has been to the sports field to watch a boxing match... are you making good progress with your studies? I am working again at the Sonnenberg where we first met, a golden wedding anniversary there tomorrow. Earlier on I am going with Mother to buy four goslings which my parents want to raise for Gänsebraten (roast goose) don't laugh, it's the truth.*
>
> *Ich hab Dich so o o o lieb*
> *Heidi*

## 21 May 1948

*1. Herewith your Travel Document, which contains an
Exit Permit to leave Germany, and a visa to enter the
UK.
2. ...await instructions as to your journey.*

Jim paid the fare – Hannover to London, Heidi received further
details.

'You will not be permitted to take RMs (Reichmarks) out of
Germany.'

Blast.   Last year wasn't it forty Reichmarks that could be
exported?   Another, but minor setback.

If the authorities kept their word, then in another six weeks Heidi
would set foot on English soil.   But have a care, there could be many
a slip between red tape and trip.   Throughout June, the authorities
remained in purdah.   Jim began to fret.   He wrote to Heidi on July 8th
suffering, 'from what seems like a nagging mental tooth-ache...
someone, somewhere seems to be failing to do his job properly.   It's a
bad show and what makes it worse is that I don't know whom to
*schimpfen!*' (scold) 'myself I suppose, if I'm honest, for not having
written earlier to get you here.'

He wrote again just two days later.

'Yesterday morning I sent off a telegram, to the Foreign Office
and so far I have received no reply.   I don't know whether to take this
as a good sign or not.   That they have not replied immediately may
mean they are making enquires...   I don't quite know whether to delay
my trip to London until Tuesday...'

For a short while calmer counsels prevailed.

"Just wait a day or two longer, son and if you hear nothing, send
another telegram."

Meanwhile, a more up-to-date (than the April) certificate of
Heidi's health had been demanded.   On 16th July, the chief public
health officer of Pullenstadt testified that one Fräulein Heidi Braun
was not suffering from any infectious disease and that the tests on her
for venereal disease had proved negative.

Jim's head understood, and fairly calmly accepted, the need for
such medical precautions in the general situation, but his heart raged
against the offensive injustice of it all in Heidi's case.

And then the impassive news that this working-class, English 'Romeo' and German 'Juliet' had so longingly ached for, arrived.

Heidi was instructed to report to the RTO (Railway Transport Officer) on Platform 5 Hannover Station between 10.00 and 15.30 hours on 18th July – with no more than fifteen marks about her person 'for small costs at Hannover' and no more than 160 lbs of luggage.

Heidi began packing her worldly belongings into two suitcases, one large, one small. Three copies of their exact contents were made out, without carbon paper, and duly stamped. Ladies' mentionables and unmentionables, all had to be mentioned – three times for each case. Such satisfaction for the red tape enthusiast.

On the same day, Jim's 'nagging mental tooth-ache' was stilled by a telegram from an highly august institution, the British Foreign Office.

*Please meet your fiancee due Liverpool Street Station London Nine o'clock Wednesday Morning 21st July – Foreign Office.*

"Yippee!" Jim's joyous yell was loud enough to be heard by the neighbours on either side.

Then followed an animated discussion between members of the wedding – wedding reception committee, Mrs Norton and son, now 'very sunny' Jim.

"If you want to make the most of the holiday you've booked, you'll have to try and get married by special licence."

"Is that difficult?"

"I don't know – but we've got just a few days to find out and to arrange a reception."

\*

Jim was on time and began pushing and dodging his way through the jostling, excited crowd on the platform. Yes, there she was, glancing about her anxiously, looking rather tired and very alone, amid shifting knots of people. He could not rush towards her, far too many pesky people were blundering about in the way. What on earth was she doing, wearing a heavy top coat in July! Of course, that was it, she was being practical, she could carry more clothes in her suit cases that way.

At last, at long last, after fourteen months of 'there's a lull in my life', his arms were firmly about her – and hers about him.

\*

"So you see, we have just three clear days to get everything ready before you become, Mrs Norton."

Heidi smiled sweetly, though she still seemed a little bewildered – and no wonder. So many new impressions in just a few short days. Such an excited babble of rapidly spoken Brummie English. Not a word of German, except for Jim's remarks. So much genuine affection and kindness shown to her, such warmth from Jim's parents and relatives, especially from that generous hearted, bright spark Uncle Les.

Jim began to dash about and to splash out – two pounds twelve shillings and sixpence for a special licence, three pounds thirteen shillings (more than a week's grant ) for the organ (but it was for a Monday service). But best and most willingly, most lovingly of all twenty-one pounds for a posh dress for Heidi. No bridal gown but a really posh outfit, bright spanking new, which could serve as 'Sunday Best' for quite some time to come.

So, on Monday 26th July 1948, Jim and Heidi were married. A hot July sun blazed down from a cloudless sky on mellow and friendly St Mary's church. Jim wore his tried and trusted grey (cocoa conversion) suit which went well with his brightly coloured undergraduate's tie. Heidi, in the beautifully tailored 'two piece', a pleated, dusty yellow, dress with matching bolero jacket, looked, well, just as a bride should look – according to Ethel M Dell and her sister scribes – 'radiantly happy'. She carried a modest spray of blue scabious and white gypsophila, freshly picked that morning from his allotment by Uncle Harold.

Jim's tubby half sister May, acted as matron of honour; Dave as personable best man. As he walked back down the aisle, Heidi on his left arm, Jim noticed Syd's aunt in one of the pews. She waved a gloved hand and gave him a warm smile. Jim was so glad and relieved to see her there.

And so to the reception in a nearby pub. Dave made a Rhein wein sparkling speech, rich with romantic imagery, interspersed with his own, highly distinctive guffaws. Guests tucked into corned beef sandwiches, spam sandwiches, a few cheese sandwiches, (the cheese ration had been cut in March to 1½ ounces a week). The trifle was popular. 'Good old Ma'. A fine, splendidly iced, three tiered wedding cake graced the top table, but not for long.

Then to Snow Hill station by taxi! Such reckless splendour for a student and a student's missus. Only two days honeymoon had been lost after all.

*

"So Heidi, with this lovely weather looking set, let's stay another, a third week in Newquay, shall we? We can just about afford it."

"Oh, please Jim let's!"

Heidi had become enchanted by the rocky coast, the crashing waves, the wheeling seagulls.

Snubs, set-backs, sneers – all temporarily forgotten. What mattered now and would continue to matter, was the poet's couplet:

> *Und doch welch Glück geliebt zu werden*
> *Und lieben Götter welch ein Glück.*

> And what happiness to be beloved,
> And to love, ye Gods, what happiness.